East Lothia**n**

0903**0**

CLAY

CLAY

Gladys Mary Coles

FlambardPress

First published in Great Britain in 2010 by Flambard Press
Holy Jesus Hospital, City Road, Newcastle upon Tyne NE1 2AS
www.flambardpress.co.uk

Typeset by BookType
Cover Design by Gainford Design Associates
Cover image: 'From a Front Line Trench' by Christopher Richard Wynne
Nevinson (1889–1946) Private Collection/The Stapleton Collection/
The Bridgeman Art Library
Printed in Great Britain by Bell & Bain, Glasgow, Scotland

A CIP catalogue record for this book is available from the British Library

ISBN: 978-1906601-19-5

Flambard Press wishes to thank Arts Council England
for its financial support.

Flambard Press is a member of Inpress.

The paper used for this book is FSC accredited.

To Jenny Newman

Was it for this the clay grew tall?
O what made fatuous sunbeams toil
To break earth's sleep at all?

Wilfred Owen, 'Futility'

What will we do with the future?
Handle it like a piece of precious porcelain
New from the clay and the fire?

William Manderson,
'The Ceasing of Hostilities'

For the spirit of poetry looks beyond life's trench-lines.
And Isaac Rosenberg was naturally empowered with
something of the divine spirit which touches our
human clay to sublimity of expression.

Siegfried Sassoon, from the Foreword to
The Collected Works of Isaac Rosenberg, 1937

1

1916

'Last leave.'

The official phrase breathed out finality. Well, the Army always did lack imagination. And now the last day of his last leave.

William Manderson strode through the new public gardens and felt aware of the dead beneath his feet. The old Liverpool Necropolis, now renamed Grant Gardens. Full, overcrowded, closed, and then the graves filled in, the tombstones removed, the earth tilled and seeded, the high walls demolished. As he walked down the central path, he glanced uneasily at the bright spring green of the new lawns, the almost too abundant flower-beds. Blossom drifted on the April wind like flakes of snow and no one lingered on the benches, not even the old men who usually sat there, staring and spitting.

He was conscious of a briskness in his step. Because of the training, the drill, the route marches, he thought, not that he'd minded PT – least of the torments. What he hated most was the lack of privacy, only random moments to himself, the frustration when isolated images and phrases were all he could manage to write down in his pocket-book. Drafts of poems he'd taken with him to the camp had remained just that – drafts.

What's that you're doing? Not now Manderson! Sergeant Gibson's pale grey eyes had fixed on him as if searching out his poetry in order to eradicate it.

Well, he was perfectly fit, if nothing else. Even Jack might agree that he'd got some muscles at last, big brother who'd always enjoyed taunting him – nancy pants, Welsh beanpole – never forgiving him for growing half a head taller than himself. Jack, already at the Front following, as he said, 'the path of duty'. Let him come through, for Elizabeth and baby Lily, and of course Mam.

He swung out through the sandstone pillars of the main entrance and caught a woman smiling at him. She was standing on the pavement about to cross the road. Ah, yes, the flower-seller from the stall on the traffic island. She held out a bunch of narcissi, white and pale lemon. He shook his head. No, he wasn't going to meet a lady friend. She gave him a wry glance and shrugged her shoulders. At least she hadn't pressed white feathers into his hand. He was wearing his civilian clothes, the favourite tweed jacket and corduroy trousers, relishing them after the stiff khaki, the rough cloth that smelt of sour milk. He'd hardly slept last night, kept seeing the brass buttons on his tunic glaring at him from the wardrobe door like a row of eyes.

Four o'clock. He'd left the house because he needed to, heading for town. It was good to get out, the atmosphere at home increasingly tense, heavy with emotion. Mam coming to him with things she thought he'd want – socks, more socks, gloves, vests, packages of biscuits, marmalade, Pears soap, Euthymol tooth-paste, a pair of pyjamas – and all the time tearful, calling him *cariad*. Dear old Pa, sitting by the fire, subdued after he'd failed to comfort Mam with his Norse legend about the wand of death. The only soldiers who die are those touched by the wand, he'd said, and set Mam weeping.

A cigarette. He needed a cigarette. He took one from his packet of Players Navy Cut and stopped to light up in front of Dawson's, the stationery and sweet shop in Brunswick Road where he'd spent his first pocket money. He drew on the cigarette, saw its glow reflected in the window, saw his face, like Pa's only thinner – the Viking look, strong nose and chin, blond hair. But was his fear showing? Fear of having to kill. Afraid of being afraid. He looked at the window display, the faded advertisements. He'd go in, buy something for little Lily. Oh, Christ! The shop was closed and a wreath hanging on the door. Which of the two Dawson boys? He hoped not both of them. He hurried on down the shopping thoroughfare where queues tailed out from greengrocers, bakers and butchers. A tram rumbled past and he leapt onto the platform, took the stairs two at a time, sat at the back. Familiar streets, the route downhill into the city, London Road – none of it seemed real, he was already at Southampton, boarding the ship. And by now Matthew would be there with his platoon – damned orders splitting the draft, putting paid to their hopes of crossing together.

He jumped off the tram in Lime Street, as crowded as ever, in spite of the war. Across the road to St George's Hall, the stone lions, his lion, on the far right, one of four crouching on their plinths at the plateau's edge. He'd chosen it when he was seven, his talisman, whose enormous front paws he'd often touched for luck – on leaving school, going for the job at Levers, placing bets that first time. And when he enlisted. And now. He couldn't leave for the Front without this sacramental moment. Both hands on one cold paw and then the other.

His last luxury, he'd promised himself this – an hour or two in the Adelphi lounge. Weren't condemned men allowed to choose their last meal? He'd feel close to Matthew in the place where he'd been the regular pianist – and where they'd enjoyed their evenings after his performance.

Two officers came out of the hotel and down the marble steps towards him. Royal Welch Fusiliers, probably from the camp at Litherland. His arm began to swing up a salute. Relax. Not a puppet on a string now, incognito in his civvies. He strolled into the lounge. He'd sit with a drink, a cigarette, and work on his poem for Aunt Mair about the Vale of Clwyd. He chose one of the leather armchairs away from the chattering guests at their marble tables, men in evening suits, women in silk gowns and fur stoles, officers with thick cigars. The luxury of this place. Like a transatlantic liner, first class of course. Airy and sumptuous, the ceilings high, the mirrors huge, reflecting tall indoor plants and ornate lamp stands. He saw the hotel set against the plain canvas of the barracks, the bare dormitories, basic latrines, the institutional dining room smelling of carbolic and stew. Of course he'd been afraid of going in, from that hot August day at Levers in 1914 when he'd seen the workforce queuing to enlist at the Gladstone Hall, seen the new soldiers, fresh from taking the oath and the King's shilling, marching in fours down Greendale Road somehow incongruous in their ordinary clothing, seen among them men he worked with in the Publications and Printing Department.

Coming with us, Manderson? Alun Davies had urged.

Later! he'd yelled over his shoulder and almost ran for the train to Liverpool, covered in sweat, back prickling with fear – the fear of going in, of giving everything up, losing his freedom, killing, most of all having to kill. He'd slunk past the recruitment Scroll of Honour every day on his way to the editorial section – but by now his name and Matthew's would have been added. Well, they'd stayed out as long as they could. It was the air raids that decided them, the attacks on London. Not honour. Not glory. Defence. They'd enlisted in the Cheshires months before conscription and tribunals and the finger-pointing at pacifist degenerates.

His drink, the whisky he'd ordered, was brought to him by a waiter he recognised – Arthur, whose limp had been acquired, he'd said, after an encounter with a shell in the Boer War.

He sipped the whisky, then lit his cigarette. Where was the grand piano? Yes, still there by the palm tree and he could see Matthew sitting at the keyboard; his wavy dark hair and impish face; how he'd adjust his cuffs, hold out his large hands, then launch into the performance, utterly mesmerising, his fingering intricate in a Chopin polonaise. Dear Matt, his playing always seemed like an act of discovery, his whole body intent on the inducement of sound and feeling, especially when he played his own compositions like 'Water Music'. Where was he now? Arrived in France? Surely they'd they meet up at the Base Camp?

Enjoy this while you can. He took out his pencil and notebook, and turned to the poem for Aunt Mair. He was immediately back at Bryn Tirion, sitting by the log fire in her farmhouse, and she was showing him Uncle Gwilym's poetry. A few more lines needed, perhaps another attempt at the Welsh ways of alliteration –

Over this sky-long, sea-long land,
Peopled as the shell-starred sand,
I see in fields of change and chance . . .

– 'change and chance', he liked the chime of the words, but not what they implied.

Seven a.m. William sat on the edge of his bed, winding on the laminated puttees. He was skilled at this now and completed the job without a re-wind. He tightened his braces, pulled on his tunic, went to the window. A suitably grey morning, clouds hurrying on the wind that had persisted all week. He turned back to his kitbag. He'd complete his packing before breakfast, select the books. Poetry . . . some Hardy, his small volume of Keats, his Tennyson and Arnold. A novel . . . Hardy again, but not *Jude the Obscure*. No, not a novel. There wouldn't be time. He flicked through the issues of *Progress* he'd edited at Levers. At least he'd made a good start in journalism, had two poems published in Wales.

On his desk lay the new notebook Elizabeth had given him. This he would pack with his dictionary and pencils, torch and other personal things. The notebook, with its blue cover and the white pages waiting to be filled. A field of snow waiting for footprints. The unknown. She'd urged him to keep writing. Don't let the Army stifle you. Keep your poems going, use the war experience. Write your journal for me. She would take care of his three notebooks with the poems and journals he'd written at Bryn Tirion – his best work so far. Lovely, her glossy dark hair held back in a velvet bow, she'd handed him the new notebook and hugged him. He'd seen concern in her hazel eyes. If only he'd had the courage to kiss her. No, he mustn't feel that way. She was missing Jack, she'd told him – but he'd noticed when he peered in their room the other day that she'd transformed it since Jack had gone. Brought out the blue-green ceramics she'd decorated at the Della Lucca Studio, displaying them on the dresser – a tall vase encircled with lilies, a jug with lizard handles, a bowl with a sunflower design. Jack calls them dust-harbourers, she'd said, laughing. She'd crowded the walls with her work. Like an art gallery – portraits of her Ma, Lily, Jack, her beloved Grandma Quecci looking very Italian in a toque hat. And she'd hung her Suffrage banner designs, the one with the cormorant like a Liver Bird and the border of sailing ships, and another of a woman like Joan of Arc breaking her chains. His own portrait, too, drawn before her marriage to Jack. He still felt ashamed that he'd never congratulated them, but then, he had found her first, introduced her to the family – and Jack. 'Young William' she used to call him – he thought for Jack's benefit. Well, he wasn't young now, at twenty-two, not the lad who used to follow her round four years ago.

He kissed the notebook and placed it carefully in his kitbag. Now he'd go downstairs and break his news. He was dreading the farewell. Mam had looked wrung out for days. Why prolong it? He'd tell them that he didn't want anyone seeing him off at Lime Street. Already he was missing them. He'd say his goodbyes, slip out through the back-yard and walk down through the new Gardens. No, not that way. He'd leave through the front door, go down the street to Everton Road, catch a tram or maybe a cab if one came along.

A last look from his bedroom, taking in all he could of Liverpool, the rooftops, spires and smoke-hazed river, and on the distant skyline Wales, the Clwydian range where Bryn Tirion lay, hills grey-blue in the early morning light. He shouldered his kitbag, took his cap from the chair. A flock of gulls, scavenging inland, soared over the back-yards with raw cries, circled, then dropped down onto the lawns of the old Necropolis.

2

22nd April 1916

A sharp Spring morning. We embarked against a
wind direct from France. I felt utterly numbed,
emotions packed away or perhaps exhausted for the
time. Grey sky and matching sea, our men silent for
the most part. Some were tugging on Woodbines all
the way over; others were sea-sick; a few of us tried
to sing but this failed, our words fighting against the
wind. The threat of torpedoes tormented me; only a
month ago the Folkstone–Dieppe packet went down.
Even though we'd been assured that U-boats
wouldn't strike, who can be sure of the enemy? The
channel waters were like a skin, with shadows
lurking underneath.

A patch of sunlight, shining on our buttons;
shining on Radcliffe's forehead, wet with fear;
shining on O'Neil's cap badge; shining on our rifles,
rifles on which bayonets will soon be fixed. But will
I be able to pierce another man's body, withdraw the
blade, jab in again? A sack isn't flesh, sinew, blood, a
man's lungs, heart, guts; and the louder Major Evans
shouts 'Turn the bugger inside out!' the less I want
to imagine the sack as a Boche. 'Kill or be killed!' –
another of his commandments. It has never seemed
real until now.

We arrived at the camp in darkness for a week of training before we're moved to the Front Line. I will be looking out for Matthew – today's his birthday, twenty-four. Catching up to Elizabeth and Jack.

Before we settled in tonight we had to remove the slugs which had invaded some of the tents – jokes about them being secret weapons sent by the Huns.

23rd April
First sight of Picardy. Green rolling fields, copses, farms, buildings with red-tiled roofs, grey walls – hardly a countryside for battle, or is it? Any countryside will do, I suppose, or any square or street corner. This landscape is subtle; the folds of fields could be used to deceive the enemy, copses to hide machine guns. The near distance, immediately beyond the camp to the south, could have been the site of a medieval battlefield, tents bright with heraldry – Agincourt, perhaps? Our tents are a muddy grey, ten men to each. Harper, from Scotland Road, is with me and one of the Foreshaw brothers from Crosby. More drill in the Bull Ring tomorrow and a grenade demonstration. I'd hoped to catch sight of Matthew today, but didn't. In uniform we all look the same, more or less, but I'm sure I'd recognise him. He must be here somewhere in this huge camp.

Outside Etaples I saw, outlined against the sunset, a long line of conscripted horses, heavy horses and light, in harnesses, tails swishing, many of them pulling carts, wagons filled with supplies, water, rations, ammunition. There were some shaggy Clydesdales like the two I used to see every day on the Dock Road. Home. I have sudden memories of places, Liverpool streets, buildings, houses, faces. Five o'clock, Mam making tea, round and neat in her flowery pinafore, Pa puffing at his pipe, in the middle of chess with old Johnson . . . No, I must resist, close the door, see only what is in front of my eyes. Like tonight's meal, the vile pressed-meat on tin plates, the earwig in my bread.

Other things: the thump-thump of distant gunfire, and at the roadside a child's shoe in the dust, covered in dried mud. And, slogging on a five-mile march, the song we sang, learning the words as we went:

Kaiser Bill went up the hill
To play a game of cricket.
The ball went up his trouser leg
And hit his middle wicket.

Poor Kaiser Bill is feeling ill,
The Crown Prince he's gone barmy.
And we don't care a fuck
For old von Kluck
And all his bleedin' great army.

———

23rd April 1916

My dear Mam and Pa
You'll be pleased to know that the crossing was calm. Many of us are seeing France for the first time – it's not all that different from England as yet, the countryside is very similar, but the houses do look 'foreign', having a distinctive shape, tall and thin and separate,

like houses in a fairy-story book. The towns have grey stone walls like the walls around the farms. The peasants mostly wear black, the women in shawls, the men all with berets, old men, as there are no young ones to be seen, only boys. In the villages they congregate around fountains in the squares, as they do at home around the pumps. As we went through one village, it was uplifting to see a crowd of children enjoying themselves playing a game similar to hopscotch. They were laughing and waving to us. Several blew us kisses as we marched past.

We are in camp among some lovely fields bordered by trees coming into blossom and new leaves, and the weather is kind so far.

Those stockings you knitted for me, Mam, they'll be ever so needed at the Front. I hear it's a huge quagmire up there, worse than any rugby pitch. Tell Elizabeth I'll be writing to her tomorrow and I'm looking out for Jack.

Pa, take extra care of my Mam.
A budget of love to you both, and no tears.
Your son, William

P.S. a song we sang on the way here goes:

Old Kaiser Bill went up the hill
To play a game of cricket.
We bowled him out, he's feeling ill
Because his team can't stick it.

—⁓—

24th April

Today our first encounter with death. At nine o'clock, after drill, we assembled at the top of the field where it rises to a small wood. An officer was coming to demonstrate how to use the new grenades. A light breeze, I remember, was filtering through the wood, carrying tangled smells of Spring. There was the hum of an airplane overhead, then the singing of larks, a silvery unwinding sound. The men were relaxed, smiling and talking, waiting beneath the trees for Lieutenant Berry. I looked at their faces, some men seem middle-aged, with jowls, but most of us are of the younger generation, like myself, going to the Front for the first time. None younger-looking though than Berry, a New Zealander and perhaps fresh from training school. I remember thinking how his tanned face made his teeth seem even whiter, his smile brilliant beneath the neat dark moustache and cap. He was introduced by Patterson, and lectured us for a while on the new methods of warfare.

A dummy hand-grenade was taken apart to show us the components. Next the demonstration, using the dummy, and stressing how quick you have to be once the pin is pulled. Then the real thing. He made us all go yards back – he was going to lob it towards the distant hedge. That moment, standing with the grenade in his hand, he paused as a flock of birds passed over, returning migrants; the next moment the explosion, smoke, pieces of him scattered over the field, against the trees. Many of us were flat on the ground. What I remember most was the acrid smell, the drifting smoke and –

I cannot continue this just now.

25th April

It's dusk and the hurricane lamps are lit in all the tents. Since yesterday I've thought of little else but Berry's death. Within moments of the explosion Patterson made us fall in, then we filed back into camp as the medical team ran past us up the field. We were given an hour to ourselves. Not a word for a while; no one seemed to want to break the silence. Finally, Rogers brought out his prayer book and we joined him in prayers for Berry. Later Patterson told us the grenade had been faulty and had detonated in Berry's hand as he drew out the pin. 'Bad luck,' he said.

My mind went back immediately to our final parade at Chester Castle and the battalion photograph which had to be taken again because Colonel Moreton's black charger moved his head at the crucial moment and ruined the picture – this upset some of the men who saw it as a bad omen.

Last night we (eight of us as Davies and Lunt opted out) smoked too many cigarettes playing cards until Lights Out. This first death was an initiation. The tension had persisted all day, men speaking abruptly to each other or talking nonsense or words of false bravado.

'Well,' says Rogers, 'we won't go to waste when they kill us. Have you heard about the Kaiser boiling British bodies down to make soap?'

'Silly bloody rumour! The Kaiser doesn't need soap,' grunts Barnes.

'Aye, maybe not. But he's not normal, is he? Deformed. That withered arm. His mind's warped too.' Rogers shuffles the cards. 'Evil he is. A Prussian devil.'

Silence. Then Jimmy Foreshaw, keen to show his knowledge. 'He's got English blood has the Kaiser. Related to the old Queen. He held her when she was dyin', it's said.'

'What, with his one bleedin' arm!' Rogers shuffles again and deals. 'Not much English in *her* either. And she married a German. That's why the Kaiser's got 'is eyes on taking us over.'

———

25th April 1916

My dear Elizabeth

If I could really tell you all that has happened since I left England, the sights and sounds, and most of all, my feelings, we would need a month. But I need to say at once that things are not as awful as you might be thinking. We haven't been sent to the Front Line yet, and I haven't had a chance to look for Jack, but can guarantee that he's been as involved as I have. Nor have I caught a glimpse of Matthew. Whatever happens, dear Elizabeth, remember always what I said to you before I left, my attitude to the war and hopes for us all.

I thought of you when I saw a line of our horses, in harness, their coats bronzed in the sunset. They were moving slowly, pulling carts along a dusty road. You would have wanted to draw them – and some of the French children we saw on the way here. Perhaps also some of the old peasants, with very interesting faces, a map of lines. On the march today we heard a village bell tolling the Angelus, and sure enough there was a group of peasants in a nearby field, standing still, in prayer, their heads bowed.

*I am well and hope you are too, and little Lily. Give
her a kiss from her Uncle.*
> *Your loving brother,*
> *William*

—◦◦◦—

30th April

Last night we arrived at the Front Line and were
installed in trenches, narrower than I'd expected, and
not deep, but enough to give us cover, with a bank of
earth in front (parapets) going the entire length.
Someone here before us made a thatched roof over
one section, using brushwood from a nearby copse.
The Boche are six hundred or so yards ahead, and
shelling us almost continuously. None dropping close
to us yet; we're told we'll get used to the explosions –
like the rats, darting along as if the trenches were
sewers, crawling across our feet and swarming
towards our rations. Foreshaw says he's going to
tame one, keep it as a pet (says he's 'got a way with
rodents'!). Patterson's going to borrow a dog from
someone he knows, to keep the numbers down.

Of all the physical discomforts so far, I most
detest this bending over all the time, having to move
head down, crouching forward ape-like, and always
alert, keeping a sharp look-out. Animals in an alien
environment. Lunt was hit by shrapnel within an
hour of settling in. It was embedded in his chest, not
deeply but enough to get him out of here and on his
way home. My cowardice hasn't been tested yet, but
I wouldn't mind having a Blighty wound like Lunt's
right now.

There was the luxury of two letters yesterday, one from Mam, one from Elizabeth. It's hard to imagine the usual Liverpool Saturday, with the trip to the market, then walking home through town. How the ordinary things seem like heaven. Here the smell of hell is all around, if you believe in hell-fire, and a stench that's not the mud but what infests it – decay, putrefaction, as though evil was taking a form. The compression on my brain and nerves is impossible to describe. It's intensified by the waiting, waiting for action, for what will come.

Running through my head today was that detestable recruitment song – 'We don't want to lose you but we think you ought to go' – I was hearing it against the crackle of machine-gun fire, thud of mortars, earth raining down. Exploding shells sing their own song; but each man will hear it differently. For me, a hissing 'Shame! Shame!' Images of dark and light – erratic light bursting across the black sky, obliterating stars.

Tonight I'll be on a scouting party. Patterson told me to get some sleep during the day – on the firestep or at the back of the trench. But I won't give up my journal. Letters are out though, now that we're going into action. Just the concession of Field Service Postcards, complete with green envelopes twice a week. These – I was given mine this morning – consist of printed formula statements such as 'I am quite well' or 'I have been admitted into hospital/ sick/wounded/and am getting on well (cross out what doesn't apply)'; also 'I have received no letter from you lately/ for a long time'. Signature only and date. Write anything else and the postcard gets destroyed.

Today I saw a magnificent horse lying on its side, disembowelled. A dark brown Shire, its legs were stiff, its eyes open, flies settling on the lashes.

Last breath by, he's done with pain
Grounded, life slit away.
First day of May
He should be in an English lane
Lit by Spring, gentled by sun.
I want to rouse him, speak his name.

3rd May
Two nights ago we went on reconnaissance, inspecting the German positions. A night of heavy cloud, no moonlight, only the occasional searchlight sweeping randomly across the dark, and now and then a mortar speeding like a comet across space. Unusually quiet, both our artillery and theirs in a lull. We went in two parties; I was with Patterson and Second Lieutenant Cooper in 'A' party, three of us, our faces blackened with burnt cork. We took wire-cutters and ladders and crawled on our stomachs, wriggling forward towards the Boche line. I nearly fell into a mine crater about forty feet deep, but Patterson pulled me back from the brink. We crept along the ladders across smaller craters and mud pools, until we reached the German wire – not easy cutting it, hands and fingers aching, the wire springing into my face like a wild cat. Slipping through the gaps, we neared their front trench. The silence and stillness unnerving, no sign of a Boche, not a gunshot. We lay there in the dark until Cooper passed the word that the front trench was deserted,

probably the result of our bombardment yesterday. 'B' party went on further while we gave them cover, and cut sections of the next line of wire, after which we crept back. No 'casualties'. I was covered in mud and felt like an earthworm, but exhilarated.

The next night we attacked after our artillery had shelled the Boche trenches. We headed for the cut wire. Now, at last, I would see a Hun face to face. Kill or be killed. The moment of truth I've dreaded. Again we crawled forward in the darkness, the first of us going through the wire. The three men ahead of me were mown down. One hung across the wire, fixed as on a gamekeeper's gibbet. I wanted to pull him off but had to keep moving forward with the others, bayonets ready. My blood pounded in my ears; my heart felt as if it was bursting as we reached the trench. I saw a Hun crouching at a machine gun pointed directly at me. 'Kill or be killed.' I was still hesitating, bayonet poised to thrust, but at that moment his head lolled back and I knew he was dead already. I fell, slipping in the mud into the trench, knocking into the machine gun as the Hun flopped sideways onto me, his face against my chest. As I threw him off, I saw his open mouth and his blue staring eyes. All the Boche in that trench had been killed by our heavy artillery. They were either lying on the ground or propped upright, awry like dolls. A few had been blown apart. I moved a helmet and blood streamed away from the head inside it. I wanted to vomit. A groan behind me. Parry was clutching his chest. He'd been picked off by a sniper. He couldn't move and blood was spurting from his mouth. I heaved him across my shoulder, struggled out of the trench and went towards our line, staggering under the weight until two stretcher-bearers took him from me. After this I went back through the smoke to rejoin the others. They were returning to our line – some were supporting each other, trying to keep going, Patterson helping to carry someone badly wounded. I heard later that it was Cooper. I was shaking uncontrollably and felt I would collapse. Back in the trench, helped by a shot of rum, I gradually recovered; but then a feeling of total numbness set in. The Boche retaliated with a bombardment and I flattened myself against the side of the trench while it lasted. Afterwards I wanted to tear my uniform off as I was smelling the sweet-sourness of Parry's blood which had soaked into my back. Fell asleep standing up.

By day, No Man's Land is hideous, a wasteland, ugly with shattered trees, stakes, coils of jagged wire. It's pitted by huge craters, mud traps, shell holes, and across it the front line snakes. By night, it becomes a different place, uniquely lovely, eerily lovely – mortars with their trails of sparks, and tracer bullets, lethal pretty things, lighting the dark, and the flares rising, descending slowly, whitening the wastes, a moonscape. Even on wet nights the show goes on, with the rain lit up, bright rods of rain curtaining us off.

5th May
Jimmy Foreshaw cheeked off Patterson yesterday and now he's got a Field Punishment – ordered to join the Burial Party until further notice, collecting

and burying the bits. Shells play cat and mouse with the corpses, blowing them up, covering them with dust, and then disinterring them, chopping them into pieces. We all feel sorry for Jimmy and wonder whether his nerves will hold out.

'Turning out the lights' . . . two lines haunt me just now – but I have no others to follow them:

I want to let the night in gently
Not hear the popping stop of gas

7th May
In action again last night. Inferno. I can't write about it, sights for devils' eyes. My hand shakes. I'm thinking of Matt. I dare to hope he is alive.

14th May
A week such as I never want to live through again. Unutterable atrocities. I have no will or energy to write.

17th May
Just to record that Cooper is dead – and Barnes, Fleming, and Harper.

25th May. Camp
We heard we were to be relieved. Incredibly, in repeated attacks, forays, working parties, I still haven't had to choose to kill, jab my bayonet into another man's guts. Firing into their line I might have killed a Hun or two, but of this I can't be sure. Very little sleep, horrific dreams, the recurring one of crawling over mutilated bodies.

Retreating to the reserve trenches, I felt stiff in every limb. It seemed that I'd been born in a trench and had lived nowhere else. Time has become a blur; days, nights have merged. We moved in darkness to the rear trenches, then marched at dawn five miles to the camp. We were like a line of old men, out of step, shuffling, bowed down with the weight of our packs, rifles slung across our backs; but we'd been lucky, only six casualties – four dead, two wounded.

The camp is in a field gently rising behind a screen of woods. We were able to wash properly at last, and tried to delouse (unsuccessfully), but at least that night we each had clean blankets. Too exhausted to sleep soundly, I again dreamt dead men's dreams, staring at the stone face of that Hun in his trench, the blue fixed eyes, grizzled jaws, open mouth. This time he wrenched my bayonet from me, using it to spear a helmet lying on the ground and swing it in the air. Inside was my head, my face gazing down, contorted. He whirled the helmet round and round and I woke up, lurching forward. I sat upright for a while, shivering, listening to the night sounds. The groaning noises from Rogers and Jimmy Foreshaw, a rustling at the corner of the tent, maybe a rat or mouse, wind whipping the tent flaps, the thud of guns. I was thankful when daylight came and with it an hour or two of warm sunshine. After stand-to, we made breakfast over a camp stove – ham, eggs, bread and tea had never tasted better.

Next morning (yesterday) the camp was swarming with men, Royal Scots, Manchesters, King's Liverpools, going up to the Front Line; others, like us, coming back. There were continuous processions along the road, and field guns and wagons. Some of the returning horses looked on the point of collapse and were thick with mud.

Our instructions came through at noon today. We would be taking Rest for three weeks, billeted at a farm near Breilly, and would leave at eight the next morning after drill.

So at last I felt relaxed enough to make some journal jottings, and today sensed the tug of poetry. A few lines only, but perhaps more will come tomorrow on the march to Breilly.

> *The woods have shoots tight-furled, breaking the soil*
> *Drawn by the logic of light, not without toil*
> *Like the worm's slow burn.*
> *Of all earth's creatures only man's insane.*

27th May
A hot day and the road to Breilly was burning under our feet. I could feel the skin shredding from my heels. Mounted officers rode alongside and tried to jolly us on, but we were subdued, no one speaking except for the occasional comment. A silence wrapped us round; the ghosts of our dead walked with us those twelve miles.

―――✺―――

Les Trois Ruisseaux
27th May 1916

My dear Elizabeth
At last I am able to send you news. I have come through my first time in action. I'm hoping your letters

will reach me soon. Our post has been held up for some unexplained reason, but we've been promised it later today or tomorrow.

We are billeted at this farm for three weeks. What a contrast to the Front Line, and how wonderful to smell the fresh earth, grass and manure. The farm has a dairy herd of golden-brown cows, hens run about and some aggressive geese.

The village is clean, a cluster of houses and farms fringing the road. We saw it first in the afternoon sunshine, the buildings all rosy, especially Les Trois Ruisseaux. The entire farm has been given over to billets, the family living in a house nearby. We're even billeted in the cowsheds which have been cleaned and fitted with new straw. Our platoon occupies two farm buildings next to the main house. We are the first platoon to arrive, others will be joining us soon. After settling in, some of our lads went off to the village to find a café, but I stayed at the farm, wanting to explore the three streams which run through it. Now perhaps I'll be able to write – a few poems are shaping in my mind. I hope to send you one or two before this rest is over.

I hope that you and Mam are enjoying these Summer days. I can picture little Lily in her sunbonnet and see you both among the flowerbeds in the Gardens. Keep up your drawing and make lots of sketches of Lily for Jack and me.

> *Love from your brother,*
> *William*

28th May

Yesterday I walked along the bank of the first stream, following it up the edge of a fallow field to where it joined another stream trickling down from a wood. The sense of peace was overwhelming but not to be trusted. Birdsong, insects buzzing, crickets singing, all nature's sounds, no hint at all of man-made noise, not even a far-distant growl of guns or nearby din of church bells. But all could be blown up in a second. I lingered on the edge of the wood, lying there in my shirtsleeves, warmed by the sun, enjoying it all, trying to disentangle the sounds, unravel the smells. Afterwards I went into the wood, a charmed place of old, twisted trees. I'm working on a poem about what I found there –

> *Today, in the heart of a wood*
> *I found the Green Man*
> *Fused to the bole of a tree.*
> *All was viridian*
> *From head to toe, and his staff*
> *On which he seemed to lean,*
> *Bright green.*
>
> *Today, when I startled the birds,*
> *Clearing a path through the copse,*
> *I found a man, green*
> *As the newly grown leaves,*
> *Phosphorescent,*
> *His rifle verdigreed.*

I was wrestling with these lines when a call came for us to go over to the farmhouse for some food. As

I entered, I heard a piano. I followed the sound to a half-opened door, guessing this to be the drawing-room of the farmhouse. I hardly dared to hope as I made out the melody – the 'Water Music'. Pushing the door back, I saw Matthew seated at a piano in the corner near a large window. He was rapt in his playing, and didn't notice me. I experienced such a surge of joy that I held back for a moment. Then he looked up, astonished to see me, stopped playing, shook his head as if in disbelief. The next moment we were hugging each other and laughing. Questions, more questions. He has a livid scar on his forehead caused by a piece of flying shrapnel. Just a cut, he says, not a Blighty wound, nor deep enough to put him in hospital, although he'd spent two days in a Casualty Clearing Station. His platoon had arrived here only an hour before, having received orders to march a day earlier than they'd expected. That evening we talked for hours, part of the time walking up towards the wood, the clear sky giving a prolonged daylight. When dusk fell at last, we could see not far away the glare of battle, the flashes and flaring arcs over No Man's Land. I confessed to him my feeling about the dead Germans, how I can't stifle my thoughts of them as someone's sons, brothers, husbands; and how I can't hate them, though I've tried to – they're acting under orders just as we are. Some of them look too young to be soldiers. He knew exactly what I meant – 'as young as our Liam, only just left school'. I asked him whether he felt love for our own men, those in his platoon. 'Yes,' he replied, 'our section's like a family.'

In the fading light I saw how gaunt he has become, the skin taut across his high cheekbones. I wanted to touch his face, feeling a great tenderness for him, but restrained myself. Then some of the others came up the field. We stood around for a while in the warm dusk, talking and smoking.

Back in the billets we sat with candles, our vests in our hands, trying to burn off the lice-eggs. Jimmy Foreshaw was enjoying catching them and cracking them between his finger-nails, making a tally of his kills. We have hopes of a change of clothing this week.

31st May
Celebration. The fresh clothing came today, and parcels and letters from home. One from Mam, a welcome few lines from Pa, and one from Elizabeth with surprising news, and also to say that she's heard from Jack by field postcard.

———

8 p.m. Les Trois Ruisseaux
My dear Elizabeth,

Congratulations! It's splendid news that you are expecting another baby. I can imagine Jack's delight on hearing this. Yes, of course I understand why you didn't tell me before I embarked. It was too early to say for sure, but now that it's official, we all have some-thing to look forward to. The first week of October – a good time, before Winter sets in. Perhaps by then the war will be over and, if not, it surely will be by the end of the year. The main thing now is to eat well, keep calm and look after yourself for the baby's sake and Lily's.

My own good news is that Matthew is here! We met up a few nights ago at the farm. Tell Mrs Riley, if you see her, how happy and well Matthew is – he's even getting in his piano practice as there's a blessed piano at the farmhouse. Today I walked with him around the entire farm until we found a little lake surrounded by trees, with an island in the middle, like the lake in Newsham Park. It was hot so we sat with our legs in the water, and just enjoyed the bliss of silence, water and sun. Also, I mustn't forget, watching the water insects and the fish – sharing Matt's delight in all this doubles my own. All was soothing and we agreed to come here for a swim as soon as we can.

I'm going over to the farmhouse tonight where we're having a bit of a party. Again, my love and congratulations.

Your loving brother, William

—⁓—

1st June

The party went on till two or three a.m. I can't remember much that happened after twelve as more bottles of wine came up from the cellar, a gift from Monsieur Marais – he, his wife and two daughters had come in earlier with bread, three roasted chickens and big round cheeses, bowls of fruit and cream. What a feast they gave us! They are in excellent spirits, not seeming to mind having to carry on their farming from the house across the fields.

After the beano, we flopped around on chairs or

cushions, drinking and smoking, while Matt played a medley of songs, rousing tunes, ones we could all sing. 'Pack up your Troubles', of course, and 'Goodbye Dolly Gray'.

—◦◦◦—

Les Trois Ruisseaux
2nd June 1916

Dear Mam and Pa,

Thanks for the parcel and letters. You can be sure that I'll thoroughly enjoy the marmalade and biscuits, rare treats. It's good to hear that you're both well and didn't catch that awful influenza. Elizabeth's news of the baby was a surprise! I hope Jack gets some leave to be with her between now and October.

I'm having a fine rest at this farm, and last night we had a party, with some of our lads entertaining us. Johnny Simms did a Vaudeville act, stringing jokes along brilliantly, some old chestnuts but also quite a few of his own – about army life. A surprise turn by Jimmy Foreshaw (from Crosby) as Charlie Chaplin, little moustache and all. He came in through the door from the kitchen, a saucepan on his head and twirling a cane, his feet in huge borrowed boots at sideways angles. Tripping over and jumping onto chairs, pursued by imaginary cops, his antics had us in fits of laughter. He pulled a string of sausages out of his pocket and one of the farm dogs leapt forward as if on cue. Jimmy fell flat on his back in true Chaplin style, the little moustache falling off and the dog on top of him. We made Foreshaw do an encore after which Sergeant Rogers got up and thanked him, saying he hadn't known before about his talent, and what a bright future lies ahead for him on the stage. We all agreed. Perhaps he'll be performing at the Hippodrome one day.

I haven't forgotten your anniversary, so look out for a souvenir I'm sending you from France.

Your loving son, William

3rd June
Today spent in drill and an unexpected route march, just to keep us fit! We groaned, but had to put on full kit and do the five miles. A visiting chaplain came this morning and gave a service, a gentle fellow with rather protruding eyes, a South Country accent and a French name – de Courcy. He offered to see us individually; some went across to him at the farmhouse, but neither Matt nor I wanted to. We both took Communion at the service, in fact everyone did.

4th June
These last three days of happiness unsurpassed, perhaps unsurpassable. I know now that the most intense moments in life are the most difficult to describe, to recapture in words. The charnel horrors at the Front. The bliss of being here with Matt.

We spend hours of each day at the lake, usually taking a small picnic of left-over bread and cheese, some fruit and wine. Swimming across to the island Matt races ahead of me, reaching the bank quickly with his energetic crawl. We sit under the willows, drying off.

I feel my exhaustion peeling off in layers. He sings
snatches of songs, arias, hums happily, then sleeps,
curled like a cat in the sun. While he sleeps I watch
him. His skin, so much darker than mine, fawn even
in Winter, and now bronzed; his hair beginning to
curl again after the last army crop, the dark brown
tinged with auburn. But the scar above his left eye is
barely healed as yet. All the dead I've seen are in his
face, his body. His face is the face of Barnes, half
sliced away, of the Hun decomposing in the wood.
A rivulet of sweat slides down his shoulder and arm.
I see his skin broken open, veins spurting blood – a
second, only a second, that's all it takes, for a bullet
to penetrate or a shell to tear apart. I've seen it
happen over and over; but although I'm accustomed
to it, I can't accept it. And there's nothing I can do to
protect him.

Today, waking suddenly, he caught me looking at
him, and asked me for my thoughts. I hesitated,
unable to express all that I was thinking and feeling.
I managed to say a few things – our time together,
how much more precious it is because of what we've
been through and what's ahead of us. Nothing in life
could mean more than these moments we have now,
all our existence gathered in, all our tomorrows
however many, however few. Our now, this very
moment, might hold eternity. Matt called me an old
philosopher, but said he liked my 'golden' ideas. 'I'll
remember them always,' he laughed, and then he
tried to distract me, quoting chunks from his Ma's
letter. I couldn't love anyone more than I love
Matthew. My love for Elizabeth is of a different kind.
She is the only woman I could love, but she belongs

to Jack. Yes, I would have married Elizabeth, and if I die and she reads this journal, I want her to know. She is my twin soul, but Matt is my challenge, my passion, as Jack is hers. I fear that telling Matt all that I feel for him might push him away. I must try to be content that we have this time together, as it might be all we have. He hasn't yet seen my poem to him, but I will make sure he has a copy before we leave.

To M.R.

We wrote our names in sand not reached by tides,
Aligned our lives to seasons and to stars.
I held you close in thoughts that banished pride
And chanced the darkness of the coming years.

Tonight he played for a few of us, the room lit by candles, played brilliantly I thought. The Brahms specially for me, rich and deep – lifting his right hand clear of the keys, long fingers suspended for a moment before plunging down to draw out the melody. He tried out some compositions he said he'd been holding in his mind, hoping they weren't a pastiche of Liszt or Chopin. It was all so expressive – quiet interludes leading me to secluded waterways, grass stirring under a Summer breeze, and then the crescendos – shelling, mortar attacks like a blast-furnace door blown open. I saw again our front-line trench, flesh spattered against the mud walls, a severed hand with a wedding ring.

11th June
Only two days left before we return to the Front

Line. The usual morning stand-to and drill in the stable yard. Captain Barrett-Hughes spoke to us about the Offensive and what lies ahead, the plan of advance, how much depends on our strength of will and fighting skills. They're calling it the Big Push. An hour of Gas Drill, what the Huns' shells sound and look like, putting on our 'improved' gas helmets, grey hoods with mica eye-holes and a tube for our mouths. Only five seconds to get them on, and there we stood looking like moths. Instructions on the dangers of the new invisible gas, the places it might linger, changes in wind direction.

We'll be making for Albert, where we'll bivouac and have our final training before moving up into position.

This afternoon was free. Matt wanted to go again to the lake. It was our last chance, as tomorrow will be drill, drill, drill and pack up your kitbags.

Lying on our stomachs on the grassy bank counting how many water insects we could find, we noticed a dragonfly that seemed to have been dipped in blood. On a reed, wings glistening, about half a finger in length, its body shone. When we tried to look more closely it flew off, a red dart skimming over the water. 'A rare breed,' Matt said. To me it seemed a portent. For days now I've been dreading the return to the Line and separation from him, the probability of the death of both of us, or one of us, and the deaths of thousands. Feeling in a trap, no power to do anything to stop the slaughter – worse than that, to have to be part of it. Kill, kill, kill! I wanted to scream, Stop! If only we could choose a champion from each side to fight it out. Like in

Arnold's poem, Sohrab fighting for the Tartars and Rustum for the Persians. No, not exactly that, not son against father, but two of equal strength and age, to save thousands. 'In single fight incurring single risk . . . The armies are drawn out, and stand at gaze.'

Matt felt my mood, guessed my thoughts. When the dragonfly flew back, hovering before us and dipping in and out of sight among the reeds, he joked about 'that ruddy insect!' Then he put his arm around my shoulder. I remember his words exactly. 'Billy, nothing you think or say or do can stop the war. We know it's lunacy. But questioning doesn't help. We're here to take orders. We don't matter as individuals.' I shook my head, about to protest, but he rushed on –

'Look. It's our fate. We were born at a time which would give us twenty years of life, some more, some less than that. It's almost as if we were being prepared, born for the war. That's it. And as the saying goes – if a bullet's got your name on it, there's nothing you can do about it.' He tugged at my hair playfully. 'Don't look into the future, Billy. What was it you said yesterday about our time together – our now? Think how happy we've been!'

The sky was darkening, big plops of thundery rain hitting the leaves. Smell of dust, wet soil and vegetation. A clap of thunder, lightning, the rain quickening, becoming torrential, tingling on our bodies. He tried to push me into the lake. I pulled him against me and we wrestled, rolling back and forth until I had him pinned down. We laughed ecstatically, laughed clinging together, clinging desperately as if never to let go.

3

As the guns fall quiet in the early hours, an eerie sound rises out of the mist across No Man's Land, a continuous screaming as if the earth itself is crying out. William shudders, huddled on the firestep of the trench, listening to the endless, nerve-shattering sound, screams from wounded and dying men, thousands lying where they have fallen.

His throat tightens, the sound cuts into his brain, he sweats with fear, certain they'll all be wiped out, the entire battalion, adding to the heaps of corpses, men mown down since the offensive began six days ago. He recalls the assurances they'd been given – that the five-day bombardment would destroy the Boche front line, their trenches, the wire, that it would put out their guns before the attack, making the first advance as safe as a walk in the park. So much for the grand plan.

Beneath the screaming, a constant groaning, the roar of a tide far out. He can't suppress the images of No Man's Land in the darkness swarming with bodies, the wounded writhing, moving like worms, trying to drag themselves back to the line before the shelling starts again and they're blown to shreds.

He feels sweat under the rim of his helmet and drenching his back, the itch of his uniform. Waiting as the hours creep towards dawn, sleep impossible. Waiting, listening to the chilling sound – he feels penetrated by it, his stomach knotted.

Six a.m. Two hours to zero. They crouch beneath the battered parapet of the trench, sandbags destroyed by German shells and bullets. Ladders are fixed in place for the short climb over the top, barbed wire taken down at exit points. His mind runs back . . . that last glimpse of Matthew, marching out with his platoon through the stone gateway of Les Trois Ruisseaux; the pact they'd made that final night not to allow themselves to think of each other once they were in action. They would seek each other out afterwards, and if the news was the worst, 'no sad songs' – Matt's command.

William takes his two last letters from his haversack, one to his mother and father, one to Elizabeth. He adds a line to the bottom of each – *You have been most wonderful parents to me* and *Thank you for sharing so much, loveliest and dearest of women*. He adds the date, 7th July 1916, folds the letters, kisses them, puts them back into the green envelopes.

The screaming invades again, this time against larksong from the low clouds. He feels his nerves disintegrating. The smell of the trench is overpowering, a choking mixture of cordite, urine, rotting waste. Nauseous, he leans against the clay wall, pretending to read his notebook. He glances to his right. Platt and Saunders, two men brought in from another platoon, sit on an upturned biscuit tin playing cards in silence, with jerky, tense movements; further on Beattie, Davies and Green are pencilling last letters, their white faces glistening with sweat; Foreshaw concentrates on his cigarette; Parker and White are on sentry duty.

Was it merely a day since they were brought up from reserve? It seems a month – trudging up the long zig-zag of the crowded communication trench, threading in single file, carrying rifles and heavy packs, sweltering in the July sunshine, followed by the supplies, ammunition, field dressings, stretcher-bearers. And passing them in the trench, the remnants of the battalion they were relieving. A straggling line of weary, dazed men who wouldn't look at them or exchange a word. Just seventy or eighty men from a battalion of nine hundred. Some were limping, stag-gering, their bandaged wounds oozing blood; some were supporting one another. Others – badly injured, mangled – were being stretchered to a dressing station at the corner of the communication trench. And a little further on he'd seen, though tried not to see, the rows of dead soldiers covered by blankets.

All the platoon had felt as he did, he knew by the grey withered look on their faces, no one smiling or joking when they reached the end of the communi-cation trench and fell in for the final inspection. And that absurd Colonel addressing them in a high-pitched voice about the privilege of serving and the honour, if it came to it, of dying for King and Country. Fat Colonel Whitely, ridiculously confident of 'a glorious victory', his cheeks flushed with the effort of bluster, wheeling his horse around and riding back to the safety of HQ at Albert.

Next, Captain Barrett-Hughes, like a Rugby team coach, had emphasised their objectives: the imme-diate one to take the first of the Boche front trenches 250 yards ahead; and then to push forward 'to secure the advantage' by taking the rising ground on the left near the town of Ovillers occupied by the enemy; and finally to push on and take Ovillers, and expect a hard fight with much bayonet work. Cold steel hand to hand, the thought of this racked William with fear, even more so when six Military Police rode up and barked their imperatives and warnings. Unquestioning obedience at all times. Deserters to be court martialled and shot. Then a list of names of those already executed, the reason, the time and place. A roll-call of the unglorious dead which echoed in their ears as each company and platoon was detailed to a position along the line.

The mist swirling across No Man's Land begins to lift. It would be better to advance under its cover, William thinks, looking at his watch. But there is still an hour to go. Breakfast is brought round – dry bread, cheese, tea in petrol cans. He can't eat or drink, feels his throat closed over, his stomach cramping. The sound comes at them again from No Man's Land, individual screams and cries now distinguishable. Then a wailing from his right, and Beattie is cringing on the duckboards, his hands over his ears. He's rocking to and fro, crying out 'Christ! Christ!' William feels himself trembling but leans down to Beattie, shelters his trembling body, pressing his head against him, trying to keep out the sound. A few moments later Lieutenant Walker arrives, one of the new officers. He drags Beattie up and shakes him, slapping his face.

'Pull yourself together, man! Come on, now. Stop it!'

Beattie howls and throws himself backwards in a fit. Walker takes him by the collar of his uniform, pulls him onto the firestep, and knocks him unconscious with an uppercut. Beattie is carried off by Walker and two of the others towards the communication trench. William slumps to the ground; Foreshaw sits with him, offering a cigarette.

'What a bloody performance,' Foreshaw scowls. 'Won't get him out of it, though.'

Green joins them. 'Poor bugger, he's had it right enough. I heard of a bloke in the Manchesters whose nerves broke like that. They said it was put on, and he was shot at dawn.'

They stand to attention for Captain Barrett-Hughes who is going from section to section giving final orders and encouragement. He exudes energy and enthusiasm, his eyes fierce above a hawk-like nose and dark moustache.

'Remember, don't slacken your pace, keep moving forward, don't stop for anyone, always forward. Eyes ahead. Mills bombs ready. Bayonets ready. 250 yards across. Take their front trench. Capture as many machine-gun posts as you can – they're the ones doing the damage. Going across you'll have cover from our barrage. Above all, don't bunch together. Keep apart. If you bunch together they'll pick you off like rabbits. Good men! You've been well-trained and you're fighting fit. Now make us proud of you!'

The order to Fall Out. Captain Barrett-Hughes moves on. His impact is immediate. The men look less fraught, primed for action. William, however, is not heartened even though he admires the Captain's qualities of leadership, doing his brave best, but already the potential target of a sniper.

A movement on the parapet above them. Perhaps

a rat, or a rag blown in the wind? It moves again, lifts slightly. A blackened hand, fingers twitching, and then a shape inching onto the parapet, a contorted face, blood-caked, one of his eyes hanging from the socket.

Foreshaw shouts as the man claws his way forward, head and shoulders now on the top of the parapet. At this moment, 7.30, the British bombardment begins. Heavy artillery behind them send shells ripping into the Boche line. The noise is a metal roar which seems suspended in the air, drowning the human sound from No Man's Land. William takes the man's arms, Green and Foreshaw lift him clear of the parapet and they lower him into the trench. He's still conscious, groaning, his breath coming in gasps. Pieces of shrapnel protrude from his face and neck. He has fouled himself. The stench of his dried blood is suffocating.

They gather round him while William pulls out a field dressing from his pack and binds the man's skull, looping the bandage as he remembers being shown in training. Davies brings a blanket and they wrap the man in it, carrying him to the bay of the trench while Green runs for the stretcher-bearers.

Red flares go up from the German line as their counter-barrage begins, shells bursting in No Man's Land, pulverising the soil, creating huge craters, but none reaching the British front trenches. The ground shakes. William feels a tremor run along the earth walls of the trench. Soon the Boche find their range and the machine-guns sweep back and forth, raking the parapets, sending soil and sand spurting.

Ten minutes to zero and Sergeant Rogers comes along with the rum, a generous ration of overproofed, treacly cupfuls which they gulp down. A wall of noise from the guns and exploding shells of both sides. William's ears hurt with the pressure, a bursting pain. He sees lightning flash and fork, but the sound of thunder is swallowed in the barrage.

Now the rain is sheeting, the trench bottom fills with water which soaks into his boots. Lieutenant Walker wades along the duckboards checking the equipment of each man in the section and the tin disks on their backs which will reflect the light, showing their gunners where they are. He adjusts William's disk, pats him on the shoulder and moves on along the trench.

'Fix bayonets!' At last the order from Walker. The clicking in unison of steel onto rifles. They wait for the whistle commanding them to go over the top. They stand in position at the foot of the ladders, two men to each, William with Platt. Again the Boche machine-guns rake the parapet, ripping up the sand-bags. William sees his mother's face; then an image of Matthew, bronzed, laughing, on the bank of the lake. He feels bile in his mouth, his throat closing over, his heart pounding with fear.

Walker, on the firestep, has his right hand up, whistle in his mouth, eyes fixed on his synchronised watch. Eight a.m. He gives the piercing signal.

At the base of the ladder William watches Platt go up, step over and arc backwards onto the parapet, blood spurting from his neck. Mechanically, William follows, parallel with Foreshaw on the next ladder. Over the top, and he moves forward across the mud, bullets zinging around him. Ahead, the swirling smoke, flames, explosions. A sensation like being out of breath after plunging into icy water. Not hit. Not killed. Not yet. He goes forward, trying to keep the pace they've been trained in, walking not too fast or too slow. Foreshaw on his left, two yards away, Green on his right. He feels naked, expecting a bullet to rip into him at any second.

Shells burst yards ahead, earth shooting up like a volcano. He moves forward, the ground uneven, every yard or so pitted with shell holes. He steps on a mound of soil, his feet sinking in, but it's not soil. It's flesh. Decomposing bodies. Christ Almighty! His feet feel bare, his skin touching the slime and putrescence. Lurching away from the corpses, he hears Walker scream 'Keep moving!' He leaps to the left to avoid a shell-hole. A hail of bullets where he would have been; one hits the rim of his helmet, glances off. Green falls.

Walker shouting, 'Go steady on the left!' A deepening of the noise overhead, airplanes flying low. The earth is a mire, pounded by rain. William slips, regains his balance. A rush of air as their heavy artillery bombards the German line, hundreds of 18 pounders hurtling to destroy the Boche. 'Keep going!' Walker shouts. Only a hundred yards now to the front trench. William glances to his left. Foreshaw is still parallel and beyond him Davies, then Saunders. Ahead, one detonation followed by another, two shells falling short, earth spurting up, five or six of their men blown to fragments.

William steps around unexploded shells from their bombardment. Not just a few, but dozens. Too many bloody duds. Then the sustained crackle of machine-gun fire from the Boche trenches tearing through their line. Davies and Saunders are hit. Walker falls, clutching his chest.

Don't stop. Keep moving forward. Walker's voice sounds in his head. William presses on. Elation. Still alive. The Boche front trench a few yards ahead. Christ! The wire's a thicket, impenetrable, not a gap in it. So much for their barrage, no bloody good. He veers parallel to the trench, uncertain what to do next. A massive explosion, and he's hurled in the air, flung backwards.

Landing in a deep hole in the earth, he's stunned, his breath shaken out. He lies against the side of the mine crater. But inch by inch he slithers down the wet earth, pulled by his weight towards the blackness at the bottom, the water rising up to claim him. He claws at the slippery soil. Nothing to grip. He grabs at his belt, pulls out his trench knife, digs it in, frantic to gain a hold, but it slices through the mud, falls from his hand, is lost somewhere below. He hears himself groaning, frightened to move as the ground vibrates. Shells wail, howling for prey before they burst. He slithers, his feet near the water now. Weariness, extreme weakness, acute pain in his shoulders, fingers numb. Can't feel. Sliding again. Christ! He sees himself face-down in the water, like a cat in a well, drowned and swollen. Desperate, he reaches up to a tree stump on the right above him, roots hanging out of the earth. He clutches the roots. They hold firm. He hangs on, slumped against the mud, feels the wet warmth of his urine soaking down his legs. A fierce thirst. Blinding rain. He tries to lick the rain from his cheeks, catch it on his tongue. He listens to the unending roar of artillery, a roar punctuated by the metal staccato of machine guns, by shrieks, shouts, detonations. He stares at a knot of worms a few feet away, wriggling in and out of the soil, brown-red-blue like intestines. They're telling me that these are my last moments, that I'll be blown to pieces any second. Worms. At least they survive when cut in half, one worm becoming two. But I'll be down there, floating in the water, a bloated corpse. He sees the worms with their blind mouths sliding in and out of his flesh, and now they're weaving towards him. Here they come! A slimy knot heaving and swinging. Medusa's head. Get away! he screams, feeling them coil around his head, one trying to enter his mouth, another licking his eyes.

Close my eyes, my mouth, don't look, don't think!

But he does think, thinks of Matthew. Christ! let him get through this. Take me, but let him live. Mustn't think of Matt, mustn't think of Elizabeth, mustn't think of love. Something else, think of something else. Can't hold on much longer, can't hold on . . . write something, occupy my mind, write it in my head . . . no poetry, just a phrase, *worms twist like barbed wire* . . .

'Billy!'

His hands are gripped, both his arms held. Foreshaw is leaning down, his beaver face covered in sweat. He feels himself being pulled upwards. Foreshaw grunts, heaves, hauls him onto firmer soil, a kind of ledge. They lie there exhausted, panting. The cool rain on his face, the percussion of the Boche shells crumping the earth, the malignant stench, the acrid air. William adjusts his steel helmet, shields his face as a cluster of shrapnel shells bursts above them, jagged metal raining down, flap flipping across the ground. Pieces fall into the crater, hit the water, sizzle.

Foreshaw nudges him. 'Close one!'

They crouch on the ledge while the counter-attack rages around them, and the crack of rifles comes close as the next wave of their men advances.

A shower of earth hits them. They lie face-down until it ceases, then sit shoulder to shoulder. William hopes the acute fear he's feeling doesn't show in his eyes.

He mumbles, 'I've lost my rifle.'

'Pick one up when we get out of this bloody hole, there's plenty lying around.' Foreshaw's slanty dark eyes are shining. 'Fucking Fritz! Our second wave's copping it now. You and me, we'll give the bastards what for.'

Get out of the crater? William breaks into a cold sweat. No! Everything within him resists, gathers into a silent scream. I don't want to fight! I don't want to kill! I don't want to move out of here! He groans, covers his face with his arms, wants to hide until the action's over, creep back later to their line.

Bullets zing-zap across the mounds of British dead. The Boche are making sure there are no survivors.

'Crafty bloody swines!' Foreshaw shouts. 'It's empty, that fucking front trench – they're all in the rear.'

He glances over the rim of the crater. Dodges down again. Bullets rake the edge, send earth spurting. The Boche machine gunner has them in his sights.

'It's that bugger over there in the second trench. On the left. We'll blast the daylights out of him. Look, I filched some grenades – I've got four. We'll bombard that bastard and the rest of the buggers. Ready?'

'Not yet. Give me a few minutes.' William is shaking as he takes two of the Mills Bombs, distrusting their casings that look as innocent as tortoise shells. He remembers Berry, grenade in his hand one moment, then bits of him hanging on the trees like flags. Mustn't fumble . . . a four second fuse! Christ!

'Now?' Foreshaw's already moving.

'What? No! We haven't planned –'

'Crawl out, aim for the second trench. If we do it at the same time we've got a better chance.'

William shakes his head. 'No. Not a better chance. It's suicidal.' His legs are weak and he's griping with fear. 'We'll be mown down.'

'Or be blown to bits if we stay here! Come on, Billy!'

'You'll go, whether or not?'

Foreshaw nods, checking his Mills Bombs, his rifle and bayonet.

'Right. I'm ready when you are,' William lies, 'but I'll need some help up the side.'

Foreshaw hauls him to the top of the crater. They ease over. In front of them bodies are mounded like sandbags, the newly killed forming a barrier, a shelter they crawl towards. William feels the viscous mud squelching, the red mud. He's wrist-deep in it and wants to vomit. Their second wave is strewn across the earth. A spray of bullets from the machine gunner strafes the dead. Foreshaw slides a rifle across to him. Wiping the mud from his fingers, William takes out the first grenade, cups it in his hand like a cricket ball. Foreshaw hisses 'Now!' William trembles as he draws out the pin, slings the grenade towards the second Boche trench, then the other in swift succession. Detonations. Silence. No retaliation.

They dash forward between the heaps of dead men. The wire of the front trench is mangled and broken. Gaps. They leap through and across to the parapet of the second trench. Foreshaw screams 'Fucking termites!' and jumps in. William follows. The machine gunner's sprawled across his station, stomach ripped open, smoke billowing from exploded ammunition. Further down the trench five or six Germans are slumped, some with head or limbs blown off, and Foreshaw is stabbing his bayonet into them, frenzied, turning and disembowelling. William's legs buckle, he's dazed, heart and head pounding. He sinks to the duckboards. The trench spins. The dead Germans spin, their dismembered arms and legs whirl in a vortex.

'They're on the run,' Foreshaw shouts. 'Dirty fucking Huns! There they go, what's left of them. Into the woods.'

'Get down, Jimmy!' William knows he's risking a sniper's bullet as he looks over the parados.

'Posh trench,' Foreshaw grins, jumping down. Solid duckboards and cladding of pine on each side give the effect of a corridor, with a neatly constructed entrance to a dug-out. Foreshaw dives in and reappears moments later lugging two German packs.

'Like a bloody hotel in there!' He drops the packs on the duckboards then crouches over them, opens one and brings out fingerless leather gloves, a safety razor, chocolate, cigarettes, a mouth organ which he runs across his lips.

'Booby traps!' William gasps the words out. Foreshaw gingerly moves away from the packs and slips the mouth organ into his top pocket.

A clammy pall of mist swirls over the trench. William wipes the wetness from his face. His hand is red, smeared with blood. He's drenched in blood, uniform and puttees sticky. Foreshaw is a blur in the red mist. Christ! William smells blood, tastes it on his lips. He's sinking, wants to let go. Foreshaw runs to him, his face a mask of blood. 'Billy!' The voice seems to come from far off; the trench is a red tunnel without an exit.

Water in his mouth. When he comes to, Foreshaw's holding him, trickling the water down his throat until the bottle's empty. Shouts and confusion, men surging into the trench, up and over, rifle cracks. The Boche? William struggles to get up.

'It's all right, Billy. It's our next wave, they're going after bloody Fritz.'

Foreshaw hauls him back across No Man's Land, at times dragging him, at times carrying him on his shoulders. He sees the ground humping up and Foreshaw's boots as he squelches through the mud. There's the familiar stench of cordite and putrifying flesh. The very air is exhausted. Choking smoke but the guns silent now. Screams and moans of the wounded, agonised cry answering cry, bodies every-where. Some are twitching, others raise themselves on their arms, fall again, some are crawling, creeping, inching their way back.

Foreshaw is panting, sweating. They rest against an abandoned supplies wagon, its wheels sunk in the mud, a dead horse slumped in the shafts.

'Billy, not far to go now. We're nearly there, lad. Think of it, just think of it, cigarettes and rum, tin-can-tea and bully beef.'

He tries to reply, but can't. He watches the clouds making their slow progression across the sky, dull grey clouds hanging low, but the rain has ceased. He's parched, pulls out his water bottle. 'Battalion bread and scrape'll do, just as long as we're in one piece.'

Foreshaw starts to sing, 'Blast the bleedin' Prussians –'

'You two all right?' Four stretcher-bearers come towards them.

'Yes, we're A1. What about 'im over there?' Foreshaw points to a man crouched on his knees nearby, his hands pressed together as if in prayer.

The stretcher-bearers run across, check him, lift the kneeling statue onto a stretcher. One covers the body with a sheet. Red Cross vans crawl over the mud, stopping every few yards to collect the wounded.

Foreshaw stands up, helps William to his feet. They pick their way through the bodies, William staring at each one they pass or step around.

'Oh, God!' He bends down. Is this Matthew, fallen face-down across his rifle, his helmet blown off? The familiar shape of Matthew's head, his dark hair. William groans, turns the man over, sees shrapnel severing his throat, stares at the dead face. It isn't him.

'Come on, Billy!' Foreshaw pulls him up. They join the men limping or dragging themselves back to the line. A watery sunlight breaks through.

4

'Parker?'

There was no reply.

'Parker.' Captain Barlow, small, wizened, newly in charge, shuffled his papers. 'Does anyone know anything about Parker?'

Silence again.

'Missing.' Barlow wrote the unofficial M next to Parker's name.

The exhausted men stood for Roll Call. William looked along the row at the remnants of the platoon. Only a dozen or so out of sixty. Captain Barrett-Hughes dead, Lieutenant Walker dead. Where was Matthew? The agony of not knowing, of not being able to find out because Matthew's platoon was further down the line.

'Platt?'

'Killed, sir,' Sergeant Taylor said promptly.

'Are you absolutely sure?'

'Yes, sir. He was hit on the parapet and died in the trench shortly after, sir.'

'Plessey?'

It seemed to William that the very names pierced the air with accusations, counterpointed by the undersound of earth being sliced and turned by the spades of the gravediggers he saw working away behind them, their bodies gleaming with sweat.

'Manderson?'

'Present, sir.'

'Norris?'

No reply.

'Does anyone know anything about Norris?'

'Missing.'

William's nerves bucked at Captain Barlow's fact-finding, his clipped tones. An officer was trained to hide his emotions, but Barlow . . . he was going too far. The bastard, so detached, cold to the suffering and deaths.

'O'Neil?'

Sergeant Taylor looked at his list. 'Killed, sir.'

'Is that certain?'

'Yes, sir. Body recovered.'

'Ratcliffe?'

No reply.

Does anyone know anything about Ratcliffe?'

'Yes, sir,' shouted Foreshaw. 'His 'ead blown off, sir. I think 'e was killed.'

Captain Barlow ignored Foreshaw's sarcasm. 'You're quite sure it was Ratcliffe?'

'I'd know his 'ead anywhere, sir.'

Some of the men gave a grim laugh, others looked uncomfortable.

Sergeant Taylor reddened. 'Enough of that, Fore-shaw!'

William saw Barlow's facial muscles tighten, his eyes flicker like a lizard's. He wrote something at the top of the page.

'Rogers?'

'Dead, sir.' Private Miller's voice was scarcely aud-ible.

'Are you sure? Where? How? Speak up, man!'

'It was 'alf way across, sir. Tim went down –'

'Rogers went down. Carry on.'

''E was shot, sir. Didn't . . .' Miller broke down, sobbing.

'Pull yourself together. How do you know that Rogers was, in fact, killed?'

Miller collapsed, weeping, screaming and shaking uncontrollably. At a signal from Barlow, he was led away by two Red Caps.

'Sadistic bugger!' Foreshaw spoke in an undertone.

William pulled at his sleeve. 'Leave it, Jimmy!'

The Roll Call continued . . . Thompson, Turner, Underwood, Vernon. Up and down the row Barlow strutted until he came to the end of the list. He stopped in front of Foreshaw, gave him a hard stare, then moved on down the line.

'Dismiss!' Sergeant Taylor bellowed.

They trudged along the communication trench as if sleep-walking. Together with men from other battalions who'd been in action that day, they were detailed to the rest trenches behind the line. William followed Foreshaw who was lumbering on and occasionally glancing back at him. Now it was their turn to receive shocked glances from troops passing them on their way up. Was it only yesterday that they themselves had marched up? It seemed another lifetime.

They emerged from the zig-zag of the trench. Sergeant Taylor led them past the Casualty Clearing Station where rows of wounded men on stretchers were waiting for attention. William paused. Matthew could be among them. A push from behind. He was forced to move on. Taylor bawled out instructions to keep together, to keep up, and doubled back to check and chivvy.

Another mile or so, beyond the supply wagons, the depots and horses, they arrived at the rest trenches in open ground. Someone had placed the home-made signs 'The Ritz' and 'Park Lane' on two of the trenches. Shallow bivouacs, like earth cradles, William thought, or graves, in which they were to sleep, the only comfort a heap of lice-infested blankets. Most men dropped with exhaustion and were asleep within moments. Others lay there with lit cigarettes, some took off their boots and tunics. William ripped off his tunic, stiff with caked mud and stinking of dried blood.

Another rum ration came round and, later, the field kitchen arrived, serving lukewarm potatoes, a dubious meat. He couldn't eat much, although Foreshaw and some others said how good it tasted. Sickening images kept surfacing in his mind, of men with their faces blown off, bodies without heads, limbs without bodies, and the sensation of sinking into dead flesh. He was still slightly dizzy and disorientated. Trying to regain equilibrium, he focused on his surroundings.

The trenches were close to a wood on rising ground, its trees shattered by shells, blasted, blackened. He could see the town of Ovillers in the distance, clustered on another small hill, and the woods to the right of it into which the Boche had retreated. A successful advance, they'd been told by Barlow, an advance consolidated by their support infantry. What were they supposed to feel about this 'success'? A sense of triumph?

A raucous sound rose from the nearby wood. As he watched, the blackened branches moved, and a wild clacking tore the air. Magpies fought each other to gain possession of something they were tearing. Human flesh perhaps, the magpies vying for the eyeballs. Higher, over the wood, a hawk was circling. If it swept down on No Man's Land, what a feast it would have. William felt the earth spin. Was he going insane? He lay down, staring at the wall of the trench.

After stand-to that evening, the men sat outside the trenches around the little fires they'd made out of ammunition boxes. Even though the evening was warm the fires gave them a cheery focal point, a hearth of sorts. Some, including Foreshaw, were chasing chats, killing as many of the lice as they could find on their clothing, running candle flames along the seams of shirts, vests, trousers. From time to time Foreshaw serenaded them tunelessly on his souvenir mouth organ.

In the glow from the fires William noticed a very young face among the men who'd joined them from the remnants of another battalion. The lad was pensive, watching them chasing lice but not laughing at the bawdy jokes.

'Are you from Cheshire?' William asked.

'No. Yes. Not really. Bury. I'm from Bury.'

'Ciggy?'

'Thanks.'

As William lit a Woodbine he saw the blond down on the lad's upper lip, the trembling fingers. He looked no older than seventeen.

'I'm Manderson.' A formal handshake.

The lad blinked, then stammered 'Sullivan.'

They talked about home, Sullivan's words tumbling out, at first hesitant, then unstoppable. William found it difficult to interject, but was rather relieved just to listen as Sullivan hurried on. He spoke of the Lancashire mill town where he'd been orphaned and brought up by his grandmother, the shock of her death when he was nine, being taken by an uncle to Chester and put into an orphanage there. The Army seemed an escape, a promise of regular food and clothing, friends even.

If I was to die tomorrow, William thought, I've known what this lad never has. Dear Mam and Pa, Elizabeth – security, friendship – Matthew. Something of Matthew in Sullivan's smile . . . yes, the way his face crinkled as he laughed.

In the near distance flares lit the dusk, guns thudded and a stray shell or two burst close by, reminding them that the rest trenches were within range of the Huns' artillery. Sullivan began to shake, his thin face shone with sweat. William lit another cigarette and placed it in Sullivan's lips.

'The buggers!' Foreshaw shouted.

Eventually the sky quietened and they turned in. Unable to sleep, William's mind returned again and again to the Boche trench. Were his grenades the ones which had killed those men? The machine gunner, with his stomach gouged out, his fingers hanging on threads of flesh, his pale face and mouth open in a last agony, his big teeth. Yes, he'd definitely killed him, sure of the accuracy of his aim, something praised during training. And those other horribly mutilated Germans, one with both legs blown off. His grenades or Foreshaw's? Now he was a barbarian himself, he'd killed, extinguished viciously, fulfilled his function. A coward, too. It was only for Foreshaw that he'd moved out of the crater. Never again did he want to put on that rancid tunic or hold a rifle, still less a rifle with fixed bayonet. He pulled his notebook from the pack and sharpened a pencil with his pocket knife.

———✺———

7th July
I can't write yet of what I've seen today. No Man's Land, like nothing I've ever known or could have imagined.

What I can write about is mud. Yes, mud.

I think there is little now that I don't know about mud. My earliest memories are of mud in the road churned by carts, mud mixed with slush and horse-dung. My second Winter, the ruts massive, deep like waves, I'm running, Mam calling me back, I'm out of control, running downhill into Everton Road, excited by the great wheels of the carts and carriages, the freedom. A large, whiskered man smelling of beer catches me up in his arms. Mam's relief, her tears, her scolding. And the innocent mud of the fields in Flintshire and Denbighshire, the ploughed fields with their splendid, corduroy lines of earth, the regularity of their pattern, and learning to walk behind the plough with Uncle Iolo, creating those lines, shaping the muddy earth. And the estuarine mud of the Mersey, with a character all its own, dense, grey-brown, contoured like a relief map, smelling of salt and urine and oil.

But the Somme mud, the mud of No Man's Land, is malign, taking into itself the very pith of human life, nourished on blood and bones. This stinking mud, I'm lying in it now, although this is where the earth has hardened. After the rain ceases, the clay has a chance to solidify, but only on the surface. There's a crust forming, but underneath it the liquid clay waits to be replenished, to receive the slaughtered, to absorb them into itself. No chance for the earth of No Man's Land ever to become dust . . . 'to dust returneth', ironical, to earth returneth. The earth beneath my fingernails, black earth and blood. Whose blood beneath my nails?

———✣———

The next morning after drill, fresh drafts were brought in to build the battalion numbers up to strength. Before regrouping went on, William made his way along the rest trenches until he recognised some men from Matthew's platoon.

'Private Riley? Private Matthew Riley?' Williams's voice was choked. 'Doesn't anyone know anything?

The men stared at him.

'Your name?' An officer holding papers came up the trench.

William saluted. 'Private Manderson, sir.'

'A friend of Riley?'

'Yes, sir.'

'I'm sorry to tell you he's missing.'

William's heart seized up.

'No other information, I'm afraid.'

'Missing,' and all it implied, all the deaths he'd seen. So many 'missing'. Slowly, William returned to his bivouac and threw himself down on the blankets. He pulled his pack across, using it as a pillow, covered his face with his hands, and lay there, a knife twisting inside him, an icy knife through his heart and stomach. Matthew could be dead or out there in agony, waiting for the stretcher-bearers to find him. William wanted to get up, go back to the Line, search the Dressing Posts, Casualty Clearing Stations, Red Cross vans. Trapped by orders, unable to move away from the platoon, he'd never before felt so controlled, so regimented. The inhumanity, the degradation of battle. Matt had accepted it more readily than he had. That fatalistic attitude – 'if a bullet's got your name on it' – helped him to keep going. But no, survival wasn't fate but chance. In battle they were like clay pigeons tossed in the air to be shot down. Yet he had to keep hoping that Matt would be found. Many of the missing did turn up. Even now their names were being gathered by the CCS orderlies.

He was in a stupor. Where was Foreshaw? He wanted to talk to Foreshaw. Looking around, he saw that the rest trenches were empty. He became aware of yells and shouts coming from a few fields away where his platoon was playing football. He couldn't bring himself to join them, couldn't read, couldn't keep his mind off the fact that Matthew was missing. Eventually two of the men, Foster and Leigh, came back and dropped, exhausted, into the trench.

'Is Foreshaw over there?' William pointed towards the football match.

'No. He's had bad news,' Foster said, frowning. 'His brother's been killed.'

William was shaken. 'Where is he now?'

Neither of the men knew. 'He'll be around here somewhere. Took it badly.'

William found Foreshaw sitting alone near the latrines. He was sobbing and moaning.

'Jimmy, I've just heard about Ben.' He bent over and put his arm around Foreshaw's shoulders. 'What bloody rotten luck. I'm so sorry.'

The sobbing became convulsive. William could just make out the words, 'Ma, poor Ma,' over and over. He tried to break through with news about Matthew but Foreshaw was beyond listening.

After five minutes he decided to get help. Jimmy needed a stiff drink. He'd find an NCO, perhaps Taylor. But there was no one about when he reached the trench. Everyone was still at the football. He hurried back to Foreshaw. He wasn't there, or anywhere nearby. The wood, perhaps he went there. William hesitated, unsure now whether to seek him out. Perhaps he needed to be alone.

Back at the trench again, William found Sullivan crouched over his kit, trying to sort it. A surprise inspection might catch the lad out, and punishment would follow.

'Here, let me do it.' He was trying to keep busy, keep his mind occupied while constantly looking out for Foreshaw. The platoon returned to the bivouacs and tea came around, a hot brew he was grateful for but immediately spilt. Damn! He stared at his shaking hands and the liquid running in long worms across the earth of the trench.

Foreshaw had not come back. Another hour passed and his absence was noted and reported by Taylor. The search party didn't take long to find him. He was on the road to Albert. And worse – he'd discarded his tunic.

With several others from his platoon, William waited near the officers' HQ.

Two Military Police came out, holding a sullen-looking Foreshaw. Then Captain Barlow and three officers, one of them a major. William's anger flared as the Red Caps dragged Foreshaw away to the Guard Room.

'Sir.' He stepped forward and saluted Barlow. 'Private Foreshaw heard this morning that his brother's been killed. He took it badly. I found him very upset and shaking. I think he didn't know what he was doing when he wandered off, sir.'

Barlow seemed not to have heard, his face a mask.

'Sir,' he persisted. 'Private Foreshaw's not a coward. He would never desert. He –'

Barlow glared at William. 'Foreshaw will have a chance to explain himself in the morning. At the Court Martial.'

'I was with him, sir. I know. I can vouch for his bravery in action. He saved my life twice. He planned and carried out an attack on the enemy, taking the trench and killing six or seven Huns. The machine gunner –'

'Enough! I've only got your word for this. I have no

report. No evidence.' Barlow raised his eyebrows. 'And even so, even if what you say is true, it doesn't cancel out Foreshaw's desertion today.'

'Sir. If an officer had taken that trench he'd have an MC by now.'

'Don't be smart, Manderson. Try it again and I'll have you up for insubordination. I'll have you Court Martialled.'

William persisted. 'Can I be a witness for Foreshaw?'

'Sir!'

'Can I speak in his defence, sir?'

'No!' Barlow smirked. 'The Firing Squad. I'll need ten from the battalion. I've just selected you. Be ready. Dawn tomorrow.'

For the rest of that afternoon William lay in his bivouac, seething at the brutality of Army procedures, wanting desperately to speak at Foreshaw's hearing, but powerless to do anything about it. Killing Huns was a duty, 'serving King and Country', but killing a friend, this he could not, would not do. He would refuse. So be it. Court Martial. He kept seeing the crater and Foreshaw's cheery face beaded with sweat, kept feeling the grip of Foreshaw's hands dragging him out of the water, yanking him from the Huns' trench and back across No Man's Land.

Unable to concentrate, he recorded the date in his journal, 8th July.

His eye was caught by a movement on the sand-bags at the top of the trench. He thought it was a small bird. Creeping nearer he saw that it wasn't a bird but a moth, the largest moth he'd ever seen. It fluttered away towards the trees and settled on a splintered branch. William watched its zig-zag flight and climbed out of the trench. He followed it into the wood because this was what Matt would have done, what they would have done together. Oh, Christ! where was Matt now! Not dead, please not dead! Images of his mutilated body kept surfacing, overlaying images of Foreshaw, blindfolded, tied to a stake. He forced himself to note the moth's markings, skull-like on its thorax, the black and orange stripes of its under-wings. The Death's Head Hawk moth! The rare moth Matthew had told him about and shown him in a book. An omen. The moth seemed to be staring back at him. It moved off, from branch to branch, a splash of colour on the blackened stumps. As he watched, the moth's wings drooped, closed up, and it fell to the ground. William turned it over, wondering at its beauty, its sudden death.

What could have caused it to wilt and die like that? He looked around the scorched leaves and twigs on the ground, intending to bury it, save it from the magpies. Beside a fallen bough he saw several shells nestled in the earth. A blurring of the air, vague smell of musty hay. God! That's it! Gas!

Hurtling back to the trench, he saw that the men had returned. He leapt in across the sandbags, shouting 'Gas! Gas!' and banged hard on the impro-vised alarm, a pan which hung from the sign 'Park Lane'. His pack, where was his pack! Panic until he found it under his blanket, scrambled out the gas helmet and pulled it over his head, pushing the grey flannel down inside the collar of his tunic. No gaps. Disorientation at first, looking through the goggles like swimming underwater. An alien sea. And there in its waves stood Sullivan, bewildered, petrified like a trapped rabbit. Clumsy with haste, he hauled the mask out of Sullivan's pack and rammed it over his head. Seizing him by the arm, he dragged Sullivan along the trenches behind six or seven others, all with masks on. Gas, at the whim of the wind, like fire. The wind a weapon, the Boche's estimate of its direction and velocity deadly accurate.

William ran, blood pounding in his ears. The lethal new gas, how long had he breathed it in? Captain Barrett-Hughes had warned them. Colourless. No visible sign, and no effects for a while. An hour at least before he'd know, before, perhaps, he'd begin to die.

They sat together on the barren earth, lolling on each other or lying flat out near the Casualty Clearing Station. About thirty or more, some of them from adjacent trenches, brought to this patch of ground by a medical orderly and Red Cross helpers. Sullivan, white-faced and shivering with fear, leaned against him. But William was unable to offer comforting words. For him, the waiting was over.

He gasped for breath. His nausea came in strengthening waves. Hot, sweating, palpitating. His stomach in violent cramps, poisonous froth in his throat, mouth, nose. Writhing in pain, choking, vomiting, he was stretchered into the tent. Lifted onto a bed, gurgling, struggling to breathe. Screens around his bed, someone – a doctor – making him bend over the side, more vomiting, spewing out bitter yellow fluid, filling a bowl, then another and another. Trying to breathe, drowning, his eyes stinging, clouding over. Oh God, my eyes! Two nurses held him down; he felt his hands being tied to the sides of the bed. Each of his eyelids was rolled back, something dropped in. Boiling water. William heard his own screams, the burning pain in his eyes intolerable. Fluid filling his lungs again, gushing from his mouth and nose. His mouth forced open, something poured in, searing his throat and chest. Smell of ammonia. The Boche were finishing him off . . .

He came round. He could see, thank God! But with each painful breath his lungs gurgled, the froth choking him. Again, bouts of vomiting, greenish fluid shooting from his mouth. A damp cloth cooling his brow, wiping his face. He became aware of a nurse sitting at his bedside. Excruciating pain in his eyes as he tried to look sideways, blurred vision. He moved his hands. Untied now. Cries and groans all around; a body carried out, covered by a sheet; more wounded brought in.

A doctor came over. 'We're going to give you oxygen, Manderson.'

Gasping for air, a bit of air. This is it, he thought. I'm going to die. They'll send my things home. Elizabeth will read my journal, my poems. Let Jack survive all this, take care of her. Dear Mam!

The oxygen mask over his face. Shapes distorting like in a fairground mirror. The nurse a white flame, her hands guttering, she is a moth flying out of the light, obliterating the light. The Death's Head Hawk moth. The ghost of the moth.

* * *

Vomiting every hour or so, pints of the yellow fluid pouring out, bowls full of it, his lungs were shutting up, he was drowning in water. Oxygen, more oxygen.

Hours, days, his breathing short and searing, he feared his heart would stop. Then gradually an easing, drawing breath less painful.

'You're going to pull through,' the nurse said, taking his pulse and smiling.

He was able to look around him but saw no one he recognised.

'The others?' His throat hurt, his voice a croak.

'You were the worst affected. They were mostly not too bad, just a few of them slightly poisoned, and they've been sent on for convalescence.'

'Sullivan?'

'That young one? Too young.' She frowned. 'He's been sent to Number 2 Field Hospital. Lucky lad. He'll be right as rain in a few weeks. He was telling me you saved him.'

Thank God, Sullivan safe; and he'd be out of it for a while. William's mouth, as he tried to smile, was acutely painful, his lips cracked.

'My pack?'

The nurse pointed to the side of his bed. 'It's there, safe and sound. Brought in yesterday. Easy now!' She pulled him back as he tried to look over the side. 'Gently does it! No rushing round for you for quite a while! Now take my word for it, you're likely as not to be sent back to Blighty. But hospital first at Boulogne.

'And, God bless you, you'll be on your way tomorrow.'

* * *

73

They placed him on a stretcher and carried him to a row of waiting ambulances and wagons draped with Red Cross banners. His eyes hurt in the sunlight, but he was desperate for fresh air. Would his lungs hold out? He feared they'd rip apart under the strain of coughing. They lifted him into an open wagon and loaded his pack up beside him. Attended by VADs, the convoy of wounded moved off along the cratered road to Albert, some of the severely injured crying out with each jolt. The road swarmed with columns of men marching to and from the front line, officers on horseback, carts loaded with supplies, guns, ammunition.

They had gone only a few hundred yards when, through the slats of the wagon, William glimpsed a familiar figure. Could it be? Were his eyes deceiving him, creating phantoms? Foreshaw, strapped hand and foot to the wheel of a gun carriage, was spreadeagled, tied by his wrists and ankles to the spokes. Crucifixion! Field Punishment Number One! William felt a surge of anger. Foreshaw had escaped execution, but this was sadism. He'd have to go through three weeks of it, pinioned to a wheel for hours every day, stripped to his vest, exposed to blazing sun or rain, humiliated as an example to others.

William tried to raise himself on the side of the wagon, wanting to wave to Foreshaw. But his strength failed and he fell back. Coughing and choking, his eyes blurring, he saw the crucified figure through a mist as the wagon moved on.

5

The convoy swung off the road near Albert and over rutted ground, stopping in front of a cluster of tents and huts. Medical orderlies and helpers thronged around, lifting the wounded out of the vehicles, placing them in rows along the soil. William felt sick as they hoisted him from the wagon and carried him on his stretcher to the earthy bank. The wounded were neatly laid out, like the rows of wooden crosses he'd seen in a wayside cemetery. At this very second, and from early morning without a pause, the individual butchery was going on, the slaughter he saw every time he closed his eyes. The graveyard of No Man's Land filling up. He wanted to weep but couldn't, and lay listening to the incessant rumble of guns, like a thunderstorm rolling around the sky. He flicked a bluebottle off his leg, one of a swarm of flies that descended on the injured.

Eventually a doctor came and examined each man. He bent over William, reading the details on the label pinned to his tunic.

'Gassed. Phosgene, possibly mixed with something else. One of the nastier of the new gases, I'm afraid. Seems you got quite a dose of it.'

He examined William's throat and eyes, checked his pulse. 'Vomiting subsided?'

He nodded.

'Right, Manderson. You'll be moved to Amiens this afternoon. Rest overnight, then Boulogne tomorrow. But not Blighty just yet.'

He marked the label and moved on to the next man. William tilted the label and saw the large C for Convalescence. He lay there for another half-hour, the flies and the heat intensifying. In the hazy distance, he could see the famous statue of the Virgin and Child leaning from the tower of the bombed basilica. Toppled, hanging precariously, parallel to the ground, at a crazy angle in this crazy war. He'd heard the superstition that if the Leaning Virgin fell the war would soon end, but the side that knocked her down would lose.

At last the stretcher-bearers arrived and carried him and his pack over to the waiting motor ambulances, a line of motley vehicles each with a large red cross painted on the roof and sides. He was taken to a converted van and slotted inside. Three other men were already in there, two more placed alongside him before they moved off, sweltering in the midday heat. Images kept recurring of Foreshaw strung out on the wheel, pinioned like a specimen moth. He'd be tied so tight that he couldn't move, not even a fraction, the greedy blowflies alighting on his face and body, crawling over him. Alive, but the cramp and pain would set in quicker each day. They'd all been warned that this was part of the punishment. Not only that, but he'd be imprisoned in the Guard House, deprived of food. Bread and water only, day after day. And, of all the lads, it was Jimmy who enjoyed Army rations, relishing anything served up. Let him keep strong, let him survive.

The stifling air of the ambulance brought on a coughing fit. William's throat was burning, he longed for cool water. He gasped like a landed fish. Next to him, a man with stomach wounds screamed every time the ambulance jolted over a rut. Jesus! Hours to Amiens.

Red Cross helpers came round at each stop, with bowls of water and cloths, briskly wiping the brows and bodies of the wounded. To William their hands were moving like flies' feelers, industrious, purposeful. Others carrying water and mugs went from ambulance to ambulance. Water. Sweet Jesus, miraculous water! He tried to say thanks but no sound came out. Like his eyesight, his voice was fading, coming back, fading.

A halt close to a farm, in the shade cast by a long high wall and a row of poplars. The farmer and two women brought out churns of milk on a cart, pulling it along the line of dusty ambulances. He watched as the injured eagerly received the fresh milk and quaffed it down. He refused it, fearing he'd vomit; thin soup and some bread were all he'd managed in recent days. Those who could walk got out and sat beneath the trees. He struggled up, propping himself against the open door at the back of the ambulance. The afternoon was heavy. He couldn't get enough air. Never again would he take breathing for granted.

Droning, a sound like heavy insects, coming closer. An airplane, swooping so low he could see the black cross on the tail and the pilot holding out a bomb then hurling it down onto the convoy. Christ Almighty! It detonated to their right, shaking the ground, opening it up like an earthquake. Then another to their left, a direct hit on one of the farm buildings. Another blew up an ambulance. Another exploded in the field that bordered the road. William flung himself down, arms protecting his head.

The roar of the plane receded. He heard a shrill neighing scream of horses. Then silence. He peered through swirling smoke and dust. In the confusion medical orderlies rushed about shouting instructions and helping the men back into the ambulances. One was trying to calm down the farmer who ran about, his hands clasped to his head, screaming hysterically.

'Two horses gone west.' A Red Cross driver peered in, checking out their ambulance. 'No one killed or injured, but one ambulance destroyed. Sheer bloody luck nobody was in it.' He wrote something in a small notebook. 'Sorry, lads, we've got to pack you together even more tightly now, being as how we're one short. Blame Fritz!'

Soon another stretcher was squeezed in alongside William. He looked closely at the wounded man, again hoping to see Matthew. The man's head was heavily bandaged, blood oozing through; one of his legs, in a makeshift splint, was obviously broken. William tried to see his face, but the ambulance jerked as the convoy trundled forward and a coughing spasm seized him. When this subsided, he tried again, lifting himself on one elbow to stare at the newcomer. He recognised the man with his heavy black eyebrows and Spanish eyes as one of their battalion stretcher-bearers.

Touching the man's arm, William rasped out 'Greaves! Tell me –'

'If I can.'

'It's about Riley, B Company. Have you heard anything . . . seen him?'

'Can't help. A hell of a lot of us are gone, you know that. I helped to bring in about fifty before I copped it. Didn't see Riley, though.'

William lay back, despair seeping through him. Images, and one in particular, kept surfacing, of Matt's face when he was playing the piano at Les Trois Ruisseaux, his rapt look, his long fingers conjuring the Water Music. The intensity of his expression, mirrored in the black wood of the piano, mirrored in the lake during their last hour together.

Amiens at last. William peered through the open rear doors of the ambulance as they wound through the cobbled narrow streets towards the cathedral looming over the grey houses. Incongruous, he thought, like a cuckoo bulging out of a nest. They passed close to its West Front encrusted with statues, its great walls padded by sandbags, and then swung down to the BEF's railhead in the field below, stopping in front of the canvas hospital.

He was deposited in the field with a line of other wounded, but Greaves and a few more were taken into the nearest tent.

'You might have to wait a while,' a slender young VAD apologised. 'The beds is all full, you see. Only the surgical cases is going in now, those as is urgent. You're in a queue, and as soon as a bed comes empty one of you gets it.'

'What you mean, lass, is when someone's Jesused!'

shouted a man with a Kitchener moustache. The VAD flushed and went inside.

William was not sorry to be left out in the early evening sun. The bite of the afternoon heat was gone; a gentle, somnolent warmth pervaded, something resembling peace, except for the midges that whirled around his stretcher, and the frenetic activity at the railhead, trains coming in packed with new drafts for the Front, khaki puppets jumping to attention on the platform, marching off, automated. High cloud gathered over the cathedral, through which the slanting rays of the sun penetrated and moved as if someone was slowly swinging a lantern. Magnificent and massive, the Gothic building was untouched by bombs or flame. What a contrast to battered Albert, the basilica now a mere shell – but the Virgin was still intact, still hanging on, leaning out high in the air, holding aloft the child Jesus. A symbol, depending on your viewpoint, of either tenacious faith or shattered religious belief. God, his glorious design for man, his mercy! A lie, at best a naive hope. How could faith survive this carnage, the agony of all those personal losses? War was a truth teller. He felt himself sinking, weak and faint now, feverish . . . if Matthew was dead he wanted oblivion.

He looked again at the cathedral in the fading light, a cliff face, an enormous grey rock rising sheer from a sea of dead bodies.

The stretcher-bearers carried him through several wards and put him onto a mattress on the floor, where he was to wait for a bed to be vacated. He was burning up now, his fever rising, his skin itching all over. A VAD washed him and took away his lice-laden shirt and vest. The bed, when at last he was put into it, was one of twelve in the ward. Pillows, soft and cool as Mam's cheeks, thin cotton sheets, now he would sleep. Perhaps an hour passed or less, when voices and disturbance in the ward brought him round. Someone in the corner was shouting. Screens around a bed, orderlies coming and going.

'Poor bugger. He's got gangrene, stinking gangrene. They'll operate now.' The man in the next bed, florid and gingery, was speaking to one of the others, but turned to William.

'You're going to be OK, lad. That sleep did you good, eh? I'm Driscoll. What's yours?'

William pushed back his sheet. 'Manderson.'

'Funny sort of name. I've never heard it before. Mine's Irish but I'm from Stepney, born and bred.'

His head ached. Driscoll's voice twanged on . . . and on.

'Watcher got in there?' He pointed to William's chest. 'Sounds like a cat purring. Kitty cat. Crackly chat. That's you, init, lad? Never mind, you're a certainty for Blighty.'

William made an effort to talk, wheezing and sweating. 'And you?'

'Thought I'd gone west, didn't they. Face-down in the mud, unconscious. Got me in the leg, see, and I passed out with the pain. An SB saved me, saw I was breathin', like. Got me out. The leg's chopped up though. Like a piece of pork. I'm waiting for them to operate, ankle shattered an' all. That's the chopping room, next door.'

Driscoll indicated the ward next to theirs, a canvas annexe. He chattered on, but kept looking nervously at the entrance to the operating room. William realised he was in a funk and talking to hide it.

A nurse went by with a covered pan. Driscoll vomited. A VAD saw him retching and fetched a mop and bucket, swiftly cleaning up the mess. Afterwards she brought fresh sheets, settling Driscoll down. He looked across at William.

'Bloody smell did it, didn't it? Putrid. It's bad enough in this ward as it is, what with the gangrene cases.'

William couldn't smell the ward. He tried to inhale the stench, sealing his mouth with his hand, sucking the air in deeply through his nose. Nothing. Not even the smell of his own hand.

He woke with a jolt, his heart palpitating. Still alive . . . frightened to sleep again in case his heart stopped. The middle of the night, a nurse walking by, carrying an oil lantern. Driscoll gone, another man in his place, bandaged, moaning.

The nurse came over to William, put the lantern down, took his temperature.

'Good,' she whispered.

'Driscoll?' he asked.

'Recovering. We operated two hours ago. He's fine. In the Resuscitation Ward.'

The glow of light through the canvas, shadowy figures moving, some standing still . . . the operating room. Working on through the night, all day and all night, every day and every night, operations in all the hospitals, many hospitals, not enough hospitals . . .

He drifted off into a restless sleep, dreaming of the dead horses, the cathedral turning into a waterfall. He kept coming to consciousness and slipping away again. A VAD crept through the ward carrying something with care, something she was holding out in front of her, something wrapped up, a foot protruding. Was he dreaming? He hoped he was dreaming. He'd seen legs, arms, heads scattered across No Man's Land, promiscuously flung. But this was more horrific, this clinical sawing off, the man held down in agony. Screams pierced the ward. No, it wasn't a dream.

Early light, a pink hue suffusing the canvas. A medical orderly drew up a chair next to him. A bowl of water, a razor were on the table. The shaving mirror. Who was this? A swollen face, eyelids puffed, lips cracked, prickly beard. The razor hurt, seemed to be scraping his skin off.

'How's that? Better?' The orderly stood up.

'Thanks. Feels much better.' His voice husky.

'You'll be on the first train out.'

He managed to eat a little bread, taking it with water, his throat painful as if filled with broken razors. An hour later and the stretcher-bearers carried him into a carriage of the longest train he'd ever seen. A light rain had fallen, the tracks were gleaming, the platform of the railhead thick with soldiers. Cries and orders rung in the air. Two enormous engines steaming at the front of the train seemed to him like medieval warhorses in armour. He smiled at his fancifulness, but was pleased that his imagination was creating an image, no matter how ridiculous.

He saw more wounded carried out from the hospital and put onto the platform. From the towers of the cathedral, the stretcher-bearers and their loads would look like ants bearing their dead. He gazed at the great building as it disappeared in the mist. He was in his stretcher on the highest rack next to a window. He'd been told they'd pass so close to the cathedral that they would almost be able to reach out and touch it. Filled to capacity, the train moved off, pulled by the two great warhorses, creaking and clanking along. When he next looked out they were gathering speed through Picardy.

6

The thin blue of a coastal sky, white clouds whisked into peaks, like skies he'd seen often over Liverpool Bay. Home. He must write home. The train crept between low hills and the darkly forested slopes of the countryside around Boulogne. He kept lifting himself on his elbows for a glimpse of the sea through the window. His body ached from lying in this tiered rack high up in the compartment. Seven tedious hours since Amiens. So many stops. And now another stop, surely the final one. He managed to drink the tea brought by helpers, tea made with boiling water from the train's engines; the pure taste, stimulating and rich after the chlorine-flavoured brew at the Front. Relief of air in the swampy heat of the carriage, doors open all along the train. He strained to breathe in the sea air, but began coughing and lay back exhausted.

The train moved off again. Two VADs entered his carriage, to ready them for detraining, when it jerked and juddered, flinging everyone sideways. He clung to the rack to stop himself from being hurled to the ground. A cry from below. Craning over, he saw blood spurting from the mouth of the bandaged man lying on the bottom bunk.

'Nurse! Quick! Haemorrhage!' William shouted.

The train was swinging wildly as the VAD eased

her way forward, followed by a medical orderly. They bent over the man. William saw wads of bloodied dressings carried away by the orderly and then the VAD stood up, looking haggard and upset. Two helpers arrived and stretchered the man out, covered by a sheet.

William lay back, closing his eyes, his pulse rapid, hands trembling, sweat pouring down his face. Suffocating. One more death. He'd seen so many yet still was affected. Palms wet, his back wet, hands shaking uncontrollably. The VAD wiped his forehead, took hold of his hands.

'Where are they taking him?'

'To the rear, the moribund carriage.'

Moribund. An appalling word – he remembered his revulsion on first hearing it at Amiens in the Casualty Clearing Station, where the dead and dying were consigned to the moribund tent. But in how short a while words like 'moribund' and 'casualties' and 'wounded' lost their impact.

Half an hour later the train pulled into the station, taking up the full length of the platform. A feeble cheer went up from carriage to carriage and a snatch of song. With what seemed to William amazing speed, the stretcher-bearers took him and the other wounded from the train and deposited them on the platform; he was in the middle section and lay there disorientated in the bright light. Seagulls wheeled above, their long-drawn calls becoming frantic. More gulls swooped in, chasing the others with ferocity in their cries. Swish of wings to his right and left, greedy beaks inches from his eyes. He covered his face with his arms. Carrion crows pecking at the dead, he could see them feasting

86

on the corpses of men and horses. Screaming, he flung himself onto his stomach, shielding the back of his head with his hands. Shaking, sobbing. A sweat of fear. Someone gently touching his shoulder.

'It's all right. They won't harm you. They've gone.' A woman's voice, gentle but firm. 'Come now, turn over, we need to get everyone on their way as soon as we can. There'll be another train load arriving shortly.'

'I'm sorry, Nurse.' He was trembling and wheezing as he turned onto his back.

She read the details on his label. 'The doctor will be with you soon.'

Two doctors were quickly examining each man and pointing those well enough to the harbour and ships, others to the hospital on the hill. Orderlies, stretcher-bearers and volunteers hurried about, lifting the stretcher cases and carrying them towards their destinations. William watched the walking wounded being helped along, many of them visibly exhausted and in pain, hanging onto the arms of orderlies. He envied those heading for the hospital ships, some wearing 'Blighty grins'.

He was one of the last to be taken to an ambulance, an open Buick, with three other wounded and a VAD accompanying them. Up a long hill, 'St Martin's,' the VAD said, from which he could see the harbour and lower town and clouds standing above the sea like a frieze. At the top of the hill, ramparts and within them a basilica, its dome towering over the upper town. The ambulance turned into a road leading onto a grassy plateau. The hospital's size surprised him; the wooden huts, red crosses painted on the roofs, were like a small town extending from the military camp.

Propped up on pillows, he studied the Hospital Redirection card issued to all new patients. *On the admission of a soldier to Hospital this card should be filled in and forwarded to his next-of-kin.*

Good, now he could let Mam and the family know he was safe. Those 'last letters', grief latent in the green envelopes, were, thank God, not needed.

Number, Rank, Battalion etc . . . Next to Sick, he wrote one word: *Gassed.*

His ward held twenty beds, ten each side of the hut. The celebration evening meal of tinned rabbit tasted metallic and he gave his to a small white dog which seemed to belong to the hospital and was following the mobile kitchen. Later that evening, sitting outside in the warm air with several others, all of them suffering from gas poisoning, he heard someone call 'Fritz', and saw the dog hurl past them, tiny legs propelling him at incredible speed after a rat as big as himself. William was surprised by the sound of his own laughter – it was a long time since he'd laughed so wholeheartedly. Exhilaration, like running down a hillside in the Clwydians, or into the cold breakers of the Irish Sea. He felt less tense but his chest and stomach ached from the unaccustomed physical effort of laughter.

22 July 1916

This camp is high above the sea and the wind searches out every corner of the hilltop. It's nickname is Ozonehove. I'm feeling stronger. Well enough today to write. My first attempt since being gassed. Wheezing less, due to sitting outside most of the day. 'As much fresh air as you can get into your lungs,' says Dr Moran, our chief medical officer. But I still have nightmares almost every night – stepping on corpses or picking up pieces of human flesh. I dread the nights and the recurring dream of being in a line of gassed men, all of us in our hoods and holding on to the shoulder in front like performing circus animals. Always I'm unable to breathe, unable to claw the hood off because it's welded to my neck – and the stench of putrefying flesh, blood and cordite, the stink of No Man's Land, is overpowering, sickening. But I'm told by Dr Moran there are no smells in dreams. Each time I wake up I have to face the fact that my sense of smell is dead – each day I'm disappointed, dismayed that I still can't smell anything at all. Yet – I must record this – no matter how horrific the nightmares are, they're not nearly as horrific as the reality of No Man's Land. Everything now, everything away from that hell, seems unreal.

Nothing can justify the carnage. But news came through today of more Zeppelin raids on England. If Germany's air power develops, no one at home will be safe. This makes me see the war differently.

Each day I look for Matthew among the new arrivals, and each day I despair. I think of times we've shared, the plans we made, but our future now seems as remote as the shrouded moon. In this despondent mood I attempted today to express how I felt after the gas poisoning, the most frightening effects, especially the blurring of my sight. Implicit in these lines, however inexpert they might be, is my hatred of the war – of all war – turning ordinary men into inhuman fiends.

I couldn't think of a title, except 'From a Hospital Bed in Amiens' –

Closing my eyes on death, I see the riddled bodies,
Torn limbs that once a mother bathed,
The matted hair she'd washed and combed.
Silent for evermore is the voice she loved.

Closing my eyes on death, I see my own.
Cloaked in the lethal gas, an invisible cloud,
A burning swamp in which my lungs drown,
I'm closing on death my eyes that no longer see.

25th July 1916

Dear Elizabeth

First, I am hoping with all my heart that you and Lily are well, and that these Summer months are not too wearisome for you – not much longer now. It's good that you're living with Mam who will look after you splendidly, as she did when Lily was born.

You will know by now that I'm convalescing at the coast. The sea air is working its reputed wonders – I'm breathing more easily and my eyesight improves each day. I've even been able to write a little and enjoy reading again. We are treated to back copies of The

Times *and* The Manchester Guardian *and issues of a new and amusing magazine written by the troops out here, called* The Wipers Times *(jolly stuff!).*

No need to say it – I'm longing to be sent home! Yet I must be thankful for this chance to rest and get well. It's a perfect haven here. One of our distractions is a Jack Russell terrier called Fritz who won the canine MC for rat-catching. I managed to take him for a walk near the cliffs – we can see England from here, enticingly near when the visibility is good. We have to be given a pass to go out of the hospital – some of the lads went to an estaminet yesterday, taken by the volunteers. I didn't feel up to it, not even for omelette and chips and vino. When I'm less wobbly I'm hoping to spend a couple of hours in what they call La Haute Ville. It's historic, goes back to Roman times, I was told by Bernard, one of our French helpers. He said his great-grandfather remembered the days when Napoleon was camped on these same cliffs and hoping to invade England. There's a fine basilica which Bernard recommends and he says I must ask to see the very old statuette of the Virgin Mary.

Would you please do something for me, dear Sis? I know you'll understand. Would you seek out Mrs Riley and ask her for news of Matthew? And write to me here at Ostrahove as soon as you've done this? A million thanks.

Your loving brother
William

—◦◦◦—

He entered the echoey interior of the basilica where groups of women in black veils chanted prayers, and some children holding hands filed down the middle aisle. Mass had not long ended, incense hung in the air and clustered candles burned in the shadowy corners. He sat in a pew near the back. A white-haired priest, shoulders stooped, shuffled by carrying a large gilt candlestick. William followed him, tugged at his sleeve.

'I'd like to see the statuette of the Virgin, if that's possible,' he said in his hesitant French.

'You mean Notre-Dame de Boulogne.' The priest spoke in English, staring hard at William. 'You've been wounded?'

'Yes. Poison gas. I'm convalescing at the military hospital.'

The priest shook his hand. 'I'll be pleased to take you. I'm the verger here, thirty years next October.'

He lit an oil lantern, selected a key from the bunch hanging at his belt and led William to an iron-bound door. They went down a flight of steps and through a labyrinth of grey passages into the cool dark of the crypt.

'She's over here.'

Behind a grille stood the small wooden statue. Around her head, like a halo, shone a coronet of gems. The verger lit three tapering candles in the stand by the grille, crossed himself and knelt. William also knelt, gazing at the faded paint, the crudely mounted precious stones, rounded, unfaceted – clearly the statue was very old. The Madonna's face was like a Russian icon, he thought, and rigid as the white faces of corpses strewn across No Man's Land, the sons of mothers crucified . . . there should be a Madonna of the Battlefields where even now Christian nations massacred each other.

'You know about the miracle?' came the verger's hushed voice.

Before he could say no, the verger continued in his trance-like tone in the spell of his own words. 'In the year of Our Lord 636, a boat was heading for Boulogne, a boat which had neither crew nor sails. It came aground on our shore and it carried one thing only – a statue of the Virgin Mary. At the very moment the boat came aground, the congregation was praying in the chapel – here on this spot where the basilica stands today – and everyone in the little congregation saw an apparition of the Virgin, telling them of her statue in the boat. They brought it into the chapel, whereon miracle followed miracle. And so her fame grew and the pilgrimage was established. This pilgrimage to Notre-Dame de Boulogne has been undertaken by fourteen Kings of France and five of England.'

'Are there many cures among the miracles?'

'Many cures throughout the centuries. See, my son, the crutches against the wall left by the crippled who prayed and were healed.'

'Are there any other miracles?'

'Why do you need miracles? Have you lost your faith?'

He was silent. Untold numbers not fifty miles away were in need of miracles. Men in his hospital ward, and the dying strewn across the battlefield, the wounded and maimed, Matthew perhaps among them – and himself, with his lungs and eyes 'still under the effects of gas'. Yes, miracles were needed.

'There are sacred relics in our keeping here,' the verger broke into his thoughts. 'Most precious of all, the Holy Blood.'

The Holy Blood. What a nonsense! He almost smiled at the priest's round-eyed earnestness and the unlikelihood of Christ's blood having been saved for posterity. Shed, perhaps, but not saved.

'How does the Holy Blood come to be here?'

'Philip the Fair brought it on pilgrimage, an offering to Our Lady.'

'Could I see it?'

'Ah, sadly I have to say no. This and all the other relics are locked away in the Treasury.'

The verger stared at the statue, his lips moving in silent prayer. To William the wooden effigy looked tawdry, like those he used to shy at on fairground stalls in New Brighton. Praying to this little statue was not much different – hoping for the prize of a prayer answered. Religion had always seemed to him so much superstition, and yet, God or not, it was needed, it kept hope alive. Never more so than in the eerie hours before battle, tension at cracking point, poignant with the prayers of men and padres; and the supreme importance of their lucky charms: Sullivan, his dead grandmother's rosary; Foreshaw, a rabbit's foot; his own, a special pebble Matthew had given him long ago, found in a riverbed when they were fishing. He'd kept it in it his pocket, smooth, warm, brown. Lost now. Where? Oh, where was Matt! Damn the war!

He looked at the statue. Why not give Notre-Dame de Boulogne a chance to prove herself?

Please let Matthew be alive, let me have news of him soon . . .

Behind the statue a tapestry hung, brilliantly coloured with flowers and leaves and threads of vines. He tried to decipher a Latin quotation at the bottom but the words became blurred and he felt himself swaying; extreme weariness in every limb, his head aching. He gripped the rail and as he stared the blossoms broke and spilled blood onto the white lettering. Faint and struggling for breath, he held on to the rail, his head down.

Outside the basilica he sat on a stone bench, still feeling faint and weak, his shirt soaked in sweat. But the air was reviving and after resting for fifteen or twenty minutes he tested himself by walking a short distance on the ramparts, looking down to La Ville Basse and the harbour where yet another hospital ship was coming in and berthing, stern first. A channel mist had rolled in; the English coast was well and truly cloaked. He tried to recall Arnold's 'Dover Beach', one of his favourite poems. He used to know the whole of it by heart and now all he could remember were isolated phrases and lines, the closing ones especially –

Ah, love, let us be true
To one another! . . .
And we are here as on a darkling plain
Swept with confused alarms of struggle and flight,
Where ignorant armies clash by night.

Two days later an orderly handed William a letter. It was from Peter Sullivan.

Dear Will

I hope as this reaches you and you'll be pleased with the news as I have for you. It's about your friend. I think it's the same Riley as you spoke of. In the Red Cross hospital at Rouen where I was I heard a nurse saying Private Riley and the man was in a corner bed opposite. This was minutes before I was getting moved so I had no chance to ask anything. This Riley has dark hair and he was bandaged across his body and arms. What I did manage was to ask the VAD who came with me to the ambulance did she know his battalion or regiment which she didn't but told me his name was either Martin or Matthew. That's all as I know. Any road, it's something as might give you hope.

Maybe we will meet one day in Blighty. I will be at Chester at the place I told you of.

Ever your friend
Sullivan (Peter)

P.S. I know the buggers got you with the gas well and proper as I heard about you from Rogers, and I know that you saved me, Will. Perhaps you'll be out of the Show now. I hope to see you again.

He read it over and over, torn between wanting to believe that the wounded man was indeed Matthew and the fear that he might be close to death. Christ Jesus! How severe were the wounds? If only Sullivan could have found out more, but the name, the dark hair – surely a strong possibility this was Matt. He would write to the Rouen hospital.

——◇◇◇——

5th August, a.m.
No reply yet from Rouen and none from Elizabeth. I wait every day. One of the lads next to me in the ward – Stephen Roberts – received a letter from his fiancée with a photograph of her, he proudly showed me. She was dressed in one of those daring off-the-shoulder gowns, a lovely girl with Mary Pickford looks. He asked me did I 'have a girl back home'. I thought of two – Elizabeth and Mam – but no other. I've wanted only Elizabeth.

But I carry in my mind, always, pictures of Matthew.

Today a reward – a lovely letter from my beloved Mam. I'm feeling stronger and have been promised by Dr Moran that I can try myself out at the beach. I'll be taken there in a few days if I keep up this progress. This is just a reminder to myself and I'll keep reading it. The sooner I can manage the beach, the sooner I'll be on one of those ships for Southampton.

8 p.m.
Some lines of poetry at last, and images, almost a sonnet! I want to express something of what it was like on 7th July, waiting to go over the top, then No Man's Land and the crater –

As here we crouch at dawn in neutral light
The sun illuminates an abattoir
Where last night's dead await us in their hour
Destroyed by mortars and by bullets' bite.
The signal sounds for our unblessed advance:
Our limbs obey; we're prey of starcrossed chance.

Worms blind as bullets searching for my skin
Twist like the wire that keeps the Boche trench barbed.
I'm in a crater-grave, trapped deep within –

I've changed the last line several times and think I prefer –

Hurled by a blast into a hole shells churned

The effort of thought and struggle with words and metre exhausts me. I think of Keats – 'If words don't come naturally as leaves to a tree, better they should not come at all.'

They climbed into the open ambulance, six of the walking wounded and a medical orderly, the burly Scot, McVeigh. The woman driver nudged the Buick down St Martin's Hill. Clear morning sky over the Channel, and the cliffs of Dover hauntingly visible. The English Channel – *'those waves that separate also connect'* – the line came to him, a surge of the old creative feeling on the brink of poetry, the closest he'd been to joy since those hours with Matthew at the lake.

They passed the harbour in a queue of vehicles,

the quay bristling with lorries, wagons, war supplies, and loud with hooting and fishermen shouting in trawlers. The driver stopped near an embankment fronting the beach and they went down the steps onto the sand, going slowly, one man on crutches. William's nerves tightened. The glitter of sea and sun hurt his eyes. The space was disorientating. He was slightly dizzy, but he kept walking. The beach ahead was strewn with large rocks, some hunched like bodies of the fallen dead. He took a grip on himself – only rocks, just rocks.

McVeigh brought a football out of his haversack, dropped it on the sand and placed his foot on top of it purposefully.

'Two teams. I want two teams. Manderson, with Roberts and Fearon, over here.' He pointed to his right. 'And Thompson, Carter and Young over there.'

'You must be joking,' Fearon shouted, brandishing one of his crutches.

'Just a gentle kick-around. Exercise is good for you. You might surprise yourself.'

McVeigh dribbled the ball, going in a figure of eight, then stopped it sharp, flicked it from his toe to knee to head, headed it at William.

Why not? He kicked the ball in front of him, lengthened his stride, caught up, kicking a little further. Good, bloody good. He went on for several yards, running and turning before he lobbed the ball back.

'Well done, long shanks,' McVeigh shouted as he picked up the ball.

'Everyone listen now. Just practise kicking gently from one team to the other so the ball is always in possession. Got it?'

Ten minutes of passing the ball back and forth and they were all grinning with the pleasure of connection. Fearon, right leg tucked up like a stork, swinging on his crutches, had managed to kick with his sound left foot.

'Rest now, lads!'

They flopped onto the sand, unbuttoning their shirts, taking off socks and boots, rolling up their trouser-legs; several lighting up their cigarettes. William moved away a few yards, wary of the effects of smoke. He wriggled his bare toes in the warm sand, enjoying the gritty texture, and closed his eyes. He felt normal, almost – just a slight tightening in his chest. Elation – he was able to move freely and breathe without wheezing. In an instant he was back at the lake, running through the trees in search of Matthew, finding him by the deliberate signal of his laughter as he dangled from a bough then leapt down. Matthew on top of him, both of them falling onto the grass, rolling over, legs entangled, then slapping each other, fighting and grappling. The silky warmth of Matthew's body. William sighed, got up. Perhaps Matthew was back in England or maybe even now was being loaded onto one of the hospital ships whose steam was rising from the harbour. The awful not-knowing. Blessings on Peter Sullivan for his grain of hope.

The white ribbon of beach stretched before him. Tempting. He walked to the tide's edge, watched the creamy waves curling over – to run again along the tideline as he used to do on New Brighton shore. But no, beyond his strength now. Go steady.

Something on the sand ahead. Purple-red, gelatinous

lumps of flesh. Pieces of muscle and sinew torn from men, sticking to trench walls, trodden into the mud. His gorge rose, he baulked, forced himself to look closer. Massive jellyfish. Merely dead jellyfish. Semi-transparent, bloodied, the red inner layer showing through. Those nearest the water rose and fell in the wash of the tide, their filaments moving like fingers hopelessly trying to grasp something.

Shivering and nauseous, his eyes blurred, he moved away. Slumping onto the sand, he was afraid he might show his fear, afraid he'd reveal his physical weakness – should McVeigh notice he most certainly would report it to Dr Moran, and this could delay his return to England.

A group of young women approached from the quay, carrying wicker baskets laden with fish. They were wearing embroidered pinafores and the sun-shaped headdress of the Boulonnaise. They waved to the men and McVeigh ran over to them, talking in particular to a tall blonde girl. Shouts of 'Oo-la-la', whoops and whistles from the men – William took the opportunity to join them while McVeigh was distracted.

'That's Amélie,' Roberts explained, 'she works in the estaminet Mac took us to the other night.'

The VAD driver signalled from the embankment: time up. The men walked back to the ambulance, bantering, teasing McVeigh. William felt more relaxed, his breathing easier, his skin tingling from the sun and salt air.

7

William stared out at fields golden under the September sun, the downs, meadows, hills and orchards of England, villages and towns on which the war seemed to have made no visible impact. But at stations where they stopped he gazed down at platforms seething with people watching the wounded being unloaded and carried to ambulances. Women of all ages pushed forward armed with flowers, some crying out and weeping; some screaming hysterically, their eyes wild like those of injured horses he'd seen lying in the mud, thrashing about in their pain. Impossible to know what griefs these women were enduring, their men dead or missing or among the wounded. And there, mocking, on the walls of every station, were the same old recruitment posters. 'Enlist Now!' and 'Be Part of the Glorious Victory!' 'Butchery' more exact. New posters, too, one of a boy looking up at his father in an armchair – 'Daddy, what did YOU do in the Great War?', the father in red-cheeked shame and expensive suit.

He was thankful when darkness descended as the train reached the Midlands. Still sick and exhausted after the eight-hour crossing, he fell into a deep sleep for the remainder of the journey.

Burton Manor, 20th September 1916

By motor ambulance from Chester Station last night,
three of us and a cheery bulldog-faced driver.
Wheezing and fatigued, yet exhilarated to be only
thirty miles from home. Turned left off the high road,
down a long lane towards the River Dee. A pillared
gateway. The convalescent hospital, a converted
country house.

Slept right through the night without waking
once. My bed is in the Main Hall, an airy room –
twenty-five wounded in here and in other ground-
floor rooms – men shuffling along in dressing-gowns
or huddled over newspapers. This morning I looked
through tall windows and was overcome on seeing
Wales, the outline of distant hills. My old yearning to
be back there, so keen it is the *hiraeth*. Pleased I am
to experience the pain of a true Welshman!

We're warmed by a wonderful fire glowing in the
grate day and night, kept going by one of the
groundsmen. A splendid Queen Alexandra Military
Nurse is in charge – Sister Jackson – imperious yet
motherly, hen-shaped. There's another nurse and two
VADs, one with a scarlet efficiency stripe. Powell, an
RAMC captain, comes to us every day, then goes to
another small hospital near Chester. Historical
footnote: the owners of Burton Manor are descendants
of William Gladstone – his third son Henry and wife
Maud – though I haven't seen them yet.

A soothing atmosphere. I know I shall get better
here – already I'm coughing less but still feel the
burning sensation when I breathe. Will I be able to

write poetry? My journal certainly. Here are wooded grounds, landscaped walks, lily ponds. Pastures. I hope Matthew's as lucky as I am, back in England and in a place like this.

———⟡———

He watched intently from a bench in the walled garden. Smoke filtered up from smouldering leaves; a gardener in old corduroys was digging up cabbages, dipping and bending, filling a wheelbarrow; a tawny cat licked its paws in the mellow sunlight.

Late September was his favourite time of year, sandstone his favourite stone, with its warm shades of rose-brown, its crumbly edges, its enduringness; sandstone all around him at Burton in the high walls and Victorian garden, and the house itself. He should feel blessed.

He sighed, got up and went inside one of two long glasshouses, touching the opulent vines with their late tomatoes plump and richly red, trying to recreate in his mind their distinctive sharp-sweet smell. He came here most days or wandered in the manor grounds, looking southwards across fields sloping to the Dee estuary. Near the marshes a row of poplars punctuating the sky reminded him of a road to Amiens.

No escape from Sunday here at home. Bells were pealing from Burton Church as insistent as a bugle call, a summons intoned over the village, over thatched cottages and the woods rising behind. Bells competed with the cawing of rooks, floating like black flags above the trees. How he detested it, the English Sunday and, as if ignoring the war, the way everything continued as before, the same calm, ordered world with its traditions and rituals – Harvest Thanksgiving, sheaves of corn, apples and pears, bread of life, village life.

He left the glasshouse and walked slowly across the yard to a side entrance of the house and into the Main Hall where he flopped onto his bed. This tiredness creeping up on him each day, his breath catching or doing its vanishing trick, left him despairing and depressed. The incessant war-talk of most of the men, how and where they were wounded, who had died in the action, details of night raids, wiring parties, over and over, wore on his spirit. He tried to read Hardy, but the words merged and blurred.

—∿∿∿—

27th September
Spilled a bowl of soup yesterday, lost my hold on it, hands twisting and moving out of control. I felt they didn't belong to me. The bowl broke on the floor. I felt a fool, ashamed. Feverish again, sweating all over. Sister Jackson checked me out, made me lie quietly. She told me my nervous system has been affected as well as my breathing. Her presence by my bed was comforting. Sleep, but again the nightmares, some the same, night after night. In one of these I'm floating above my own body, looking down at myself lying dead among other corpses, and Red Cross orderlies are lifting me, removing my identity disk.

Then I'm standing on a beach watching naked swimmers coming out of the waves. They stagger, some falling on their knees, struggling, getting up.

On they come, nearer, nearer, out of the sea, dead men, gashed, mutilated, decomposing. I call out. Wake in a sweat. And see, always, the silhouettes of men still sitting at the card table by the fire. All day and every evening the card table. And in a wheelchair by one of the windows a man sitting, never moving, never talking, staring straight ahead.

2nd October

A poem at last, and drawn from my dream after lunch today. I'd been thinking back to other centuries – the wars, the sameness of violence and slaughter. I dreamt I was in medieval Wales in the army of the Prince, Llywelyn the Last, fighting the English and being pursued by Edward's soldiers. Delirious, I was lying in a tent. The poem came spontaneously, flowing freely. Too easy, probably. No struggle with words. No rhyming.

These images came first:

This fever's black maw,
Its burning paws and hydra head.

Then more unbidden lines –

In reptiled sleep I rest, yet constantly I roam
Listening to the wind's warnings,
Hearing of Llywelyn's last encounter,
His death-wound in the bladed woods
A chorus of doves moaning a new meaning.

Images crowded my mind, one after the other. I selected these:

I see Llywelyn's head piked high in London,
A crown of mocking ivy around his brow,
Llywelyn's head in the wind, in the rain,
His hair flowing like a banner,
His noble face a gargoyle in the air.
Again I burn and rage; my fever flares.

The poem seemed to round itself off – I was indeed burning up by the time I'd finished.

―⁓―

He sat under the arcade of the Fountain Court wrapped in his greatcoat and blankets, sheltered but in the open air. Sister Jackson's orders to spend an hour here each day were paying dividends. His breathing was easier, his cough less racking. And it was inspiring in the little courtyard, uplifting; the chessboard floor of black and white marble tiles, the plants and shrubs in pots around the edge, the square of sky above.

He flicked through his notebook, dissatisfied with last night's poem; it seemed far less effective this morning. Probably another poem he would abandon.

'Private Manderson. Sorry to disturb you, sir.' The young housemaid flushed as she handed him a letter, then hurried away.

Postmarked Liverpool, 28th September. He ripped open the envelope.

―⁓―

Dear William

This morning I saw Mrs Riley going into the Post Office on Everton Road, so I asked after Matthew. She looked strained and was abrupt. Just a few words – he's in a hospital down south. I wanted to ask more but she turned away and made it obvious that she didn't want to talk. At least this is some news. What you've been waiting for, though not enough. I heard from Jack. He's got no hope of leave and with the baby due any day now I miss him unbearably.

If I was not in this condition I'd get across the Mersey to see you. Somehow I'd manage it, Will, be sure of that and of my constant thoughts and love.

from
Elizabeth and Lily

—◊◊◊—

Matthew definitely in England. William felt intense relief mingled with anxiety. How badly was he wounded, and in what way? Should he write to Mrs Riley? Would she post on a letter? An agony of indecision. He began writing and destroyed several attempts.

The following day a second letter arrived from Elizabeth, and one from Mam.

—◊◊◊—

Dear Will

My baby was born, 1st October. We are both well. She's Gwyneth.

Our love
Elizabeth

3rd October

Dear William,

We all look forward to the day when you'll be home, also Jack. If it was possible I'd come to see you, but I'm needed here, so much to do. I know you'll be wanting to hear about the new baby, a dainty girl, blonde like Lily, but unlike Lily she cries a lot and as I write I can hear her grizzling. Elizabeth is doing as well as can be expected. She sends you her love and has asked me to tell you that your friend Matthew Riley has had one of his arms amputated because of gangrene. She heard this from Mrs Costello who called to see baby Gwyneth – you might remember her, she lives in Lloyd Street two doors down from Mrs Riley.

The war seems never ending, prices of everything going up from week to week. So many deaths in the paper. We are putting together a parcel and will send it this week, remembering no Woodbines this time.

Your own Mam

＝〜〜＝

His hands shook and he dropped the letter on the floor of the ward. Everything around him receded, disintegrating. He was reeling in a chasm, the one appalling fact obliterating all else. Matthew's arm amputated. Gangrene. Was his life still in danger? Oh God!

He found himself running through a wood at the side of the Manor and down a flight of stone steps into the deep underground chamber of the ice house. He heard himself screaming, the screams amplified, echoing from wall to wall. Dark wings all around, cloaked forms, dozens of them, bats disturbed in their roosts, now circling, soaring. He sank down against the chill wall and let out one long scream, a howl of pain for Matthew. The horror of mutilation, what they'd both dreaded most. The agonising irony, to lose his arm, his hand and fingers, his career as a pianist, perhaps his life. Gangrene, the creeping killer. William felt helpless, enraged. He would have given his life for Matt yet now could do nothing. He wanted to lash out, punch, kick, but lay there weeping until he lost consciousness.

The blaze of a huge fire. Shapes of men sitting at a table. Faces above him – Sister Jackson, Captain Powell.

'You were seen running from the house. Lucky we found you down there,' Sister Jackson tutted, placing her hand on his forehead. 'You'd have frozen to death.'

That evening he stood at the window beside the silent man in the wheelchair, always looking out and never speaking. The moon in a swirl of navy cloud was like the iris of an eye with a white pupil, a blind eye staring but not seeing.

'We're almost certain your friend will be at Roehampton. They specialise in disablement and artificial limbs.' Sister Jackson spoke in a brisk tone, pulling up a chair and sitting beside William's bed. 'He'll be receiving the very best treatment and he'll be surrounded by men like himself – and those even worse off – some will have lost all of their limbs, many there will have had both legs blown off or amputated.

There –' she broke off as she glanced at his hands clenching and twisting.

'Captain Powell,' she called across the ward, and Powell came over, his thick sandy hair youthful above his middle-aged face, its deep lines running into jowls.

'Can we contact Roehampton?'

Powell held his stethoscope to William's chest and he responded automatically, breathing as deeply as he could.

Powell listened. 'Again.'

William took another chest-aching breath.

'Mm. Better today, Manderson. You can be up and about tomorrow, but keep away from ice houses.' Powell smiled. He spoke slowly, precisely, tasting each vowel. 'I've got a couple of old friends serving at Roehampton. It should be possible to trace Riley but we won't get an answer for a few days or more. If he's there or if he was there and has been moved on, they'll tell me. His recovery will take many months, possibly years. It's important to understand the deep trauma of an amputation.' He knocked on his left thigh with his knuckles. 'You see, I know only too well what it's like to lose a limb.'

Ten days later, Sister Jackson placed a piece of paper in front of William at the dining table. 'This is the full address of Roehampton Hospital. Captain Powell heard from his contact – and Private Riley is there and will be for another few weeks.'

'Did he hear anything else – about Riley?'

Sister Jackson hesitated. 'Yes . . . it was his right arm. But he's clear of gangrene now, out of danger.'

Dazed by the news, William read the address, not taking it in. He mumbled his thanks, adding 'Please tell Captain Powell I'm very grateful.'

'Don't expect much from Riley. Remember he'll still be in a state of shock.'

—◆◆◆—

20th October
My third letter to Matthew and as yet no reply – I had hoped he'd send word through a VAD. He must be suffering in so many ways, not just physical pain. I wish it had been my loss not his, as I think I could cope without my right arm, could still be a writer, a poet. Pathetic wishes. All I can do is wait, think of him, hope he'll be sent home, dare to hope that one day I'll be able to look after him.

Last night's dream . . .

Matt and I are lying side by side on stretchers in the hold of a hospital ship. The metal wall might burst open at any second and it does, but there's no explosion, just the snout of a torpedo coming at us, and in a moment it changes into the snout of a whale. We're lifted onto its back, its skin is shiny and soft and we cling as the whale swims towards the coast. The cliffs are white slabs like sliced cheese. The whale beaches and we're hurled onto the shingle, lie there exhausted, crawl towards each other. Matthew is whole.

—◆◆◆—

Burton Manor,
Cheshire
22nd October 1916

Dear Mam and Pa,

I had my examination by the Medical Board yesterday. It was at a camp just outside Chester where four of us were taken from Burton by motor ambulance. Three doctors. One examined me, listened to my chest, tested my reflexes; another took notes; the third did nothing but read the notes and pronounce me unfit. I've been given another four weeks convalescence but ordered to do light duties outdoors, helping the gardening staff here at the Manor. Then, after this, another Board.

I start my outdoor duties tomorrow, and today was introduced to the ten gardeners, men too old for army service but otherwise very fit, as I soon will be, they promise! In particular I'll be helping with the kitchen garden – all the food here is home-grown and the baking is done by the Gladstones' own cooks. Last night there was a short concert, Henry Gladstone sat with us and his wife played brilliantly on her Stradivarius – what with the candlelight and firelight it was an hour of enchantment.

If you're still busy knitting, Mam, I could do with some gloves, scarves and anything else you can send me for the outdoors! My eyes are considerably improved but get blurry when I'm in a bright light or if I get too anxious. It's good to hear news of Gwyneth – I'm longing to see her – and all of you.

Your loving son, William

21st November

Tired, but a healthy tired, aching all over due to the
physical work. Allowed out of the Manor for a short
time now and then, when not needed by Parkin.
Yesterday I discovered some graves in the woods.
Parkin tells me they're the graves of Quakers. Very
little written on the gravestones – laid flat on the
ground. My mind went directly to the Somme, the
new raw graves and unaccountably, after so many
deaths, to Berry blown apart by his grenade.

> *Fallen leaves*
> *Medallions*
> *Medals*
> *Crushed underfoot*

I wrote these images after returning from my
walk, and then spontaneously these lines, recalling
my train journey from Southampton –

> *So here are the fields of home, the perfect grass*
> *Unravaged downs, orchards, meadows –*
> *All's steeped in golden Septemberness.*
> *I should rejoice, but hear the screams and groans*
> *Across earth washed red in slaughter grounds*
> *Where I saw wonder on a dead man's face,*
> *Agony in a smile.*

———

He looked up from the rows of Brussels sprouts as
Parkin loped over from the stables. With his long
face, keen eyes and side whiskers, he looked like a

gamekeeper or poacher, not that William would ever tell him so. Parkin prided himself on being assistant head gardener.

'I need help over in the copse by the lake. We need brushwood and kindling. Wrap up.'

William fetched his greatcoat, securing the neck where buttons were missing with a soft woollen scarf Mam had sent. He pulled on his cap and waited in the yard by the walled garden until Parkin reappeared, cloaked in several layers of sacking and wearing an old fur hat. They set off, each pulling a wheelbarrow, crossing the pastures to the south of the house, sheep moving away from them in clusters as they approached the copse, the lake a strip of pewter behind bare trees.

'Collect what you can here at the edge.' Parkin banged his hands together several times, then took an axe out of his wheelbarrow. 'I'll work further in.'

William pulled out a knife and set to, cutting away loose twigs and fallen boughs of birch, making a pile like a bonfire. Satisfying work. He imagined large fires blazing in the manor grates. From inside the copse came the bark of Parkin's axe.

In reddish light, with the sun blurred, the copse became a tangle of silhouettes. Each twisted tree was a Boche listening post; he was back in the devastated wood near Ovillers, the death's head moth settled on his shoulder, and overhead shells ripping the air. He heard a whoosh of wings. Only a V of Canada geese flying towards the estuary. He tried to laugh at himself for being unnerved, but the pastures remained eerie in the half light. He occupied himself by filling his barrow; rustling and crashing branches told him that Parkin was still working. But as he waited for the gardener to emerge, the warmth from his own exertions faded, his fingers began to feel numb. The cold intensified and a moaning wind filtered through hedges, swept across the pastures, dead leaves eddying in the air. Then the first flakes, large and wet, hit his face; ice crystals on his tongue.

At last here was Parkin, pulling a laden barrow.

'If we hurry, we'll beat the snowstorm,' yelled Parkin. 'It'll be dark earlier than ever tonight, due to this damned Summer Time.'

'Aye,' William called back, the chill air hurting his lungs. 'Ridiculous, mankind trying to control time.'

Visibility lessened, thickening flurries became a curtain of falling snow. He reached the shelter of a large shed in the stable yard where he deposited his wood. Snow gleamed along the sandstone walls, on the dark leaves of evergreen shrubs, on the rows of cabbages, the furrows of the kitchen garden. The glasshouses were white-canopied, but this loose wet snow would probably be gone by morning. Snatch the magic, the moment, before it dissolves; how many more lives would be destroyed by daybreak?

They went in through the Servants' Hall, stamping the snow from their boots. William took off his greatcoat and hung it on a peg near the door. In the kitchen he stood warming his hands over the oven.

'News for you, Manderson.' Sister Jackson approached. 'The Travelling Board arrive here tomorrow. Six of you are going up.'

21st November

Dreamt last night of No Man's Land under snow. Images: iced snow covering the mud, our men frozen effigies lining the trenches.

Today I carried a holly bough,
Beads of blood dripping on snow.
I have never seen white as white
As dead men's faces until now –
Until they blacken, like day into night.

A memory of the first Winter of our friendship, a heavy fall of snow, Liverpool transformed. We made our way through silent roads to Sefton Park where Matt wanted to go tobogganing. Afterwards his fingers were numb, so I caught his hands between my own, warmed them, his big hands, the breadth much wider than mine. He laughed. And then he gasped when the pain came, and I held him.

—∿∿—

'Private Manderson.' Captain Powell opened the door of the Medical Inspection Room, a sheaf of papers in his hand.

'Sir!' William saluted him, entered and approached the long table where the three RAMC doctors were sitting. He saluted again. His head was aching viciously, his entire skin felt tender, his wheezing was audible.

The Senior Medical Officer, in the centre, looked up from some forms. His face was like a ferret's, sharp-featured, hungry for the kill.

'Strip off! Quick about it, man!' A shrill, high voice.

William put his clothing on a chair and stood naked in front of the table. The SMO's glittery eyes scanned him up and down.

'No wounds.'

Statement or question? William wasn't sure. 'No, sir.'

'Just gassed.'

'Yes, sir.'

He took a stethoscope to William's chest, listened for a few moments and stepped back.

'Open your mouth.' He held William's tongue down with an instrument. 'Wider!' A cursory look and he returned to the table, writing something rapidly and passing the note to the other doctors.

'Get dressed! Quick as you can. We haven't got all day!'

William scrambled into his uniform and stood again before the doctors. Why was Powell looking so worried?

The Senior MO wrote on a form, signed it and placed the pen back into its stand. He picked up his pipe, lit it, leaned back in his seat and puffed out a cloud of smoke. William choked, coughing uncontrollably. Powell handed him a glass of water.

'Manderson. Not too bad.' He sucked at his pipe then held it in his hand, giving William an icy stare. 'We're sending you to a Training Depot. The camp will get you fit again, you'll work up from Category 6 and in no time at all you'll be ready for active service. Transit is arranged for tomorrow at noon.'

William returned to his bed and lay there. Retraining. He could scarcely believe it. He'd never stand up to the rigours of active service. It would bring him to death's door, he knew it. Depression began to set in with the realisation that this was the end of his time at Burton Manor. He'd felt himself coming to life again, but that wasn't what the Army wanted, this 'softening', these individual feelings and thoughts. He was the Army's property, its creature, his body no longer his own. And they were after his mind as well. He'd never let that happen, never. He'd hide his thoughts, they couldn't have those, he'd cling on, keep going with his journal, his poetry.

The morning after the Board William sat under the arcade of the Fountain Court for the last time, writing to Mam with news of his posting. He'd said his farewells to Sister Jackson, Nurse Foster, the VADs, other staff and the men in his ward, and left a letter of sympathy for Parkin who'd just had news of the death of his son at the Somme.

He picked up his kit and made his way to the yard. One by one the other five men who'd gone before the Board joined him outside. They stood in silence, waiting for the Army lorry. He was shivering, his throat on fire, his whole body aching.

8

The North Shropshire camp was as crowded and noisy as Lime Street Station. William's nerves jangled at the crackle of musketry from the practice butts, the tramp-tramp of marching, shrieks of NCOs and instructors on the parade ground. As a transport truck rumbled past, throwing up dust, he choked, too late to cover his mouth and nose with his hands. The drabness of the place, its uniformity, the ruler-straight roads lined by wooden huts, the gates and sentries – a prison.

Inspection followed within half an hour. Thirty of them assembled in front of the dormitory huts. He shivered in the bitingly cold air, enduring the bawling and bullying from Kelly, a puce-faced pig of an NCO.

'Yer buttons, Manderson. Sew em on! Yer hair, Manderson! Who d' y' think yer are, Goldilocks?'

He waited for his turn in the shearing hut where three barbers worked non-stop. How sheep-like the queuing men seemed, submissive while the Army reduced them to a number and a rank. What else could they do? How could they show their anger even if they felt it? Clip, clip, clip. A helper was sweeping up mounds of hair and removing it in bucket loads to the incinerator. Brown and black and blond, all strands from living cells yet the dead hair of men, dispensable. His turn. The cool fingers of the barber against his ears, lifting his hair, lopping it off; the rasp of the razor up the back of his neck.

'Less for the lice, lad,' the barber grinned.

He joined the queue on the path outside the canteen. Wind siphoned through the avenue of huts. A sensation like icy water poured down his neck, waves of shivers, his skin tender, his cough racking. But to report his condition would be to invite the accusation of malingering.

The doors opened and they filed inside, lining up at the counter for stew plopped from vats into enamel bowls by a team of women. He looked for knives and forks but there were none, merely hunks of bread on the long trestle tables. Men sat tipping the bowls to their mouths or licking up the gravy like hungry dogs. Those who snatched the bread tore it into lumps which they used to mop up any stew remaining in their bowls. No cutlery, an Army tactic to pull them down, humble them.

'Here, have mine.' He passed his untouched bowl to the man next to him.

'Thanks!' The man seized it and gulped it down, gravy smeared across his cheeks, dribbling down his chin.

Wind found its way through gaps in the wood and ill-fitting windows of the dormitory hut. The men for retraining were packed side by side, settling down in narrow camp beds. Most of them were eager to tell each other their story, but a few lay silent and looked as ill as William felt. He drew his blanket over his head and closed his eyes.

'I'm Baker, Lancashire Fusiliers.' The man in the next bed pulled at William's blanket.

'Manderson. Cheshires.' He managed to raise himself on one elbow.

'My bloody leg's only just mended, they're bloody well taking anybody back because there's hardly anyone left over there, that's what this is all about.' Baker's voice rose to a shriek, his eyes staring wildly. 'They think we don't know. Convalescence! Bloody hell! Of course we fucking well know!'

'What's this then, chitter chitter!' Sergeant Kelly banged the door back against the wall. 'Settle down! Reveille's at six o'clock sharp!'

William drifted in and out of sleep, in and out of delirium. He saw writhing men, their faces torn away. He saw Matthew on an operating table, his arm hacked off, nerves, sinews, veins hanging in a mesh of blood and flesh. He saw a nurse holding up Matthew's arm in a pair of forceps.

He came to, hearing the thump-thump of guns. No, not the Front. The guns were in his head; a banging headache, fever, his body sore. All around him came groans from men reluctant to rise. Then Kelly bawling, 'Show a leg!'

In the grey light of dawn they were led down the dismal avenue of huts to the training ground Kelly called the Bull Ring. William shivered as a chill wind ripped across the flat fields, but after fifteen minutes of PT he was soaked in sweat, his muscles trembling, legs wobbling, his chest aching, on fire. Gasping, he fell on his knees.

'Get up, Manderson!'

'I can't, sir.'

'Get up, I said! Try harder!'

He tried, but fell forward onto the ground.

'Lift him!'

He felt himself being hauled up and laid on the grass at the side of the Bull Ring. He was panting, clutching his chest as each breath seared. Kelly's shouts, relentlessly putting the men through exercises, came from far away. One man, then another, and another, were placed next to him, each of them rolling in pain.

Gradually his breathing grew easier and he sat up, but the world spun around him. Lie down, don't move . . . beaten . . . the whirling clouds . . .

'Dismiss!'

He heard the men hurrying away to the canteen and breakfast.

Kelly stood over him, bulky, scowling, his pale close-set eyes like stones.

'I'm going to have you examined, Manderson. We'll soon know whether you're faking.'

Two RAMC officers questioned him in the medical hut. When had he first begun to feel ill? Why hadn't he reported it when he arrived? The interrogation made him sweat profusely and want to vomit. Next, the examination, his temperature taken, the ends of stethoscopes like large cold coins pressed against his skin. The doctors consulted behind a screen. He could hear what sounded like a dispute. Surely they believed him? If they didn't there'd be some physical punishment, hours of sentry duty or heavy work lifting supplies. One of the doctors emerged and came over to him.

'A mild attack of influenza. A couple of days rest and you'll be fine. We'll keep you over here in the isolation ward.'

A bed with mud-caked blankets and sheets stained with old blood. He slid inside, grateful to be left alone, then lapsed into a feverish sleep, hour after hour, unaware of day and night, delirious, seeing over and again a figure on the rim of a hill – Matthew, his body silhouetted against the light, then dissolving in the light.

Four days later, temperature down, he rejoined his unit. Almost too weak to walk, he stumbled into the hut. The men who came in after evening stand-to were mostly strangers; so few of those he'd started with were among them. He was glad to see Baker's bony face.

'Where have they gone? Not France already?'

Baker scowled. 'Shouldn't be surprised. They've been moved up the grades bloody quick. I'm still in the lowest – my leg won't work, y'see. Twisted.'

'I've been graded six as well. Training starts tomorrow morning.'

'Training? Hardening, you mean! As Kelly said, what we need is hardening.'

* * *

The NCO's bark. 'Clear a space over there! Forward!'

William's unit moved to the side of the Bull Ring as a company of maimed men advanced into the centre, walking stiffly but managing to keep in step. They reminded him of jointed wooden puppets. Behind them, clinking forward, another half dozen on crutches.

The shrill command cut the air; as one, the maimed men halted.

He watched as the mutilees began their exercises. They looked pitiful with their awkward movements, some trying to bend over, others swinging rigid arms, a few gasping with pain. Why were these men not discharged? Why were they being put through this? The Army's barbaric methods. And then he saw that they were all officers, some of the few who'd survived so far, evidently determined to stay in to the end.

'Manderson!' bawled Kelly. 'Gassed over here!'

He joined his unit in the corner of the Bull Ring and each of them was issued with pack and rifle.

'A test march. Three miles! Form up!'

After a short drill they marched out of the camp in drizzle and a light mist. Again he felt the hypnotic effect of moving in unison, a piston of a large machine, a mechanical creature with many feet. How easy it would be to give oneself over to it, lose identity; there was something oddly comforting in being part of this collective metronome, this physical pattern. But no, he must resist, must use the rhythm, make it his own, hang on to his individual thoughts –

march, counter-march
wheel right, wheel left
about turn, form squads
unable to think
legs hurting, back hurting.

'Hold yer 'ead up, Manderson, can't yer!' screamed Kelly.

They turned into a muddy lane rising uphill, bordered by bare birch trees. His boots seemed to be lead-lined, his pack full of bricks. Chest aching, the burning pain when he breathed. Keep going. Recite Longfellow, like he used to do on his bike, cycling uphill from town to Everton . . .

Tell me not in mournful numbers
Life is but a waking dream . . .

The lane stretched into the misted distance. One man ahead of him collapsed and was dragged to the bank. He tried to suppress his cough but couldn't . . . a dense, dead feeling when he breathed as if his lungs were filled with putty. A few more yards, then another spasm of coughing. He felt as if his lungs were tearing apart.

'Now then, Manderson, trying it on again!' Kelly came at him down the line of men. 'Get that cough under control, double quick!'

He felt the power of Kelly's huge fist hitting his back, once, twice, three times. He keeled over but was immediately hauled up and Kelly pushed him back into his position in the line.

He was out of step, clammy with sweat, fearing

another coughing fit. He heard the chink of harness as a troop of military police in greatcoats swept by, their horses' hooves flicking mud which lashed his face. Pollarded trees lined one side of the lane, their branches stripped of bark, like white hands dead-fingered; some thin and sharp like snapped bayonets. A fallen tree, fissured and lichened, became a khaki, headless body. Dizzy, his every footstep a torture, heart thumping, blood pounding, breathing razors . . . can't breathe; no air; can't . . . must be death. Redness flooding. Blackness.

Ticking of a clock. He turned his head. White flowers at the bedside, flower hands like the hands of the pollarded trees, held up in protest, hands held up to be counted . . . shadowy forms, uncontrollable shaking, every breath excruciating, bringing tears to his eyes. The sensation of levitation, then floating, his body being lifted and lowered again. Cool hands. Cool sheets. A glass filled with water, water filled with glass. Splintering pain on both sides of his chest.

'Where am I?'

'Ssh!'

'Mam?'

'No, I'm not your mam. But she's been to see you, and your father with her. They'll be coming again soon. Don't fret.'

His ribs felt as if each one was snapped, his chest caving in. Sleep . . . let go.

* * *

Grinding of cartwheels, motor horns, street criers, was he imagining the sounds, and the long windows, the high ceilings. Where am I . . . how long have I been unconscious . . . this weakness, can't even lift my hands . . . blurred sight . . . throat sore.

Hot waddings around my chest . . . the searing pain.

'Is it Tuesday?' His voice a whisper.

'No, not Tuesday. Friday.'

Not Tuesday. He wanted Tuesday, his favourite day, a blue day.

'What . . . ?' and again 'What . . . ?' He couldn't remember the question he was wanting to ask.

'He's through the crisis, Mrs Manderson. His fever's gone.'

'William . . . '

Mam's voice from far off, like someone calling from floors up in an empty house. Was he dreaming? Perhaps this was death, to see your mother at the foot of your bed, a last glimpse of the person who made you, of the flesh from which you came, a final glimpse before your own flesh dies. And this gnawing, this hunger for all the unremembered days . . .

'William! *Cariad*!'

Unable to open his eyes, deeper regions sucking him down. But again her voice.

'William!'

She was smaller, looked older . . . was this really her?

'Nurse, he's awake!'

They brought extra pillows, propping him up. The comfort of Mam's hand holding his . . . gazing at her for countless minutes. Still the sensation of floating, images drifting. He is himself yet not himself . . . he is the small boy running into the muddy road, and Mam is scolding, her eyes sharp with tears . . . he is nineteen, bringing Matthew to meet Mam for the first time, and she is looking at them both with questioning eyes . . . he is at Les Trois Ruisseaux, lying at the lake side and Matthew is on both elbows looking down into his eyes, almost mockingly, saying over and over *our bubble now, our now* . . . and he is in No Man's Land, seeking Matthew, turning over the dead soldier and looking into his glassy eyes, eyes with no future. Now, in this moment, in this pinprick of time, he is looking at Mam, at her eyes sharp with tears, her questioning eyes.

They'd come with a VAD in a little group from the Chester Royal Infirmary, shuffling along to a teashop in the Rows. A chintzy café packed with soldiers and their relatives, girlfriends and mothers, fathers too old for the Army. The fuggy warmth and cigarette smoke choked him. He lurched out of the door and leaned on the balcony rail at the end of Eastgate Row, weak, sweating and trembling. He looked up at the black and white gables and the triangles of uncanny blue between them and loathed the unseasonable heat. The very brightness of the day was a mockery in this war.

Dark wood of ages, Tudor and Stuart, alleys, Roman stones and walls, Chester – a city permeated by the past. The past swallowing the present, consuming it at the very moment of its inception, like war consuming young lives. His life belonged to the Army. In a few weeks he'd be allowed home, but only for a short leave, then after his leave another Board would tell him he was fit to retrain. The Army would never let go.

The raucous cry of a newsboy cut through him.

'Chronicle! Latest!'

By the ancient stone cross and St Peter's Church a queue for the newspaper was building up, people drawn by the billboard shock. *Ramsgate Shelled From The Sea*.

He looked down Eastgate Street where women were lining the pavements on both sides, crying and wailing as a stream of motor ambulances approached, passing one by one under the sandstone archway of the Jubilee Clock. The vehicles, carrying yet another train-load of wounded from the station to Red Cross centres, seemed aware of their load of pain, going at a speed which might be thought reverent; perhaps the speed of a cortège which might have passed this way bearing a dead Roman; certainly at a speed slow enough for the women to throw flowers onto the roofs and bonnets. White blossom crushed under the wheels. Spring blossom like white feathers. How many of these weeping, black-veiled women had urged their men to join up? He thought of Freddie Barton breaking down when he received a white feather through his letter-box, Freddie loath to leave his crip-pled mother, Freddie dead at Ypres.

A distraught, grey-haired woman broke through the crowd, attempting to hurl herself in front of an ambu-lance and nearly succeeding but for a policeman who caught her and swung her clear. The driver had to pull up sharp, causing the six ambulances following him to brake hard – he leaned out of the window, railing at the woman. William heard his own voice joining a chorus of others – 'Bloody fool!' Didn't she realise that even the slightest jolting would hurt the wounded men inside, perhaps cause a haemorrhage.

The crowd quietened after the incident and the ambulances lumbered on into Watergate Street.

———

25th May 1917
The last few weeks have set me back, with pleurisy and bronchitis. The medical officer calls it a relapse. More convalescence and my leave cancelled.

2nd June 1917
I have lost the Spring, but perhaps will survive and stumble through another year – reading A.E. Housman has been my consolation. Elizabeth sent me *A Shropshire Lad*. How could she afford it, and what did she go without in order to buy it? Her intuition of my needs, her faith in my talent, sustain me.

For her I must write, or attempt to write. There is much I want to say. I've been preoccupied with thoughts about the durability of stone and the brevity of flesh, about the tombstones of Romans – soldiers marching, dying in a foreign land – and about this war, how it infects everything like a disease, like poison gas, like bacteria, like the pneumonia which nearly killed me. I want to write poems about Matthew. But no poetry will come, not a spark, not an image.

3rd June 1917

News today of Matthew. He's in Liverpool. Mam
had word from Mrs Costello who says he was home
with his mother for a while, but went back into
hospital. She didn't know why or which hospital,
except that it's in Liverpool. That's all! Infuriating
not to know more. And still no reply to my letters.

4th June 1917

Now, at last, I'm declared well enough for leave.
Tomorrow! Already my mind runs forward and I
can scarcely wait to find Matthew and be with him
again, yet at the same time I'm fearful. So severely
wounded – how will it have affected him? I haven't
forgotten Captain Powell's warning.

To be home after fourteen months that seem like
endless years. Home to Elizabeth, her children, Mam
and Pa. A postcard's been sent to let them know. I'm
giddy, must steady myself, think of Mam, her
unchangingness (is there such a word?) – this
morning she'll have put on her coat, the light brown
coat she takes out of the cupboard every year in
Spring and folds away in September. She'll be
heading for the shops in Brunswick Road, or is
already there, queuing. There'll be a tram at the top
of the hill, people shoving on and off, old men like
fixtures on the park benches. There'll be that stout
woman with orange peel cheeks and her daughter,
the one with yellow hair, selling flowers at the corner
of the traffic island. The daughter will be winking at
men at the tramstop, offering them buttonholes, and
each flower she offers will be white, as white as
bandages and dead faces.

June. Liverpool. On days like this, I'd open the window of my room, breathe in the tang of sea air filtered through city soot. I'd hike down to the ferry and board it and marvel at the browny-grey river that will outlast me.

9

At Chester General Station William lowered his kitbag to the ground and studied his ticket. Leave included free travel so he had enough change in his pocket to buy a mug of tea at the kiosk and the morning's *Manchester Guardian*. Nine a.m. He shivered, and the yellow-brick of the Victorian station took on a sickly hue, the arches grubby with layered soot. Cradling the mug to warm his fingers, he glanced at the milling crowd, many of them soldiers and their families, some clasped in a final embrace before departure. Only hours before he'd be home, before he'd be with Matt – he'd search the hospitals until he found him.

His train steamed in and passengers poured onto the platform. Better push on to secure a seat, he didn't feel strong enough to stand in the corridor all the way.

He found a compartment with three vacant seats, and loaded his kitbag into the rack. Before he could sit down a small elderly woman in a silver-grey coat bustled in and claimed two of the seats, thrusting her suitcase and matching holdall onto them. Drat, he'd wanted that corner seat by the door but now had to sit in the middle of the row. Still, she seemed a pleasant little lady, whose bright brown eyes stared at him in a penetrating way, scrutinising his hospital blue jacket and red tie, his cap with the Cheshire Regiment badge; she flashed him an admiring smile, her cheeks shaping into lovely curves. He smiled back. She must have been very beautiful once, and still was beautiful, but what a ridiculous grey hat, a pork pie with a horizontal feather poking out of it.

'Here! In here, Olive,' she called to a youngish woman in the corridor, who came in and nervously straightened her skirt and jacket before sitting down. Obviously her daughter, with the same close-textured skin, the same pert mouth and high cheekbones, but with clear blue-grey eyes. He pictured his own lovely woman, Elizabeth – no, not his. He rebuked himself for the thought but was unable to banish it.

As the train drew out of the station, two of the three men in the other seats thumbed tobacco into their pipes and unfolded newspapers. Out into the overcast June day, the train gathered speed, shedding the ragged suburbs and patches of industry. Could green be as green as this, he asked himself. After months in sterile grey and white, he'd forgotten how bright and luminous was the green of new growth. The train ran through the flat fields of Cheshire, fields depleted of horses, farms drained of men. He noticed groups of women working (were they planting or gathering?), herds of black and white cows, the distant gleam of the Mersey estuary. Every mile was bringing him nearer to Matt, nearer to Matt, nearer to Matt . . . he caught the rhythm of the train . . . closer to Matt, closer to Matt, closer to Matt.

Outside Runcorn the train stopped for a signal; five minutes passed before it jerked forward. He began to cough, choked by the air in the compartment, thick with incessant pipe and cigarette smoke from the three middle-aged men. He wanted to claw his way out to the corridor, but this, too, was smoke-filled, packed with soldiers.

'Here, young man.' The elderly woman produced a flask of water and a cup from her holdall. He drank gratefully but the coughing spasm continued, deep racking coughs as though his lungs were collapsing.

'You!' she snapped at the other passengers. 'Stop smoking! Open the window! Give him some fresh air, for goodness sake!'

One of the men pulled the window down, took a last urgent draw on his cigarette and tossed it out; the others tapped out their pipes, grunting and sighing. This was a carriage near the front of the train: through the open window the roar of the engine drowned all other sound and smuts of soot drifted in like black snowflakes.

His coughing subsided at last and William lay slumped in the seat for the rest of the journey, his eyes closed. The train slowed and halted at several small stations before it creaked to a final stop. He opened his eyes and saw the familiar long bays and glass roof of Lime Street Station. Home. He held back his tears.

'Is anyone meeting you?' the woman asked. She and her daughter were gathering their luggage; the three men sped away.

'No, I didn't know what train I'd be catching.'

'Then you'll need some help, laddie. Olive will find someone from the Red Cross. They're always here meeting the trains. We come regularly to Liverpool to see my son in the Royal Hospital.' She sighed. 'He's recovering from an operation. Wounded at the Somme.'

Olive came back at once, accompanied by a Red Cross worker, a tall man who shouldered the kitbag and helped him along the platform to an ambulance.

'I can't thank you enough,' William murmured to the two women as they began to edge away. He watched them go until they were swallowed in the crowds at the station exit.

'Sit in here, son. Breathing problems. Aye, we see a lot like you. Steady there. Just lie back. We're not going yet – dropping some others off at hospitals. Convalescents.'

No, not another hospital. 'Please could you take me home? Everton?'

His street, the row of houses unchanged, the same cracked paving slab he'd tripped over when he was twelve, skinning both knees. Mam, Pa and Elizabeth at the door with the Red Cross volunteer. Damn this wheezing. He longed to run to them, but could hardly stand. Must get out of the ambulance.

'Careful, now!' the volunteer caught him as he swayed towards them, supporting him in strong arms. 'Take it easy, lad.'

Their faces a blur. Mam crying out. Pa and the volunteer half-lifting him up the steps to the door.

'Bed's what he needs now, Missus. He'll be fine after he's rested.'

'Thanks,' he managed to say as the volunteer left them.

'Can you manage the stairs, Will?' Elizabeth took his hand. How pale she looked, and weary.

'Here, lad, let me help you. Up we go.' Pa gripped

him around his shoulders; they took the stairs slowly and reached the first landing.

'We've got your bed ready and aired,' said Mam, with a tremble in her voice.

His bedroom. Mam helping him out of his coat and holding him to her, cuddling him. The pillowy warmth of her body. He sank down onto the bed.

Elizabeth undid his bootlaces and began to remove his boots; he noticed the anxious look in her eyes. 'That train journey was too much for you, Will. You'll need to rest for a few days.'

'I need to know about Matthew,' he burst out, 'then I can rest. Do you have any news of him?' He heard his own shrill tones.

Mam tutted. 'Never mind Matthew Riley. It's yourself you should be thinking of. The state of you – you should still be in hospital.'

'But you don't understand. I need to know how he is, where he is –'

'We'll find out what we can tomorrow,' Elizabeth cut in. 'Try to rest today.'

Cries of a baby, muffled at first, then strident, rose from a nearby room.

Elizabeth looked agitated. 'It's Gwyneth – she's teething.'

A light squeeze on his shoulder and she was gone.

Pa came in that moment with the kitbag over his shoulder. He swung it onto the floor, next to the tall oak wardrobe. 'Good to have you home, lad.'

'Thanks. I've –' William stopped, his wheezing giving way to a fit of coughing.

Mam poured water into a glass from the jug on the dresser. He drained the glass and handed it back to her.

'There now. No more talk.' Mam pulled the blanket up over his legs. 'You look exhausted. Rest now. I'm making you a nourishing *cawl* for dinner.'

He saw her wiping tears away with her hand as she and Pa left the bedroom. Within moments he slipped into the long, sweet sleep only home could give.

10

He'd got this far – and without having to stop. Good. Just one long street, then a shorter one and he'd be at Matthew's house. He turned into Everton Road, crowded with handcarts and horsedrawn vehicles. He paused, looking downhill to the river and across to the skyline of Welsh mountains, blackly purple, seeming much nearer than they actually were – a sure sign of rain. Moel Famau and the whaleback ridge of the Clwydian hills: would he ever again be well enough to walk those heights? Probably not, but he intended to try. If he could make it to the slopes, perhaps just lie in the grass by the track to the summit, he'd look down on his Eden – the Vale of Clwyd – see again its veil of blue light, the distant sea-line.

Now the first drops of rain, a welcome wetness to damp down the dust churned up by wheels, the lethal dust. He walked past shops he'd known before the war, recognising the names and tradesigns; many were shuttered. Two, he knew for sure, would not open again. And there, a few yards further on, was Bradley's the Tailors, where he'd had a tweed jacket made after joining Levers.

He felt the feared tight sensation in his lungs, then came the wheezing, the short painful breaths. If he could reach Bradley's. He sat gasping on the step, leaning against the old grey wood of the entrance, trying to fight off the feeling of suffocation, eyes misting over again, please not that, keep calm, it will pass like it did last time. He kept his hands clenched in the pockets of his greatcoat to prevent himself rubbing at his eyes. Swooning almost, he was back at the Casualty Clearing Station with his hands tied to the bed, his eyeballs searing. How much more painful Matthew's suffering must have been, and probably still was. How close to death had he come?

Resting in the doorway, he saw the notice 'Closed' and was relieved not to be disturbed by customers. People hurried along as the rain became a downpour, the gutters not coping. He watched the rivulets running across the sooty pavements. Gradually his wheezing lessened and the blurring cleared like mist on window panes. He dragged himself up and went slowly on, pausing frequently, until he reached Lloyd Street and crossed over to the pavement on the left. Matthew's house was halfway along the red-brick terraced street whose slate roofs shone in the rain. He could never see it without hearing Matthew singing 'It's Irish invaders we are, we are! It's Irish invaders are we!' – his joke about his family living in a street with a Welsh name, put up by Welsh builders in the last century for Welsh immigrant workers. If only Matt was here now. He lurched up the street. Would Mrs Riley be in? If not, he'd try Mrs Costello or one of the other neighbours. Which hospital? Why had Matt been readmitted? The dread of knowing, the torture of not knowing. And why no note, no word in all these months?

He leant against the wall of the Rileys' house trying

to recover his breath and steady himself. Many of the houses had blinds down or curtains drawn, some had wreaths on the doors. What were the names of the lads who'd lived there? Faces came to him, one lad in a grubby jersey, Bobby James, and his friend Marty. They lived a few doors from each other. Was it Bobby's house with the wreath?

Rain sluiced from the gutters and became a continuous heavy curtain. He straightened up and, heart pounding, he lifted the knocker and gave two taps. Mrs Riley came to the door immediately, as if she was expecting a caller.

'William!'

He remembered the tight smile, her raven-black hair, now streaked with grey; she was thinner, shrugged into herself.

'Come in, come in. Take off that soaking wet coat.'

She hung the heavy greatcoat and his cap on a coat-rail in the long, narrow hallway; he followed her into the parlour, stooping as he entered, relieved to slump down onto the couch. Holding a handkerchief to his face, he tried to stifle his wheezing.

'Rest there. I'll get you a drink.'

She returned with a glass of water. 'We heard you were gassed, that you nearly died?'

He gulped down the cool water. 'Well, I suppose that's true enough.' He drained the glass and again pressed his handkerchief across his mouth and nose.

Mrs Riley perched on the edge of the couch. She took the glass from him.

'Let me get you some more –'

'No. Really, no, it's all right, easier.'

'Are y' sure now?'

He remembered how pressing she could be, how insistent, how she'd repeatedly come into the parlour reminding them of how late it was. *'Matthew, shouldn't William be getting back?'* or *'We've got to be up first thing.'*

'When did you get home?'

'A week ago. This is my first time out. I was in a hospital at Chester for months. Pneumonia. Mam managed to get across to see me a few times.'

'You've heard about our Matthew?'

'Yes. That's why I've come, Mrs Riley, for news of him.'

She looked at him sharply. 'Matty was home for only a month, you know. A month. Then the doctor sent him back to hospital.'

'Was he –?' William's question, one of many he was bursting to ask, was cut off as she went on.

'We were luckier than them opposite, at least.' She crossed herself with the crucifix on a silver chain around her neck. 'They lost all three sons, the Barneses. And next door, the McEvoys – their Brian missing now, and Gerald killed at Loos. Regular Army, one of the first to go across, Gerald was. They had the telegram about Brian last week.'

He recalled the ginger-haired boy who liked to gamble on anything, even the next day's weather, and how he astonished everyone at school by his uncanny wins.

'They're hoping Brian's a POW. Every day hoping for news of him.'

He nodded. 'Well, I've heard that the Huns treat their prisoners quite decently. Perhaps Brian's luck was in.' He thought of the thousands of men blown apart, bits of them shovelled into sandbags, and the thousands more uncollected corpses decomposing in the mud. Missing forever.

'I've written to Matthew several times. But he's never replied –'

'Jesus, Mary and Joseph! You obviously haven't understood how he's been.'

'Then tell me how he is, Mrs Riley. Please. I want to know –'

She ignored his pleading, gave him a sharp sideways look. 'They haven't discharged you yet, then.'

'No, not yet,' he managed to smile, and tapped his blue coat. 'They hang on even to crocks like me in the hope we'll be fit to go back. I was sent to a camp, made to do some training, would you believe? The Instructor took us to the parade ground and shouted – "Gassed over here. Quick march!" Half of us fell down after a few steps and had to be transported back to hospital.'

Mrs Riley laughed, with a tilt of the head so like Matthew's that William's feelings surged.

'How is –'

Again she cut him off. 'I'll make us a pot of tea.'

'No, please, I've come for news of Matthew. I must know how he is. The amputation. Why he's back in hospital. Can't you –'

'There's no "must" about it, that's for sure. Matty's business is his own – and mine. I'll not be giving details to anyone.'

'But I'm not anyone, I'm –'

'I'll get the tea.'

'Mrs Riley –'

He got up intending to follow her into the kitchen,

then thought better of it. Let her make tea for them, he'd talk to her gently, soothe her down, win her over.

It seemed incredible to be back here in the Rileys' parlour, their best room with the flocked green wallpaper and the framed photographs on the wall, one of Matthew aged about three, standing with a ball in his hands, impish, chubby. Another photograph of him in uniform. Next to that one of Liam, serious in his cadet cap. And against the wall Matthew's beloved black Rushworth's piano, the lid closed. William felt his throat constricting. He touched the lid and the sheet music strewn across the top. Beethoven. Chopin. Liszt. He gathered the sheets together; underneath were manuscripts, Matthew's own compositions dated 1913, 1914 and one dated 1915 with corrections, and beneath this an Army document. A Medical Case Sheet. Matthew's. William picked it up and began reading, his hands shaking.

MEDICAL CASE SHEET (copy)

432818   Pt Riley, M. 1/13 Bn Cheshire Regiment.
Age 25
Disease: G.S.W. (shrapnel) multiple wounds
Wounded: 7.7.16

Extensive and penetrating wounds of right arm and hand.

Two smaller wounds on right thigh, front, and several superficial wounds of right shoulder and neck. Skin of right trunk and leg peppered with tiny fragments of shrapnel. Removal of shrapnel in France.

18.7.16   Secondary haemorrhage from wound in right forearm, artery ligatured. Lividity of right arm from elbow downwards.

20.7.16   Increased lividity of forearm. Temp 103. Whole arm warm.
No tactile sensibility in hand. Brandy 3 p 4 hrs

23.7.16   General condition bad. Forearm gangrenous, much discolouration as far as elbow. Temp 101–103

24.7.16   Amputation through arm at junction of humerus and elbow.
Flaps drawn down. Saline given. Oxygen given. Morph 1 / 4.

25.7.16   Saline injections 2 hourly for 6 hours.
           Adrenaline given with the first.
           Patient in poor condition. Frequent
           attacks of vomiting. Mild haemorrhage
           from the stump.

18.8.16   Patient is generally wasted. Wound
           healing slowly. Sloughy.

27.8.16   Unhealed surface at the end of stump.
           Second operation.

26.9.16   Small unhealed surface. Scab covering
           terminal scar. Considerable puckering of
           the skin.
           Condition of wound satisfactory. No
           deformity of stump.

6.10.16   Admitted to Roehampton for artificial
           limb

14.12.16   Admitted to Alder Hey Hospital,
           Liverpool.

12. 3.17   Recommended for discharge home.
           Discharged from Regiment.

M.R. Richardson
Capt. RAMC

—◦◦◦—

William sank back onto the couch, still holding the Case Sheet. His mind was reeling and he felt faint. He could scarcely focus on Mrs Riley when she came in with the tea tray, but her voice pierced through him.

'Where did y'get that? It's private – you've no right to be reading it!'

He flushed. 'Of course. You're right. I'm sorry. I was looking at Matthew's piano pieces and found it there. I wanted to know –'

'I always knew you for a nosy journalist. Don't think you can go writing about Matty. Snooping around here to find out about his amputation. You know you've read what you shouldn't have!'

She plonked the tray on a table. 'Give it to me!' Without waiting for him to hand the Case Sheet to her, she snatched it out of his hands.

'Matty must never know it's been read, not by any-one.' She placed it back on the piano among the music sheets with a show of care for the accuracy of its position.

He was still reeling from the shock of the medical facts, the horror behind the clinical details, Matthew's extremity of pain in all its forms.

'Lost your voice, have you. Now, let's get it straight. No writing! D'ye hear me?'

'Of course I won't. I simply want to know as much as I can about Matt – to help me to understand –'

'Listen. No one but me can really understand what he's been through, how he's been changed by it all.' Her eyes were fierce.

He controlled his sudden anger and remained silent, twisting his signet ring round his finger. The tea tray on the low table in front of them, so civilised, was like a sneer.

He felt he could cope no longer with either his own feelings or the intensity of Mrs Riley, her accusations, the protective wall she was putting up around Matthew. He broke out in a sweat, his spine seemed to be disintegrating. Was he going to pieces, like Beattie, like Foreshaw?

'Matty's life was saved by the amputation, don't ever forget that,' she snapped.

He managed to rasp out the question he'd come to ask.

'Why is he back in hospital?'

Mrs Riley stood up, moved across to the window, staring out. He expected another rebuke, and was surprised when she turned and replied to his question.

'The pain. His arm – the stump – gives him so much pain. And the depression. Moping about, day after day, refusing to do the exercises, won't practise using his left hand, hardly eating, staying in his room.' Her voice became low, strained. 'Saying over and over he wished he was dead.'

He was unable to speak or think of any consoling words, but sat awkwardly, wheezing, exhausted.

She poured out the tea, put milk in and handed him the white cup. 'Y'see, it was hearing him cursing, cursing that he'd ever been born. Cursing the shell for not killing him outright.'

'I used to think like that too, most days, wishing I'd been killed rather than gassed. It'll take time, a long time –'

'Well, he's got me. I'm the only one he wants to see.'

William longed to contradict her but instead tried to swallow his tea. He found himself blurting out words she wouldn't want to hear. 'Matthew and I became very close out in France. I'm sure he'll want to see me.'

'Jesus! Didn't I tell you! Listen. That was then. Now's now! He'll not want to see you. Not you or anybody. Think what he's been through, what it's like for him now.'

He gulped down the rest of the tea and made a movement to go.

'Another cup?'

He jerked up from the couch. 'No, thank you.' What hypocrisy. Another cup of tea after being flayed.

To get out of the suffocating atmosphere, be out of the gaze of this woman, her accusing eyes, her bony sallowness. To feel the rain on his face, the cool rain. He edged over to the parlour door, taking a last glance at the dead piano.

'I'm very sorry, Mrs Riley.' He took his greatcoat and cap from the coat-rail. 'Can you tell me which hospital he's in?'

'No, I won't.' She went ahead down the hall and opened the front door. 'He won't want to see you. He won't see anyone except me. Keep away from him. Do I have to tell y'again! You'll only upset him – after all, you're still in one piece aren't you. Once you've got over the gas you'll be back to normal. He'll never be normal again.'

Her words were an icy cut. He'd heard other people say the same, not understanding the effects of gas poisoning. But worse was the appalling comparison she'd made between himself and Matthew, the barrier she was putting up between them.

As he stood on the step in the rain she closed the door without a word of farewell. He turned up the collar of his greatcoat and set off down the street.

11

The VAD pointed to a lawn where wounded soldiers sat with their visitors in the afternoon sun. William's heart raced. Which one was Matthew? He crept from group to group and then towards a quiet corner shaded by tall trees, and a bed-chair in which some-one was lying, a blanket across his legs and his left hand holding the blanket. Matthew. His eyes were closed.

William stood still. Even though he'd tried to pre-pare himself, he was overwhelmed – that cruel space where Matthew's arm had been, the empty sleeve pinned up, flat and neat, to his shoulder. And his left hand, the length of his fingers, the hand-span he'd been so proud of, now a reminder of all he'd lost.

That last time together at Breilly, the lake-side under the willows, Matthew's eyes shining as he spoke of 'after the war', of playing in concerts again, composing. Most of all, composing. William felt his heart would burst.

The scene around him seemed unreal, like a paint-ing by an artist intent on the effects of light and the arrangement of groups – the wounded and visitors, the crutches and wheelchairs – all lit by June sunshine, the light a gloss, covering the suffering, the pain. A counterfeit.

Sounds intruded – murmurings and laughter, forced jollity, the rattling of a tea trolley pushed by a VAD. The chinking woke Matthew. He looked up, startled.

'Billy!' He began to weep.

William knelt beside him, wanting to hug him but restraining himself, unable to speak, grinning, choking back his own tears.

Matthew spoke first.

'I got your letters. Sorry I didn't write back.'

'Don't worry.'

'But I did write to you – in my head. Couldn't get it down. Meant to send word through one of the VADs, but didn't. Somehow I was swamped by all of this.'

'Matt, it's all right,' William muttered. Anything he said would be totally inadequate to express what he was feeling and thinking. 'We're both here. Incredible isn't it, both of us alive?'

He noticed the silver at Matthew's temples, the many tiny scars in his neck, his extreme thinness, even more than when he'd last seen him in France.

There was so much he'd planned to say; he couldn't stop looking at Matthew, couldn't resist touching his hair.

The VAD arrived with her tea trolley and handed a cup to William. He drew up a chair and sat down. She placed a beaker of tea for Matthew on the small table at his left side. He grimaced when she'd gone. 'Now see how clever I am – or am not.'

He lifted the beaker.

'Look! A child's learning-to-drink beaker, with a spout in case I spill the tea.'

'You're doing fine,' William said.

Matthew slammed the beaker down on the table.

'You don't know how I'm doing, Billy. No one does. Not Ma, even. She thinks she knows, but she doesn't. Treats me like a sick child.'

'She's trying to –' William stopped, confused by the outburst. Then he mumbled. 'I went to see her the other day, to get news of you. She wouldn't tell me which hospital. I guessed it would be Alder Hey and took a chance on it. I was desperate to find you. But I can't say she encouraged me.'

Matthew sighed. 'Well, you know what Ma's like. I can't stand it at times and want to scream at her. Sometimes do. But she was so sure I'd be killed, you see. Living in fear from day to day, expecting a telegram. Now that she's got me back she's . . . ' He hesitated, looked unsure.

William quelled his impulse to say something about Mrs Riley. Wiser to change the subject.

'How's Liam?'

'He was frightened when he saw the stump.' Matthew frowned. 'Wanted to pull out of the cadets. When he told his friends, they turned on him – he was bullied, beaten on his way home. Tries not to be around if I'm downstairs and that makes me want to be anywhere but home. I'm happier in here with those like myself, those who know what's it's like over there.' He threw back his blanket and sat on the edge of the bed-chair. His eyes looked wild. 'I'd go back tomorrow if they'd let me. I hate the war, but I'd rather be dead than have to live like this. I wish that bloody shell had finished me off.'

'I understand,' William murmured, miserable, hiding that he was shaken by this glimpse of Matthew's personal hell. No point in mouthing homilies such as 'things will get better', no point in speaking of the future they'd planned. This was not the right time or place to be talking intimately; and Elizabeth's words, 'don't expect much of Matt today', rang in his mind.

He noticed a soldier sitting on his own under the trees nearby, staring at them over the top of his newspaper, watching intently as Matthew described the deaths of Rogers, Hurst and others in his platoon.

'We were moving towards the ridge when this happened.' Matthew indicated his right shoulder. 'The shell burst directly over me. A piece like an axe sliced into my arm. I fainted with the pain for I don't know how long. You remember Tommy Jordan? When I came to he was lying next to me, decapitated.' He stopped, his voice choked. 'I dragged myself back as far as I could towards the line and lay there until some SBs picked me up and took me to a dressing station. From there to Rouen, Number 2 Field Hospital. The worst was when gangrene set in –'

He stopped talking, his expression curious as he gazed at William, as if seeing him for the first time.

'Tell me about yourself, Billy. About the gassing. Everything.'

Until then William had managed not to wheeze, but now felt his breath catching, a tightening in his chest. He hoped it would pass, that it was just temporary, brought on by the tension of these first minutes together.

'It was after the advance on Ovillers,' he began. 'We were in the back area, in the rest trenches –'

'Mind if I join you?' The soldier who'd been watching now stood over them, blocking out the sun.

William did mind the interruption, of course he did,

but what could he say to stop it? Especially as Matt was smiling at the man, evidently someone he knew, a sergeant, dark, with a small moustache and older than them by about ten years.

'Sidney Kempton.' He introduced himself to William, pulling over a chair. 'Cigarette?'

'No thanks, Sid,' Matthew answered for them, and introduced William.

Kempton took a silver lighter from his top pocket and lit his cigarette, sucking in the cheeks of his long, aquiline face. He blew out the smoke, looking directly at William. 'Mine was just a Blighty wound.' He pointed to his neck. 'I was lucky. Severed tendons. That and a shattered shoulder. Not nearly as bad as it could have been. Nothing like as bad as young Riley here.'

'Or poor old Mitchell over there!' Matthew gestured towards a soldier in a wheelchair. 'Both legs blown off.'

Kempton went on about his own wound, caused by a trench mortar at the Ancre. 'Ended up here in Alder Hey,' he smiled and again inhaled, his fingers cupped around the cigarette. 'Riley and I were admitted in the same week.'

Was Matt merely being polite? Surely he resented this intrusion? If so, he wasn't showing it. Why wouldn't Kempton shove off? There he sat, dominating the conversation, stabbing the air with the cigarette he held like a pencil, banging on about the war, newspaper reports, what a disaster the coalition was, how despicably Lloyd George had manoeuvred Asquith out.

Damn it! He wanted to contradict Kempton, defend LG, but didn't have enough voice, enough strength.

And why was Matthew keeping silent? After all, he was an admirer of LG, or used to be.

'So you'd have known Jimmy Foreshaw,' Kempton prompted. 'I met him before the war on an engineering job in Crosby. Someone told me he'd copped it for cowardice. Ran off. Deserved the court martial.'

'No, that's wrong!' William was stung into speech. 'Foreshaw certainly isn't a coward. I know from experience, he —'

His voice was drowned by Kempton's, again butting in. 'He was lucky not to be executed.'

'That's unfair —' William choked as Kempton's cigarette smoke caught his throat. Eyes streaming, he felt ridiculous. Dizzy and faint, everything receding, he could hear his breath rasping as if it was outside his body.

Matthew struggled up, yelling for help.

A nurse ran across the lawn. 'Lie down!' she ordered. William slumped onto the grass.

'That's it, as flat as you can.'

Soaking a towel in water from a jug, she placed it over his eyes. 'Breathe in slowly and deeply through your nose. Keep your mouth closed. This will control the attack.'

He fought against the drowning sensation.

'Stay still. Try to relax, beginning from your toes upwards.'

He did as she instructed and felt his tension receding. She chatted on, telling them how she'd specialised in gas patients after Loos. When she removed the pad from his eyes there was no blurring. He could see Matthew. Thankfully, Kempton had gone.

'Lie still for another ten minutes,' she ordered,

folding the damp towel. 'And come up to the ward for a check-up before you go home.'

'Thanks,' he whispered, and lay there, eyes closed against the sunlight.

He felt his hair being ruffled, Matthew bending over him.

'You gave me a fright, Billy lad. I didn't realise how ill you are.'

'A lot better than I was,' he managed to say.

Matthew flopped back on the bed-chair. He lay there, silent. What was he thinking, William wondered, swamped by a feeling of abject failure, angry with himself for having the attack. He should have been cheering Matt up or distracting him with chit-chat like Kempton's. Perhaps if Kempton hadn't come over, he wouldn't have had the attack. But it was important for Matt to understand that he, too, was maimed. No, not visible injuries, but if Mrs Riley repeated her vile comments about him being *in one piece*, Matt would know better, know what the gas had done.

'The bloody Generals!' Matthew shouted for all to hear. 'They should be killed off themselves. Send the lot to the Front Line for twenty-four hours and we'd get rid of them!'

'Matt!' William pulled himself up onto a chair.

'I'd be out there if I could, seeking a "glorious death" or whatever else they call it. An unglorious death more like!' He looked desolate.

William knew what he meant. He'd heard others say the same, in hospital at Chester particularly. And the contrast between life at the Front and life at home was hardly believable. Everything in him cried out against the war. He never wanted to see the Front again.

That obscene hell. Home was like coming to heaven. And though his head wasn't clear, his energy low, he had hopes of improving, of being able to concentrate again, even write a little.

'Have you done any writing lately, any poems?' Matthew seemed to have read his thoughts.

'Just a few jottings when I was convalescing. I haven't been able to focus or think straight.'

Matthew leaned forward, looking at him intently. 'How close to death were you? Tell me the truth, Billy.'

'There was a time – forty-eight hours – when I was sinking, unable to breathe – it was touch and go then. My heart held out.'

'You always were strong in that quarter, Billy boy.'

Words William would hold onto. He was unable to see Matthew's expression as he'd turned his head away.

The afternoon sun slanted through leaves lifting and falling in a light wind. Rooks cawed in the chestnut trees, where generations had roosted before them. Good to have this oasis of green sound. William listened gratefully, letting the atmosphere seep into him, relieved to be with Matt again, relieved that his breathing was easier. At five, a gong rang out and visitors began to leave, while the VADs wheeled the wounded back inside the hospital or helped those on crutches and others who shuffled along.

How much more vulnerable Matt looked now, shrunken and frail, as they went across the lawn.

'There's the workshops.' He pointed to some large wooden huts where a few disabled men were coming out. 'Curative workshops they call them. Colonel Jones' idea. To keep the mutilated from going insane. Usefully occupied, work for body and soul, what-ho!'

'Work? What sort of work?'

'There's a few choices, depending on what limbs you've got left.' Matthew jerked his head towards the end hut in a row of three near the hospital entrance. 'I work in that one. Just now and then. Making splints. Rather do that than stamp designs on leather. Splints for the poor buggers who'll need them. Not that I can do much, but every little helps.'

'Perhaps I could help? That's if I get discharged next time.'

'Surely they won't be sending you back?'

'That's what I thought at Burton. Then the retraining! But I'll know soon. The Board –'

They'd reached the hospital doors. Matthew went through and led the way along a corridor to his ward. 'This is my corner,' he said with a wry grin.

William looked and smiled, but felt hollow.

The bed near a window, a table, and on it a thick block of white paper and some pencils.

'For practising writing with my left.'

A small pile of books and magazines. And propped against the wall, an artificial arm with leather straps. Matthew picked it up by the gloved hand. 'I'll never get used to this.'

He glanced at William. 'Customised! I was measured for it at Roehampton. A good fit. But it can't even lift a piano lid.' He tossed the arm onto the bed.

'Oh, Christ!' William moved towards him but Matthew turned away to the window and stood with his back to the ward.

'Private Manderson. Your check up.'

Damn! He didn't want to leave Matt but the nurse stood waiting. He followed her to an examination room. A doctor, a stethoscope, the familiar tests, deep breaths, a torch shone down his throat and droplets put in his eyes. The usual advice about rest and fresh air.

Thanking the doctor he left eagerly, wanting to get back to Matt.

Blast! Kempton was hogging Matt again, perched on the edge of his bed, Matt lying out, his head on a mound of pillows. They were deep in conversation and didn't look up as he approached.

'Listen, Kempton!' William blurted the words out. 'Do you mind? It's been almost a year since I saw Matt.'

'Sorry, old man. I'll leave you to catch up.' Kempton swung down from the bed and shuffled off. Then he turned around. 'See you later, Riley.' With that, he lit another cigarette. William saw insolence in the hooded eyes.

'Here, Billy. Sit here.' Matthew indicated a seat next to the bed. William was stung. Only next to the bed, not on it. He remained standing, stunned by Kempton's evident intimacy with Matt.

'What did the doctor say?'

'I'm going to live,' he grimaced. Disorientated, wrung out, his voice stiff, he could only repeat the doctor's advice, not think of anything else to say.

A VAD came up the ward. 'Private Manderson. The ambulance is outside now.'

'When shall I come again, Matt? Shall I come tomorrow?'

Silence.

William was bewildered. 'Do you want me to come tomorrow?'

Still no reply. Oh God, what was it? What had gone wrong? They walked down the corridor and out to the hospital entrance.

'Matt –'

'Not tomorrow. Ma's coming tomorrow.' He spoke slowly.

'The day after?'

A hesitation. 'Yes, come then.'

As the ambulance pulled away through the lodge gates and along Alder Road, William looked back at the hospital behind its long sandstone wall. Clearly, it was Matthew's sanctuary. But eventually he would have to leave and where could he go from there? Surely not back home under the consuming eyes of his mother. Yet, without money how could Matt live elsewhere?

He would find a solution, he'd work out something for Matt.

12

Two days later, William climbed the stairs to the attic with his breakfast mug of tea. He sat in the old wicker rocking chair and took a sip of the hot liquid. Ambrosia, compared with what had passed for tea at the Front. For a moment he was back near Ovillers in the rest trench and someone was brewing up on an old primus.

Sparrows fussed about in the eaves and he relaxed, receptive to their chittering, gently tipping the rocker back and forth. He would start out soon after eleven for the hospital. He'd get there early, head Kempton off. He'd need privacy to put forward his plan to Matt.

In the excitement of the thought, he sprang up and opened the window of the attic, letting in the morning air and breathing it in as deeply as he dared. Today, for the first time, no wheezing, no snatching of his breath. With his spirits high he looked out over the city, its smoky pall thinned by the wind. Scudding clouds, rooftops catching unexpected light and shadow, spires and tall buildings in the commercial heart of the port. Tall masts of ships forested the Mersey and, on its opposite bank, the Wirral peninsula spread out like a frieze. And beyond this, the long horizon of hills that drew his gaze, hills that made Liverpool seem part of the Celtic land, hills whose mood altered with the light but which, for him, were always bright with promise.

His love for this place, this dirty port, was matched only by his love for Wales. Into his mind flashed shell-torn Albert, the blackened husks of buildings, toppled spires, blasted trees. He'd marched past a row of shattered houses, their fronts blown off, open like dolls-houses, every floor exposed. He'd seen women weeping, others picking about in the ruins, one woman putting a kettle on the hob and taking it off again, mechanical movements; a woman like Mam, someone's mother, and Albert, someone's town. He pitied the inhabitants. If Liverpool had been bombed like that . . .

Every day he spent some time in this attic, his 'studio' Elizabeth called it, his homecoming surprise. She must have taken weeks preparing it, decorating and furnishing. The deal table was from her own room, and on it she'd placed some books, including Shakespeare and a dictionary. A lamp, her treasured lamp from home, with the elephant feet. A pot for flowers from her Della Lucca days, decorated with vine-leaves. The rocking chair, given by Pa, fresh with linen cushions she'd made from old curtains, an orange and lemon design. And a bed, set against the wall, in case he needed to rest.

He crossed the room to the table on which he'd arranged his pens and pencils in a jar and his note-books in two stacks, roughly chronological – an encouragement to write, when he felt stronger. He sat and ran his fingers over the antique inkwell Elizabeth said she'd found in Pa's trunk, made of horn and brought from Sweden. As yet he'd not managed to write anything new in the studio, only sit and think, and during the last two days think about Matt, his predicament, the bleakness of his prospects, his vulnerability. He kept returning to those hours at Alder Hey, his first sight of Matt under the trees, the empty sleeve. He would offer him a room here, at No. 80. There were several empty rooms, including the other attic and a furnished room on the second floor. It would mean freedom for Matt, a chance to find his way again. And they'd be fulfilling the plan they'd made for 'after the war', their plan to live together. Then the closeness would return. He was sure it would return and grow. Yet his heart was heavy with the realisation that their time at Les Trois Ruisseaux had not been the lodestone for Matt that it was for him; Matt hadn't clung to the memory the way he had. And what was Kempton to him? Just a hospital friend?

'Unca Will, Unca Will!' Lily pushed open the door and hurtled towards him.

He jumped up from his chair, caught her in his arms and managed a twirl around the room.

'Show Molly the window.' She held out a rag doll and he went into the game of talking to Molly, holding her at the window to see the birds and clouds.

'Unca, take me to the park.'

'Let's see what your Mam says.'

'Mam's here.' Elizabeth came in, carrying Gwyneth. Slightly out of breath from the climb up two flights of stairs, she seemed relieved to sit in the rocker. She soothed the baby, who'd begun to grizzle.

How lovely Elizabeth looked in her pale blue morning robe, her dark brown hair loose around her shoulders. Must stop gazing at her.

'I've had a letter from Jack this morning. He says he's in Reserve and recovered well from a touch of trench fever. Asks for news of you, Will.' Elizabeth adjusted the baby's shawl. 'No mention of any leave. You know, it's hard to believe he's never seen Gwyneth.'

'Hard for both of you.'

'Yes, that's probably true. But I must be patient.' She lowered her voice. 'So many children will never see their fathers again. As long as Jack survives . . . '

She lifted Gwyneth higher on her lap and bounced her lightly to a nursery song she chanted in a low voice. The baby's little face, a miniature of Jack's, her sheen of new flaxen hair, sad blue eyes – she stared at him and thrust out her fist for him to grasp. He knelt in front of the rocker and placed her fingers around one of his.

'What a year to be born in.' He kissed Gwyneth's tiny hand and looked up at Elizabeth. 'No wonder she cries. She senses your fears for Jack.'

As if in agreement Gwyneth broke into a more sustained crying.

'There now!' Elizabeth rocked her and quietened her with a dummy, then glanced at William, that quick intuitive look he loved. He picked up a colouring book Lily had dropped and sat with her on the bed, turning the pages, reading the story.

'You're looking better, Will. Less exhausted,' Elizabeth said. He felt her scrutiny, knew she was mentally drawing him, recording every detail of his features, every expression. Had she already made some sketches of him? What a wreck he must have looked when the Red Cross brought him home two weeks ago.

'Pa's right. He keeps telling Mam and me that you've got the Manderson strength and he's perfectly certain you'll make a full recovery. You'll soon be writing again, Will.'

He glanced at his notebooks on the table. 'I've been copying out the poems I wrote at the Front. Bringing them together, though some are just fragments. I don't think I'll ever complete them.'

'Unfinished poems are still poems.' She shrugged. 'Just as uncompleted drawings are drawings. How can we tell if an artist thought he needed to do more to his work, regarding it as unfinished, when to our eyes it looks as though it is?'

'Yes, but with language –'

'They're still poems. Read one to me, Will.'

He selected a notebook. Not suitable, he thought, turning page after page. Too bloody true. Not this one either, not with Jack at the Front. Perhaps this one . . .

'I wrote this after the gassing. My sight kept fading and I thought – I feared – I'd be blind. It was like a miracle being able to see clearly again. Didn't get far with this though –'

'Come on, Will. While Gwyneth's quiet.'

'It's called "Rechristened Eyes". Well, here goes –'

As if for the first time
I watch leaves riding their own tide,
Waves claiming the passive land.

As if for the first time
I see clouds disperse, gather, glide
Under the wind's invisible hand.

I look with rechristened eyes,
Can distinguish twilight from night . . .

'That's as far as I got. Nothing else would come.'

'Those last lines are strong. Just give yourself time. Don't fret. It will all come back.'

'Focusing is difficult though. I think the gas has had a permanent effect on my brain.'

'Nonsense. You're still exhausted, physically and emotionally. You're expecting too much of yourself.'

'And as soon as I'm better I'll be packed off to the Front again.'

'Surely not! The Board will discharge you next time. Have you heard anything from them?'

'No, but they'll be after me any day now, and it might be a different Board. More ruthless. At Alder Hey the doctor said I need further convalescence and, in his opinion, should be discharged from General Service.'

Elizabeth said nothing, but looked worried.

A hooter sounded in the corporation yard at the top of the street. William stiffened.

'See now, you are getting stronger. The other day you leapt out of your seat when that old hooter went off. Knocked your tea over. You were all hollow-eyed, staring as if you'd seen ghosts!'

He laughed. 'It's being up here that's made the difference. Good for my nerves, no doubt about that.' He changed his tone. 'Seriously. I mean it. And, Elizabeth, I want to ask you something, something important. Do you think we could let Matt have a room here? He needs a place of his own – it's intolerable for him at home. What do you think?'

Elizabeth got up abruptly, holding Gwyneth to her shoulder. 'You'll have to discuss that with Mam.' Her voice was tight as she turned away, fixing the baby's shawl. 'No doubt she'll like the idea – she's always saying how empty the old house is, with all her lads away.'

'I'm going to tell Matt about it today. He'll be delighted, I know.'

She stopped at the door, calling Lily. He noticed the tired lines around her eyes, a sadness in her expression, probably due to lack of sleep and her concern for Jack.

'I'm all right, Will.' She'd read his thoughts. 'Don't worry about me.' Moving Gwyneth to her other shoulder, she turned to go.

He put his arms around them, caught into their sweet almond scent. At last his sense of smell was becoming keener. The joy of it, the piquancy it brought to being alive. He lingered, breathing in the warm biscuit smell of baby flesh and the fragrance of Elizabeth's hair; found himself nuzzling into it, kissing it. He pulled away, feeling a flush rise up his neck and face.

Elizabeth looked surprised. Then she drew him to her and kissed him on the mouth. A kiss that stopped thought, that shook the ground, made the room spin.

'Unca, can we go?' Lily whined, flinging a cushion to the floor. 'Are we going to the park now?'

'Ssh!' Elizabeth bent over the child. 'Just for a short while, then.' She glanced up at him. 'If that's all right for you, Will?' Her eyes revealed nothing.

She'd closed herself off from him; it was as though nothing unusual had happened. He stood there, dazed.

'Will?' She touched his arm. 'It'll help me. I want to give Gwyneth a bath.'

'Yes. Yes, it's all right. Just – just half an hour.' He pulled up his braces and took his coat from the back of the chair.

William and Lily walked down the path, which bisected the new Gardens and the lawns covering the filled-in graveyard. He still couldn't see this as a park, only as the Necropolis, and his childhood fear surfaced, fear of the ghostly cemetery he'd stared at from his bedroom window, stretching into the distance, thick with stone monuments and memorials, angels and crucifixes above the overcrowded dead. And now, overlaying this, he saw the newly dug mass graves near Albert, the raw earth, the makeshift wooden crosses.

Lily skipped ahead, clutching Molly and turning frequently to smile at him. That smile so like Elizabeth's. The kiss . . . undoubtedly a mistake, a loving impulse she evidently regretted. Not a passionate kiss, but tender and gently seductive. He was surprised to find himself aroused, more so now than then, as he relived the feel of her lips on his. If she had kissed him like that five years ago – but the thought was disloyal to Jack and he felt ashamed.

As they walked towards the flower-beds, two munitionettes wearing trousers and turbans approached up the path. One woman smiled at Lily, said something to her friend and they stopped at a bench where they put down their shopping bags and lit their cigarettes.

'Your little girl's lovely,' said one.

'And her dad's not bad either,' said the other.

William held Lily's hand firmly as they passed the women.

'Who is my dad? Are you my dad?'

'No, Lil. I'm your dad's brother.'

Lily looked puzzled. 'Why did the lady —'

He distracted her, pointing to the pansies. 'Look at their faces. They're like Spaniel dogs.'

'But they're not barking!' Lily laughed, high, tinkling.

William helped her onto a wooden bench and sat next to her. An undertow of sadness, a physical sensation, pulled at his stomach. Lily threw Molly onto the flower-bed. Immediately he leaned down to pick up the doll and saw beneath it a skull protruding from the soil. He broke into a sweat and his fingers trembled as he shook the earth off the doll. When he looked again the skull was gone. Steady yourself, breathe slowly, from your stomach upwards.

The Gardens sloped towards the main road where trams and other traffic passed by continuously. Directly opposite the park loomed the Royal Hippodrome Theatre, a big friendly presence. He tested his eyesight, straining to read the billboards. Between the stone pillars at the park entrance came a familiar figure, head slightly tilted to one side. For a moment a line of dead soldiers marched towards him, this special one leading the others up the central path, coming nearer, nearer, and then Matthew shouted.

'Hello, Billy lad! A surprise eh?'

William stuttered. 'I was coming to the hospital today —'

'I know. But I've been discharged. Some bad cases arriving. They need the beds. I was on my way to tell you.'

'When did you –'

'Get home? Last night. By ambulance, with all my things. Ma's delighted, of course.'

William was astonished. Not only was Matt home, but he seemed pleased, cheerful. 'Naturally your Ma's delighted. But how do you feel about it, Matt?'

'I'll tell you later.' He bent down to Lily who'd jumped from the bench and was trying to pick a wallflower. 'Lily. This must be Lily. Hello, Lily.'

William lifted her back onto the bench and she sat between them. He couldn't fathom Matthew's mood, his almost elated air, or why he'd come from the opposite direction to Lloyd Street, on the other side of the park.

'This is Molly.' Lily put the doll on Matthew's lap.

'Hello, Molly,' he laughed, dancing it on his knee. 'Funny dolly Molly.'

Silent, Lily frowned at him, staring at his jacket sleeve pinned back to his shoulder. She snatched Molly from him and hid her face in William's coat. 'Unca,' she cried, 'where's the man's arm? Why is he hiding his arm?'

He tried to quieten her. 'It's all right.'

But it wasn't all right. Matthew looked as though he'd been hit.

'I'm sorry, Matt. She's only young and doesn't –'

'Don't apologise. No need.' Matthew snapped. He shrugged and stood up. '"Out of the mouths of babes and sucklings" . . . something I've got to get used to.'

Lily continued to squirm, looking anywhere but at

Matthew, and hid behind William's legs when he set her on the path. As they walked up the park, she trudged, dragging her feet, holding William's hand tightly. Christ! How could he stop her shouting something else? What could he say to help Matt?

'She doesn't realise about war, but when she's older –'

'Leave it, Billy! Bloody hell, haven't I told you!'

Stupid, he chastised himself for Matt's distress. They walked on in silence. A breeze had sprung up, whisking fallen petals across the lawn. The munition-ettes were gathering up their bags, evidently about to go, but now they loitered. Damn! No hope of evading them, cheeky things.

'Aah, here's our lovely lad,' one called to him. 'Don't you look grand in that blue coat. Where were y'wounded then?'

'Bet ye're proud of yer dad,' the other said to Lily.

He flushed and tried to hurry Lily along. She held out the doll. 'He's not my dad. He's Molly's dad.'

'Oh, lord luv 'er.'

As they passed, the women stared hard at Matthew, nudged each other and went silent. He hoped Matt hadn't noticed, and perhaps he hadn't, striding on ahead.

As they left the Gardens, a bi-plane roared over from the direction of Aintree, flying so low they could see the pilot in the cockpit. Matthew stood trans-fixed, watching it into the distance as it curved through the clouds, heading out to the Mersey and the sea beyond.

'I'd hoped to get into the RFC,' Matthew spoke at last as they reached the yard door of number 80. 'An

NCO at Etaples told me that if the war continues long enough they'll be looking for trainee aircrew. I'd have liked that, Billy, reconnaissance –'

'You never told me.'

'I'm telling you now, aren't I, idiot!' Matthew grinned and playfully punched him on the back. What a relief to see Matt smiling again.

He led the way down the stone steps and through the door into the basement. Their eyes adjusted to the darkness of the back kitchen and they ducked under the sheets and washing hanging from a pulley. Neither Mam nor Pa at home, the kitchen empty, but a fire smouldered in the hearth and the kettle steamed on the hob, presences giving life to the room. Lily left them, rushing upstairs without a word.

The table was laid, as always, with clean bowls, teacups, saucers, plates, as if visitors were expected. This was Mam's habit, from the days of what she called 'a full house', all the family at home. William loved this continuity, loved the way she left a loaf upended on the bread-board and, close to it, the butter – margarine now – with 'tramlines', the serrations of a knife, running across it. Matt, he could tell, was already beginning to relax in the comforting atmosphere and had taken off his cap and coat.

'Here, Matt.' William drew two armchairs towards the fire. 'Tea?' He was aware of Matt watching him intently as he took two mugs from the dresser and poured the hot water into the teapot. Matt sat down, giving him a deep, almost questioning look, but saying nothing.

Footsteps on the stairs, the door pushed open, and Elizabeth ran across the kitchen followed by Lily.

'Good to have you home, Matt!' She kissed and hugged him, then sat next to him chattering about the baby and Jack. Thankfully she was tactful, not asking him about the amputation; thankfully too Lily was quiet, preoccupied with making Molly a bed on the sofa cushions. How light and dancing Matt's conversation – he was his old bantering self today. No sign of depression. No mention of wanting to go back to the Front to be finished off. This sharp change of mood and attitude – not an act he'd put on. But perhaps these unpredictable moods were to be expected after all he'd been through.

'Sounds as though Gwyneth'll be a leader.' Matt responded to Elizabeth's description of the baby in one of her imperious attitudes. 'That reminds me, I saw a friend of yours this morning. One of your Suffragettes – Amy O'Connor. She was driving a tram and waved to me as she went by.'

'Good for her! I always knew Amy would take the wheel one way or another.'

William heard a tug in Elizabeth's voice that belied the buoyancy of her reply. He noticed her face darken. She looked away, then got up. 'Would you like to see Gwyneth? I need to check on her. She never sleeps for long.'

Afterwards, William took Matthew up to his attic. Now the moment had come, he would surprise Matt with his plan, like unwrapping a present. They stood at the open window. In a flurry of wind the long muslin curtains billowed out and wrapped around them. They struggled, netted and laughing, then disentangled themselves. William closed the window and picked up some sheets of paper blown off the table.

'It's marvellous what she's done for you here, Billy.'

'I know. I'm very lucky. But how are things for you, Matt – at home? I mean – your Ma? You seem to be more cheerful now about being home.'

'Well, yes. But I wanted to explain –'

'Listen, Matt. You can live with us! You can have the other attic. We'll do it out, make it like this one. And Matt, we'll be together!'

Matthew looked astonished. 'I can't.'

'Why not?'

'Because I've already accepted an offer from Sid Kempton – his house in Newsham Park.' He pulled from his pocket a bunch of keys, an enrapt look on his face.

William's legs went weak, his heart lurching. He sank onto the bed.

'I thought you'd gone back to your Ma.'

'Indeed I have. Just for a few weeks. Sid's still in hospital but he's expecting to be out any day now. It'll give Ma time to get used to the idea that I'm moving.'

William's mind was reeling. Matt going to live with Kempton. Now he understood that insolent look Kempton had given him, and Matt's elation. He felt an unexpected rush of sympathy for Mrs Riley.

'You've definitely accepted then?'

'That's what I've come to tell you. First thing this morning I went along to check on the house for Sid. It's been empty since his sister married. Six bedrooms. Sid said I can choose any of them, whichever takes my fancy.'

'I see.' William tried to steady himself.

'Aren't you pleased for me, Billy? It'll solve a lot of my problems.'

'I'd hoped to do that for you. I'd set my heart on it.'

He found himself on the landing outside the other attic. Matthew's room. Empty. The creak of the door as he swung it back, dust on the floorboards, the imprint of his footsteps in the dust. Shattered, he stood at the window, hearing over and again Matt's words, half excuse, half promise – 'no time to talk about it now. Tell you next time I see you' – then the flippant 'Got to go!' And there he was, striding along the street below, turning into the Gardens, down the central path, and ahead of him someone getting up from a bench, walking towards him. Kempton. They strolled together down the path.

The sensation of falling from a great height into a chasm, his body disintegrating until nothing was left, only an aching void where flesh and bone had been and where hurt burned and burned. He reached the bed in his room and slumped onto it, covering his face with his hands.

A touch on his shoulder startled him, and Elizabeth's voice. 'I met Matt downstairs on his way out. He told me his news.' Then her arms around him, cradling him, the warm softness of her. She stroked his hair. 'I understand.'

His sobs, when they came, were for his own despair and disappointment and for more than that, for his bottled-up hatred of the war, what it had done to them, what it had done to others.

She held him tenderly, soothing him, continuing to

stroke his hair. 'Remember, the best way to hold a bird is with an open hand. Give Matt that freedom. He'll love you the more for it.'

He quietened, taking in what she said but not believing it to be true.

13

William opened the low gate of the vegetable garden in the yard. The wood was pulpy and rotten and falling away from the rusty hinges. He would mend the gate and the broken fencing and clear the patch, overgrown with tough grass and nettles. At the market he'd buy seed potatoes and plant them with other root vegetables and lettuces. This would help Mam and Elizabeth. He set to with a pair of shears, clipping the bearded grass. Nettles toppled, releasing their sharp aroma. He rolled up his shirt sleeves, grateful for his returning strength, though otherwise empty and drained. The morning was pleasantly warm with a breeze which fanned his hair and cooled his sweating body. It reminded him of his days at Bryn Tirion and he was back in the grey stone farmhouse and the sloping fields in the lap of Moel Famau. If the Army discharged him he'd return to Wales, ask Aunt Mair for work, leave Liverpool behind except for occasional visits to the family – and Elizabeth. But no, he couldn't leave Elizabeth.

The latch of the yard door lifted. He looked up, expecting to see Mam returned from shopping. Matthew came in and stood there, grinning, his cap on the back of his head. He shut the door and leaned against it.

'I see you're busy, Billy, but I had an idea this morning – would you come with me to Alder Hey? The workshop? You did say you'd like to help out. I told them I'd do a couple of hours this afternoon. We could have a drink at Gregson's Well before catching the tram. What do y'think?'

They sat in a corner of the pub, where smoke hung in the air. Bearable for a short time if he didn't begin to cough. He waited for Matthew to speak as they took their first long sips of beer.

'I'm still with Ma.' Matthew darted a look at him then hurried on, his voice thin and strained. 'But I've told her I've had this offer from Sid and she's begun to accept that I'll be moving. At least I won't be far away, she can come when she wants to, even do some cleaning there from time to time.'

William had struggled through the last three days, tortured by questions. Now he'd ask for answers.

'Is Kempton besotted with you?'

'I remind him of his close friend Larry.' Matt paused, gulped his beer. 'Larry was killed at Thiepval. Sid saw his body on the wire, hanging there until a shell blew him apart.'

'But –'

'No buts! I know Sid seems possessive. You must remember he's been like a father to me.'

'Nothing more?'

'No, nothing more.'

'Then why are you going to live in his house?'

'Sid's on leave now and after that there'll be retraining. Then he'll probably be going back to the

Front, unless he gets a home posting. He wants to do something for me, give me a place of my own for as long as I need it. I'm going to look after his house and garden – a kind of caretaker. He's drawn up an agreement with his solicitor. If he's killed –' Matthew hesitated, his voice husky '– if he's killed, the house will be left to his sister. Sarah will let me continue there if I want to, even if she decides to move in. She runs a secretarial college in town somewhere and lives on the premises.'

'I see.' William felt chastened but relieved, telling himself to say no more, to hold back. Even so, he couldn't erase his intense dislike and distrust of Kempton.

In the large wooden hut, men were bent over long benches, others carrying or stacking the splints. William took in the happy atmosphere, the bonhomie and joking, some of it crude. While a few men bore no outward sign of their injuries, most did – some with bandaged heads, some in plaster casts and others, who had lost either one or both legs, worked in their wheelchairs at special benches.

He immediately liked the instructor, Ted Whalley, a sandy-haired cheerful Red Cross volunteer who treated him and Matt as a team and showed them how to work together for maximum output, adding with a grin, 'But take your time'.

From a heap of wood, already cut into assorted lengths, Matthew selected a piece and placed it on the bench. William then sawed it to the required size. They soon set up a rhythm, and worked for a half hour or more, until he noticed Matthew wearying. How pale he'd become, his face tight, his expression clenched; and with an air of silence rather than silence itself as he continued to respond to the jokes flying about.

'Can we have a rest? I need to stop.' He pretended for Matt's sake. 'Any chance of a cup of tea?'

'Over here, lads.' Whalley called them into his store-room, piled high with long boxes filled with splints.

They took their mugs of tea outside. William led the way to a tree in a secluded part of the lawn. Matt lay on the grass and fumbled at the buttons of his jacket. 'Billy, help me to take this off.'

William pulled the jacket off and folded it as a pillow. Matt sank back on it, groaning. His shirt sleeve was folded back so that his stump was uncovered. How vulnerable the bare flesh, rounded, pink, like something newly born, and the end gathered into a small seam. The pathos of it. William managed to hide his reaction, turning away as he took his own jacket off, then lying down.

'It's aching today, worse than usual,' Matthew gasped. 'Any practical work's an agony. I can feel myself doing things yet I'm not doing them.' He drew in his breath as the pain caught him. 'It's as though the ghost of my hand's taunting me to touch, lift, pull, but there's nothing here, nothing to do it with.' He stared at the stub of his arm. 'Useless remnant! It's the nerve ends, Billy. They're still raw, they feel like sharp teeth gnawing and gnawing.'

'Can't something be done?'

'Yes, but I refused to have a third operation. Meant taking more off. They warned me, the pain could go on for years, perhaps for as long as I live. And –' he stopped.

The leaves above them filtered the sunlight and dappled their faces and bodies. William leaned over and gently took Matt's stump between his hands. He wanted the warmth from his own flesh to enter Matt's, hoped that somehow it would ease the pain. No words from Matt, no telling him to leave off. He stole a glance and saw tears on Matt's face.

'No one's done that for me before.'

On arriving home, William was greeted by Mam coming towards him with a copy of the *Liverpool Echo* in her hand. Spectacles on, her voice rising with excitement, she read

'"The 1917 Welsh National Eisteddfod to be held in Birkenhead." Well now, isn't this wonderful news!'

William smiled. 'Astonishing news! In Birkenhead – the Welsh National Eisteddfod! Why outside Wales?'

'Because of all the Welsh living in Liverpool and Birkenhead. It says, "The Eisteddfod looks after the interests not of Wales alone, but of Welshmen and there are more Welsh around here than would be found in any similar area in Wales itself." And likely it is that Lloyd George will attend. Gwilym, isn't it amazing?'

He laughed, delighted at Mam's delight and her rare use of his Welsh name. 'When will this be?'

'Early September. There'll be thousands coming, choirs from all parts of Wales, music and poetry contests, the Chairing of the Bard, think of it! A big festival's just what we need to buck us all up. I can scarcely wait!'

She folded the newspaper and propped it against a vase on the marble dresser. Still ecstatic, she left the kitchen, singing in Welsh one of her favourite hymns, '*Calon Lân*'

William sighed. Come September and the Eisteddfod, would he still be home, or back at the Front by then, or dead.

Mam reappeared, holding several letters. 'These were delivered while you were out, Will.'

Familiar handwriting on two of the envelopes . . . Dennis Gray from Levers, Charlie Thompson. And a brown envelope. William ripped it open, read the letter and flung it on the table. 'The Medical Board. I'm due next week.'

Mam's expression changed to apprehension. 'You'll be discharged this time, surely to goodness?'

'Oh, I'm not sure at all. They're desperate to fill the ranks.'

William crossed Lime Street in the late June sunshine. He needed to visit his lion. Half an hour to go before the Medical Board, before he'd learn his fate. He'd touch the lion's paws as he had before embarkation. Well, he'd come through hadn't he, just about? He'd need all the good luck possible today, ironically one of those rare days when he felt back to normal, breathing without a hint of a wheeze. No coughing, no tightening sensation. Probably due to the recent brisk winds from the Irish Sea clearing the air of smoke; and this bright but not hot morning, conditions which suited him. Yes, he'd pass as fit, he was sure – the Army wouldn't let go. He broke out in a sweat, his stomach clenched at the thought of retraining and, if he survived that, a draft to the Front Line. A return to 'kill or be killed'. Yes, he was a pacifist in his heart and mind, but didn't have the courage to be a conchie. Well, he'd have to face up to the Board, there was no escape, and if he didn't turn up he'd be arrested for desertion.

Before setting off, he reached up and performed his private ritual, placing both hands on the lion's left front paw and then on its right. How comforting the warm stone under his palms. If ever good luck could be transmitted, let it be now.

He entered the Central Hall headquarters in Renshaw Street and stood in a queue of soldiers at reception. Ten minutes to go before eleven. An elderly sergeant with sad, tired eyes ticked his name on the list. 'Private Manderson, you're next. Strip and wait over there.'

In the drab corridor outside the cubicles he sat on a bench with two other naked men. One trembled continuously and dribble fell from his open mouth onto the floor; the other man, emaciated, with staring eyes, twitched and jerked his limbs like a marionette in a puppet show. Compared with them, William knew he looked a perfectly healthy specimen.

Five long minutes passed before an orderly summoned him into the hall. Three grim-faced RAMC officers sat at a desk, none of whom he'd seen at previous Boards. Ridiculous to be saluting them when naked. Blasted army protocol.

The orderly measured his weight and height while the three MOs each studied a set of papers.

William stood in front of them. Still no wheezing or catching of his breath.

'Gassed at the Somme, Manderson.' The balding officer in the middle, a Captain, spoke with a strong Lancashire accent. His tone invited a reply.

'Yes, sir.'

'You've done well to recover. And you've gained weight since your last Board. Good. Let's examine you then.'

William stood stiffly while the MO prodded him, listened to his chest and pressed around his stomach.

'Right. Get dressed Manderson and wait outside.'

He dressed in the cubicle and awaited recall. Ten minutes passed on a clock with noisy fingers above the door. Why was the decision delayed? Had the MOs disagreed? The two naked men still sat on the bench, trembling and jerking. He saw a batman go into the hall with a tray of tea.

Another ten minutes and the orderly reappeared. 'Private Manderson.'

At last. Heart lurching. Now, only now, damn it, was his breathing tight, rasping.

The senior MO, who'd examined him, passed a sheet of paper to the other officers who signed it in turn. He looked directly at William.

'Manderson, you were severely gassed. One of their experimental cocktails. Phosgene certainly, with other gasses. The fact is, your lungs are permanently damaged. And – you need to know this – they can only get worse. You should be prepared for further deterioration.' He paused and cleared his throat. 'Manderson, you'll be sorry to hear we've decided to discharge you.'

* * *

William was light-headed as he walked back along Renshaw Street and took the tram. The shock of release disoriented him. He was out of prison but in a turmoil, at one moment floating on a thermal, the next about to drop into a dark ocean. The implications of the discharge began to hit him – his lungs likely to deteriorate further, the ominous tones of the MO. So the Boche had done for him after all. But he'd keep this likelihood to himself.

Mam hugged him and wept tears of relief, Pa shook his hand. He looked for Elizabeth but she was out with the children. Carrying the mug of tea Mam had poured for him, he dragged himself up to his attic room where he slumped onto the bed.

Drifting in and out of sleep, he saw the Death's Head Hawk moth beating at the window, fluttering, banging, beating. His head ached, whirling with the instructions he'd been given: demobilisation papers to be signed, what he could keep – was it his uniform, helmet and greatcoat ? – what he would be paid. And he needed to tell Matt. But could he force himself to call at Kempton's house? It was a week now since Matt had moved in. He was tired of making silly excuses to avoid visiting him, even though he knew Kempton had been posted to Ripon. But he dreaded seeing Matt in Kempton's home, the atmosphere of Kempton wrapping him round. Damn it, he'd have to face that test sooner or later – for Matt's sake and his own – and it might as well be on this day of ordeals.

* * *

With a curious sense of detachment, as if his body was somewhere else, William walked into Newsham Park. He tracked along one of the curving drives bordered by three-storeyed houses, his steps automatic as he knew every corner of this park, a favourite boyhood playground. The early evening sunshine lit vast open spaces of grass where the leafy branches of old oak trees and horse chestnuts cast shadows that bowed and tossed in the breeze. He needed to focus, shake off the sense of unreality, look for the house named, Matt said, after a place in Ceylon near the tea plantation where Kempton had lived with his parents.

And there it was, 'Jaffna', written in bold yellow lettering on black, the nameplate on the gate of a substantial red-brick house with bay windows in a row of similar houses along the drive. He stopped, took deep breaths, chided himself, tried to summon up his courage. He couldn't rise above his loathing of the situation. Jealousy, he kept warning himself, corrosive, like poison gas.

Someone was gardening – it was Matt, bent over, digging a border. William watched from the screen of the hedge as he plunged the spade into the soil, forced it in further with his foot on the blade, levering and turning the earth. How well he managed with his left arm, grace and energy in the rhythmic movement.

'Matt.'

He spun around.

'Billy! I was going to call at yours tonight to see how it went –'

'They've discharged me.'

Matt threw the spade down. 'So they bloody well

should. Let's have a drink to that.' He nodded towards the open front door. 'I've got a jug of beer.'

William hesitated. 'No. I just wanted to let you know. That's all. I'd better be getting back –'

'What? Come on, Billy, it's not the lions' den. Anyway, I thought your second name was Daniel.' Matt gave his puckish smile and went towards the door.

William followed across the tiled floor of a wide hall, noticing the oil paintings on the walls and a large brass gong near the oak-panelled staircase.

'My rooms.' Matt wheeled around. 'I've taken all these on the ground floor – kitchen, bedroom, parlour and Games Room.'

Nonchalantly said, but there was a look of apprehension in his hazel eyes, a look William interpreted as concern about his feelings this first time in Kempton's house, a look which reassured him, brought a spurt of joy.

'Oh, and behind the staircase there's a bathroom.' Matt laughed. 'How about that, an indoor lavatory?'

'Good,' William said, smiling. 'Luxury.'

'Let's have that drink. Cain's bitter, no less.'

In the kitchen Matt poured the beer from an enormous brown jug into two tankards on the rectangular deal table. 'Here's to you, Billy lad,' he said, handing one to William. They clinked the tankards together and drank.

William took in the spacious room with its high ceiling and tall windows looking out on a small rear lawn and wooden fencing. A dark oak dresser dominated one end of the kitchen, holding blue and white dishes, shining brasses and a carved ivory Buddha. Over the wide fireplace hung photographs – Kempton in uniform; young Kempton, age about ten, with father, mother and small sister, all wearing pith helmets, posed in bright sunlight before a verandah; another in the tea plantation with servants and workers; Kempton at boarding school; Kempton in shorts holding a hockey stick; Kempton on horseback.

William felt that Kempton was in the room with them, listening and watching. How bizarre it was to be with Matt in this house, a house filled with the presence of a man he hadn't known until a month ago, a man he didn't want to know. He heard Matt say something but missed the words.

'What did you say?'

'I said I want to show you something. Now, before we have another drink.'

William followed him across the hall to a door which opened into a long room overlooking the park. In the bay window stood a piano shrouded with a dust sheet: for a moment he hoped this might be what Matt wanted to show him.

'The Games Room,' Matt announced.

A billiard table stood in the centre, and against one of the walls a mahogany table with chess pieces set out, the blacks outnumbering the white pieces on the board, as if the game had been abandoned. On the wall facing the window hung a darts board.

William leaned in the doorway watching as Matthew placed his tankard on a glass-fronted cabinet filled with gleaming silver cups and trophies.

'Watch this, Billy.' He stood before the darts board, three darts in his left hand: placing two in his trouser pocket, he held the third between thumb and fore-finger, then eyed the target for several moments before aiming one dart after another. Each little shafted arrow hit the board with a satisfying thump, two in the bull.

Matt grinned. 'Strengthening my left.' A questioning look. 'What d'ye think?'

'I'm astonished!'

'Want to play a set?'

'No, definitely not.' After the initial chill and bite as the beer slid into his empty stomach, a warmth ran through his veins. The room tilted.

'Not this time, Matt. I'm out of practice.'

'Next time, then! Let's drink to the next time.'

William lurched into the yard and down the cellar steps. As he expected, the kitchen was in darkness, Mam and Pa upstairs in bed. Good. He didn't want them to see him in this state. He'd sleep it off and be fine in the morning. 'Positively nappoo.' He laughed and said it again, louder this time. 'Positively nappoo,' adding, 'Tickety boo, where's my shoe?' and stifling his laughter. Who was this, waiting at the bottom of the staircase? Elizabeth held him as he swayed. Her arm around his waist was firm, supporting him up the short flight of stairs and onto the landing.

'In here, Will. Come on. Quiet now.'

She led him into her rooms, made him sit on the couch. She closed the door of the children's bedroom, then turned up the lamp on the side table.

'Here, let me take your coat.' She pulled on each sleeve as he struggled out of it. 'That's better.'

She undid his tie and the top buttons of his shirt, and plumped up the cushions behind him.

'Lie back there a while until your head's clearer.' She knelt on the floor by the side of the couch. Her lovely face, so close to his. If he could reach out, kiss her. He saw tears, her eyelids raw from weeping.

'What is it? Is it Jack?' He was conscious of his words slurring.

'No. Not Jack. It's not that!'

'What then? One of the children?'

'No. No matter. It's just me.' She tried to laugh. 'A good weep.'

But why that stricken look? He was puzzled. Must be his fuddled brain. Fool. The room spun. He felt the pressure of her hand on his.

'I heard your news. Mam's so relieved you won't be sent away again, bless her. She's been so happy this evening.'

He sighed.

'There's more, isn't there? More that you haven't told us. Why have they discharged you?'

'Just that – gas poisoning.'

'Yes, but what did they say?'

He turned onto his side. Why was she so insistent? All he wanted to do was close his eyes, sleep.

'Will! Tell me what they said.'

'Deterioration . . . my lungs permanently damaged . . . can only get worse.'

He hadn't intended to tell her. Now she was kissing his hand. More tears. Then a blanket was tucked around him. Again he felt her hand, this time smoothing his hair. He needed to sleep, a long sleep.

* * *

192

At dawn, his eyelids hurting, his head fuzzy and aching, he crept out in the grey light, and along the corridor to his bedroom.

14

In a freshening wind, gulls followed the ferry as it steamed across to Woodside on the Wirral bank. William and Matthew leaned on the rail of the crowded top deck. Visibility was good, and they could see as far as the river-mouth where New Brighton Tower loomed, tall and spindly. The brown waves of the Mersey surged in a strong tide, skimmed by a flock of shining birds. 'Goldeneye. Rare visiting birds from Iceland,' Matthew shouted. 'On the way to their wintering grounds.'

William's spirits lifted. A fine Thursday morning in September, and here he was, sharing an excursion with Matt. These were moments carved out of time and in spite of the war. Yes, they were both damaged, but they'd also been lucky. They'd survived. Escaped. He wanted to share these thoughts with Matt but kept them to himself rather than risk provoking one of his rages. He could hear the bitter protest, Escaped! No, we haven't really escaped at all. We're prisoners in our bodies! – and the repeated cry, I'm only a part of what I was! Yet glancing at him now, he saw Matt's face transformed as he watched the flock of Goldeneye. Instead of the pinched look of misery, here was the ecstatic look he loved but hadn't seen since France when Matt played the farmhouse piano: a look of intense pleasure and involvement. If only he could rekindle Matt's interest in the natural world.

The ferry approached the Woodside terminal crab-wise, tawny froth like beer churning around the stern, the hooter blowing. He felt a thrill of anticipation. The Eisteddfod. Today, the highest bardic honour – the Chair – awarded for the best long poem in strict metre. He was keen to hear the adjudication of the winning poem and how this year's set theme '*Yr Arwr*' (The Hero) had been interpreted – he would need to con-centrate, testing his understanding of Welsh and Welsh poetry. And at last he would see Lloyd George.

Although the Chairing of the Bard was an afternoon event, they'd set out mid-morning, intending not to take the tramcar from Woodside to the Eisteddfod in Birkenhead Park, but to walk, a distance of about four miles. William's aim was to walk a little further each day. While he didn't remember the detail of all their pre-war walks, the precise route and directions, these being Matt's concern as navigator, he did remember the writing afterwards, poems mainly, often evoking the atmosphere of a place – Formby shore in the mist and the hidden highway of ships, or that walk to the beach through scented pine woods, or some small incident such as meeting an old cobbler who remem-bered Matt as a baby, or a personal detail, like the time he'd slipped on seaweed covering the rocks at New Brighton and was winded and Matt had yelled his concern against the roar of the tide. He'd hoped to find inspiration on their walks that summer. No success as yet, preoccupied with breathing not writing.

He'd agreed with Matt's planned route to the park via Hamilton Square which he hadn't seen for years –

the Gardens, the fine Town Hall and houses, and on the corner the former studio of the Della Lucca Pottery. His mind slid back to the hours he'd spent waiting nearby for Elizabeth to leave work; how when he saw her he'd lack the courage to approach, and would hide, feeling ridiculous with his cheeks hot and heart pounding; how one time she'd spotted him and he'd lied that he was just passing that way to the ferry from Levers.

'Look at that!' Matt's voice jerked him back. Decorations hung in profusion from the balconies, and a large white platform was being erected in front of the Town Hall. 'You'd think there was something to celebrate,' Matt called to the two workmen putting finishing touches to the platform. 'What's it for?'

'The Prime Minister tomorrow,' one of the men shouted back. 'The Freedom of the Borough conferred by the Town Council.'

'Bloody carry on!' Matt spat the words out. 'Councillors! They've no idea of what's going on at the Front! They don't want to know! Half of them are on the make, getting fat on profits while out there the lads are being blown to shreds. Lloyd George should have turned it down!'

William both agreed and disagreed. He still clung to his admiration for LG and didn't object to him receiving the freedom of the borough. But perhaps the honour should have been delayed until the end of the war was in sight.

'Bloody waste of money, all this!' Matt shouted.

William pulled him back to the kerbside as motors rushed towards them. Matt never lost an opportunity to rail against the complacency of people at home, the way they carried on their lives regardless of the butchery across the channel. He too detested such callous disregard when the papers gave lists of the dead each day. He imagined tomorrow's scene: the Prime Minister smiling on the platform as crowds cheered him; lines of munition girls, VADs, a guard of honour from the Cheshire Regiment, the Mayor and members of the Town Council, no doubt rows of cadets, boy scouts, school children, wives and mothers in the crowd. And all this while their men were being slaughtered. Murdered. How many more years would it go on? He recalled an officer's courageous protest against the war that he'd read in the *Manchester Guardian* a month or so ago, a 'Statement' made 'on behalf of soldiers' by one who'd 'seen and endured the sufferings of the troops' – he remembered the exact words. The name too he'd recorded. *S. Sassoon*. A lone voice. Where was Sassoon now? Undoubtedly he would have been court martialled, imprisoned, silenced. How much truth was there in his accusation that politicians were prolonging the war unnecessarily, aiming for conquest rather than negotiation?

They reached the huge arched entrance of the park. A printed notice gave directions to the Eisteddfod at the west end, in the ground of Cammell Laird Football Club. Already leaves were turning red and falling; the park was heady with the sweet scent of wallflowers, and the paths filled with people going in both directions, but mostly towards the Eisteddfod.

At one of the stalls, William bought mugs of tea and they ate their packed sandwiches while strains of singing reached them, carried on the wind. They threaded their way through the crowd on the field towards the enormous pavilion and joined a long queue to enter. There was Mam ahead of them, with members of the Liverpool Cymrodorian Society. She looked flushed and happy, years younger, like a girl on a Sunday School outing, and wearing her best hat. William waved but she didn't see him, talking excitedly to a luxuriously whiskered man beside her.

Seated at last inside the massive tent, he felt his chest tightening in the humid, close air, the smoke from hundreds of cigarettes. No, not an attack here, he told himself. I refuse to have an attack. Take deep, slow breaths. He made himself relax, look around. About seven thousand people in the audience, he estimated, and numbers of them were men in hospital blue and army caps, like themselves, and VADs and soldiers. Some no doubt would have been attracted by the promised presence of the Prime Minister. But there was a predominance of Welsh, from all parts of Wales as well as locally, many who'd obviously taken part in the morning competitions, dressed for the occasion in the colours of their choirs.

William rejoiced to hear the language spoken all around him. He was alive to the chatter of the crowd, the expectant atmosphere, the buzz of a bluebottle, the grass trampled to grey strands, trodden lifeless into the mud by thousands of footsteps. Mud. He saw duckboards over the mud, endless duckboards at the bottom of trenches, dead men sunk into the clay, and parts of dead men, agonies and mutilation going on even at that moment as they sat here in the Eisteddfod pavilion. His throat constricting, he was relieved when trumpets heralded the start of the ceremony and the procession of Archdruid and Druids in their white, blue and green gowns – these, he explained to Matt, were the Gorsedd of Bards, an association of men of literary, musical and artistic achievements.

Cheering, loud and prolonged, greeted Lloyd George as he strode onto the platform, energetic, bird-like, his fluffy grey hair and moustache familiar from the photographs. He was followed by his wife and daughter, and Lord Leverhulme, looking deeply serious – a smaller and more rotund figure than William remembered (was it three years ago they'd paraded before him at Chester Castle?). Other local men occupied the rows of seats on the stage; all of them looked beyond army age. More cheering and the song 'For he's a jolly good fellow!' rang out as Lloyd George stepped forward to the dais to make his speech.

William hung on his words, delivered in a clear, bell-like voice, disappointingly without a trace of Welsh accent. 'I will try to speak a little in both languages and not too long, I hope, in either,' Lloyd George promised. He'd come to 'the calm of the Eisteddfod' as to 'a city of refuge'; he valued the 'lessons of the Eisteddfod', talked of the role of little nations, of national unity and British patriotism.

The applause subsided and the Chair was brought to the front of the platform for the adjudication cere-mony. William remembered other bardic chairs he'd seen, but none compared with this, its rich oak elab-orately carved with crested dragons.

Archdruid Dyfed and the Gorsedd Recorder stepped forward and stood by the Chair. More trumpets; a clarion call to announce the winning poet.

'Fleur-de-Lis, will you answer the call?'

Again: 'Fleur-de-Lis.'

No one came forward.

And again: 'Fleur-de-Lis.'

Still no one acknowledged the nom-de-plume. William turned in his seat, looking back across the audience. Nobody was coming forward. Murmurs broke the hush.

The Archdruid spoke first in Welsh, and William was able to follow most of the sad speech, spoken again in English in the same grave tones.

'I have to tell you that the winner of the Chair has answered a greater call than mine. The young man who sent in the best composition has paid the supreme sacrifice. Thus there will be no Chairing ceremony today, nothing beyond the calling of his name. He was Private Ellis Humphrey Evans, his bardic name Hedd Wyn, a shepherd from Yr Ysgwrn, in the parish of Trawsfynydd. He sent in a composition last July, after arriving in Flanders with the Royal Welch Fusiliers. Now he rests in a foreign land.'

The silence which followed his words was palpable. William found himself rising to his feet with everyone else while the Archdruid unfurled a black cloth and draped it over the Chair. A wave of shock and sympathy ran through the audience, and then subdued weeping and murmuring.

William glanced at Matthew whose eyes were closed. Not that the death of a soldier was surprising. But the fact of this soldier winning the Chair when newly dead and never knowing of his triumph – the triumph of his poetry – was tragic.

He thought of a rowan tree he'd seen on a

Denbighshire hillside, a solitary tree, its berries exotic, orange-red, its boughs slender and smooth. He recalled how he'd sat beneath it and looked down on a lake hidden in the cwm and watched sheep moving along the side of the cwm with a shepherd. He thought of Hedd Wyn's flocks on the moorland above Trawsfynnydd and how he should be there now in the Welsh peace.

Matt's eyes were still shut during the plaintive singing of a soprano, Madame Laura Evans-Williams, her song a traditional air, lamenting a soldier-hero. Tears were running down the faces of the people around them.

Afterwards, pushing through the solemn crowds, William and Matthew headed towards one of the park lakes. They walked in silence until William spoke. 'Ellis Evans. I hadn't heard his name until today. "Hedd Wyn" translates as "white peace".'

'Well, he's got that now, Billy. Had no choice, did he? Not peace either. Death's not peace, it's oblivion.'

'Yes, you have to be alive to know peace. He would have experienced perfect peace sometimes at Yr Ysgwrn,' William sighed. 'I've known it at times in the Clwydian hills.'

They stopped at the lake, circled by rushes and waterlilies.

Matthew knelt at the edge and looked into the green water. 'Perhaps that's why he chose Hedd Wyn as his bardic name. Wales has lost a great poet. No wonder LG went on about love of Wales being compatible with British patriotism.'

William didn't want to discuss LG's speech or the politics of the war. His mind was filled with Hedd

Wyn. 'To win the Chair and never know it! Never to write again, never to enjoy life as he should have, never to return to Wales.'

They were both quiet for a while. William wanted to say, look we've survived, we weren't touched by the wand, it's our fate, accept it, you the fatalist, instead of wanting to be 'finished off'. He wanted to say let's be grateful for what we've got, think of Hedd Wyn, the empty chair, the thousands of empty chairs.

Matt took a stale sandwich from his pocket and broke it into pieces which he hurled into the lake. A duck made a swift vee across the water, quacking and determined to be first at the feast.

'That's a female mallard.'

'How can you tell?'

'The quacking. Only the female quacks,' Matt said, and grinned.

They devoured the meal Elizabeth had left for them in the big black saucepan on the hob: a hot pot without meat. A note was propped on the table –

Save some hot pot for Pa when he comes back roaring hungry from his bowls match. We've had ours and I'm playing with the girls upstairs and settling them for bed. Mam said she'll be back late from the Eisteddfod.

The grandfather clock struck six and, as if on cue, Pa entered the kitchen, his cheeks flushed, his sandy hair dishevelled. He beamed and nodded a greeting to Matt.

'You won!' William got up and patted him on the shoulder.

'Aye! Now we've beaten the Netherfield team three times in a row. It's getting monotonous,' he chuckled, lifting the lid on the saucepan.

'We've left you plenty, Pa.' William gave him a clean bowl and he spooned in the hot pot up to the brim, spilling some as he lowered it to the table.

'Did you see your Ma over there?'

'That we did. She was thoroughly enjoying herself, we could tell – in her Welsh element.' William laughed. 'But the Chairing –'

The door bell rang, three, four rings in quick succession, William leapt up to answer it, but stopped on hearing Elizabeth run along the hall. Moments later, she rushed into the kitchen.

'Matt, it's someone for you. Sarah Kempton.'

Matt hurried upstairs, followed by Elizabeth. William poured a mug of tea for Pa, his hand shaking. Matt reappeared with Elizabeth and a tall, elegant young woman, her features aquiline like Kempton's, finely boned. She struggled to control her tears.

'Sid's been killed.' Matt's voice was taut, his face ashen. He held the telegram. 'Sarah heard this afternoon.' His words triggered Sarah's sobs and she held a handkerchief to her face.

'Sit here by the fire.' Elizabeth took Sarah's arm and led her to Mam's chair by the hob. She quickly poured a cup of tea, stirred in two spoonfuls of the children's sugar and handed it to Sarah.

Matt, slumped on his seat at the table, stared at the telegram. What was he thinking, feeling? He looked devastated. William's stomach knotted with anxiety – the shadow of Kempton had fallen between them again. He was conscious of Elizabeth's guarded scrutiny of his face as she leaned over the table gathering the used dinner plates and cutlery.

'I'm sorry.' William heard himself saying. But immediately he felt hypocritical.

Sorry. Did he mean it? He'd tried not to look ahead to what the situation would be when the war ended and Kempton returned; and he'd never discussed it with Matt. Yes, he'd wanted Kempton out of their lives. But not killed. He hadn't wished for Kempton's death. Matt and Sarah were grieving – all war deaths, every death, means something to someone, the removal of a person, loved or hated or even only slightly known; each death leaves a silence that affects someone living. 'No man is an island.' But all that evening, after Matt took Sarah home, he couldn't suppress his sense of relief and struggled with mixed feelings of guilt and shame.

15

4th October 1918, 9 p.m.

This morning I wanted to write about Autumn,
linking the death of leaves with the loss of life in war,
the one a natural process, the other an unnatural
cutting off. With this intention, I was about to go up
to the attic when the bell rang and the post delivered
a letter and package for me from an army chaplain,
the Reverend John Farrell. A shock. Peter Sullivan
has been killed – news which I'm still taking in. I've
thought about him all day as fierce wind tore
through the trees and harried the dark grey clouds.

The chaplain says that he buried Peter, killed
during the counter-attack at Amiens. And (words
intended to be of comfort) that he was 'well-liked
and a credit to the battalion. He died trying to help a
wounded officer.'

Peter named me in his will as the person to whom
his belongings should be returned. These were in the
package and included a letter I'd sent him from
Boulogne, torn at the edges, blotched with rain and
dirt. A pair of mittens I'd given him, caked in sour
mud, were wrapped around his grandmother's rosary
beads. Not that these 'lucky beads', as he called
them, had saved him from death. What kind of a
death I don't know – and can only hope that it was a

swift cutting off by bullet. 'A bullet with his name on it.' Peter was superstitious but didn't share the comforting fatalism of many soldiers.

Tonight I wrote two poems. The first took me by surprise. I was cleaning the mud from his rosary beads and thinking about superstition.

Some cling to a four-leaf clover,
A special button, a dented coin –
Not holy relics, not a saint's thumbnail,
A splinter of the True Cross, or three hairs
From the head of Saint Peter.

I've seen a rabbit's foot soaked in a soldier's blood,
A black cat brooch with ruby eyes
Held by a Hun while his fingers stiffened.
I lost my smooth round pebble
When I choked in poison gas.

Some cling to a four-leaf clover.
Some clutch a crucifix.

This came spontaneously and is, as yet, a rough-hewn piece.

I took longer over the second poem and struggled with some of the lines. It's not quite what I want to say, or good enough, but will have to do, as I cannot work on it any further.

To Private Peter Sullivan
Died 9th August 1918, Amiens, age 19

I saw your face, as pale as this frail flower.
Our lives had intersected in that hour.
You were my khaki angel, bringing hope,
Grim hope, a casualty in that landscape.

Though starved of love, you had the love to give.
Now here am I, your friend, the one who'll grieve
Remembering how your light shone true for me
Illumining my dark anxiety.

If you had lived, I would have come to you –
The brother you had longed for, never knew.

10th October

I spoke to Matt today about Peter's death and he
read my poem of tribute. We were in the attic. I was
able to tell him at last how devastated I'd been when
he was reported missing at the Somme, my fears for
him, the overwhelming sense of loss and despair as
weeks passed without news. And then I brought out
the letter Peter had written to me after the gassing,
when I had all but given up hope. After reading it,
Matt went very quiet. I asked him did he recollect a
little lad called Sullivan in the hospital at Rouen. At
first he was definite that he couldn't, but then told me
he had a faint memory of a boy staring at him from
the opposite side of the ward – a blond boy, very
thin, very young. But he couldn't be sure, as it was a
time of pain and confusion and he'd had morphine.

 I want to think that Matt did see Peter. I would

have told him this and why, but he went on to talk about Kempton, and his death at Ypres. Sarah has been told by Kempton's CO that he was killed by a bullet in the head. He died instantly.

10th November 1918. Last night's dream
I am in the new Gardens. A mist clings around the trees, which have lost almost all their leaves; the grass and paths are covered in shades of brown. I cross the lawns, crushing the leaves underfoot. I am treading on bones, crunching them like shells, the bones of the unnumbered dead, surfaced from a mass grave. Skeletons, once temples of spirit, flesh and passion, reach up, reach out for what they have lost. I want to leave but cannot. There is no path and the mist is thickening. I'm aware now of the trees watching, waiting; like Boche listening posts.

11th November 1918
I was in the vegetable garden, digging, when I heard the tumult – bells of churches and schools ringing out, hooters from factories and, on the river, ships' horns and sirens and steam-whistles giving out their cock-a-doodle-doo. Cheering and shouting as people ran into the street as if they couldn't stay indoors and needed to be with others.

Matt arrived in the late afternoon and stayed for dinner. Pa brought out his treasured bottle of Glenmorangie for a toast. What did we toast? Not 'Victory'! The end of the war at last. No rejoicing, but a sense of relief. Some men are saved from death at the eleventh hour by this laying down of arms; others will have died in the dying minutes of the war.

Mam was tearful as she'd just heard that Mrs Cullen's son, David, has been killed. The news of his death came this morning, of all days surely the cruellest.

Elizabeth and Matt came up to the attic with me to look out at Liverpool on this first evening of the peace. Dusk was falling and street lights came on all over the city, houses and buildings lit, blackout torn down, the windows liberated. It was as though the earth and a starlit sky had been reversed. Where before there'd been a vast dark pool, now all was starred and shining. As we watched and talked of the years since 1914, the lights seemed to me like candles lit for those who'd been killed. And not enough candles. I thought of Berry, Captain Barrett-Hughes, Lunt, Walker and especially, Peter. Peter, that night by the fire when we met, his frightened face, the glow of a cigarette.

Later, when everyone had gone, I wrote a poem provoked by the headlines in the *Evening Express* –

11th November 1918

'The Ceasing of Hostilities' –
Such sibilance in the polite phrase,
As easy as a handshake
Ends a falling-out of friends.

And now there's a haunted silence,
Fear creeping away like a rodent,
Guns dumb, with empty mouths.
Now earth can reclaim the trenches;
There'll be time to groom the turf
Over the slots for shattered bodies.

What will we do with the future?
Handle it like a piece of precious porcelain
New from the clay and the fire?

Strip back the black.
Let the green of Spring be only green
Not the signal for an offensive
When innocent buds become bullets,
And flowers chalices of blood.

12th November

Tonight I showed Elizabeth my new poem with some trepidation, although I did want – no, I needed – to share it with her. I explained that I'd written the third verse for her. She liked it, and verse three particularly, but suggested one or two slight changes – the last verse could be more hopeful, more positive if it really is the closing one? Or perhaps I would write another verse? I told her I cannot be hopeful at present, I haven't got it in me, and I have to be truthful. But she is right. The poem needs an ending. So I've decided to repeat the line

What will we do with the future?

as the last line of the poem. This is the question that looms large in all our minds.

Elizabeth went to check on the children, then reappeared with a surprise for me. A 'peace present', she said. My portrait, in pastels, wearing my blue hospital jacket and red tie, cap pushed to the back of my head. Well, she laughed, at least you recognise yourself. I confessed I like it better than that earlier

210

sketch when I'd just come home after convalescence. I don't look as ghastly thin, and my hair is quite long again. But those worried eyes – I hadn't realised I look so anxious!

Her lavender blue dress set off her olive skin and she'd wound her long hair in a decorative silk braid, a style I haven't seen before. I wanted to hold her. In truth, I wanted her. But I rambled on, telling her how pleased I am with the portrait.

During this last year we've become closer than I ever thought to be with anyone, except for Matt.

But she's made it perfectly clear that the one kiss will be the only kiss. All her talk is of Jack's return now that the war is over. She uses his name like a shield. I know she would never betray him.

16

Elizabeth clutched Lily's hand and wove through the crowds along Lime Street. As drizzle fell, greasing the pavements, they ran the last few yards into the station. Trains and trolleys clanged, steam hissed, whistles and shouts reverberated under the grimy glass roof. She scanned the Announcements Board. Damn. Jack's train running late, a crowd building up behind the barrier. She joined the waiting throng and protected Lily, her arms around her as people pushed forward. No escape from the stench of wet clothing and body odours. She remembered the peppermint sweets in her bag, took out one for herself and another for Lily.

At the next platform a train huffed up clouds and flakes of soot from its engine. Smuts speckled Lily's pale blue coat and smudged her forehead. Elizabeth rubbed at them with her handkerchief, too vigorously, Lily wincing. Would the fingers of the station clock never move off 5.30 – they seemed to be stuck, the huge dial staring down like a moon. This waiting was a version of Purgatory, man-made, and they were trapped in it. Through her mind all day had drifted lines from Dante that Grandma Quecci used to quote, proud of her translation –

Through the river of fire I've come, and see
That day I longed for at last in my view . . .

She yearned to see Jack again and hold him, be
stunned by his smile, the shape of his head and neck,
caress him in bed and make love. For three years she'd
lived with the dread of a telegram saying he was dead
or missing – and now this, at last, the day of his return,
his safe return – and her apprehension at his return.
How would they get on? Would he have changed?
Oh yes, she loved him, but he'd find that he couldn't
order her about like he used to do, watching where
she went, wanting to know who she spoke to, telling
her what to think – or trying to. No surprise he'd been
made an NCO. But perhaps he had become more
tolerant. She cursed herself for being an ungrateful
wretch – so many widows, so many children father-
less.

A drawn-out ten minutes and here it was, the black
engine panting into the station. She let the crowd push
ahead of them, fearing that Lily might be crushed.
Khaki figures poured onto the platform, indistinguish-
able from each other, among them a sprinkling of
men in demob suits. Jack would be in khaki; he'd told
her in his letter that he'd taken the 52 shillings and 6
pence instead of a suit. So had most of them, he said,
amused at the army's grandiose gesture: 'every man
deserves a suit'.

Her panic rose as the first soldiers hurried through
the barrier while others were still descending from the
train. Was that him leaning from a carriage door, then
jumping down? Yes, definitely Jack, with his bouncy
walk. Nearer now. He'd seen her. His way of waving,

from side to side, his hand like a raised flag. A family edged forward in front of her – a bulky man, his bulky wife and two other women of identical girth. Where was Jack? Her heart lurched. He was at her side. He pressed his face against hers. The coldness of his cheek, bristle, his mouth, his familiar taste. A long, urgent kiss. Then release. She was breathless, unable to speak, unable to remember the words she'd rehearsed.

'Jack –'

But he'd bent down to Lily. 'My lovely big girl!' A kiss. Lily, shrinking back, tried to hide herself in Elizabeth's coat.

He stood up and she saw the left side of his face. A raw scar jagged across his cheek from his nose to the corner of his jaw. His face, ripped open, had been crudely sewn, leaving stitch marks like boot laces. Another scar ran above his left eye towards his hair-line, how far she couldn't tell with his cap pulled low. Dear God! What other wounds did he have? Her stomach heaved. What agony he must have suffered and then to find himself disfigured like this. Pity whelmed up and she hugged him to her as tight as she could manage, her hands clutching the rough greatcoat and not letting go. No hint in his letters of being wounded, of scars. Now she understood why he hadn't objected to being sent to Cologne, demobbed at last, seven months since the Armistice. This horrific wound – he must have come close to being killed. Jack always so vain, so touchy – what should she say? She continued to hug him until she felt him pushing her off.

'Where's Gwyneth?'

She was slow to answer. 'Home. At home with Mam. Too wet, too late to bring her –'

He hitched the kitbag over his shoulder, put his arm around her and they moved down the platform towards the queue for cabs. He kept on her left, steering them through the crowd. Lily clutched her hand and held onto her coat in the queue.

'Come on, take Daddy's hand.'

Lily screamed and spun away from him, squirming against Elizabeth.

'Shush! You silly girl! Stop it!' Her angry commands brought louder screams from Lily, a paroxysm. People stared at them with expressions of annoyance or concern.

'It's me! She's frightened of me!' Dismay and panic in Jack's voice.

Her heart wrenched, knowing it was true. Bringing Lily had been a mistake, but she hadn't known about the scars. How awful he must be feeling now. She wanted to protect him.

'She doesn't remember you, Jack. It's been almost three years.'

'I know how long! No need to remind me or make excuses! Do you? Do you remember me?'

'Jack, what are you saying?'

'You don't seem overjoyed to see me. Lily's terrified. Have I changed so much?'

'Of course not! That's nonsense.' She busied herself wiping Lily's wet face.

They joined the queue for cabs. A soldier hoisted his little boy onto his shoulders and hugged his wife to him. Another couple stood kissing, oblivious, wrapped in each other. The babble of reunited people all around made her feel more alone. How was it that everyone else was happy, even rapturous? Her throat constricted.

He pulled her to him and kissed her, harder this time. She felt anger in the kiss. Three cabs drew alongside and the queue was swallowed into them. The fourth cab was theirs.

'Where to, Sergeant?' The driver leaned forward and they climbed in.

'Cresswell Street, thanks. Off Everton Road.'

The cab swung out of the station into Lime Street over the wet cobbles. Jack had again positioned himself on her left, with Lily between them.

'These buildings, St George's Hall and the others. Bloody wonderful!'

As the cab crawled along he gazed out of the rain-splattered window at the spacious plateau, the statues and lions on their plinths, then the Steble Fountain by Wellington's Column, the art gallery and circular library. He kept looking out as they passed the shops in London Road, lit like grottoes.

'Jack, why didn't you tell me about the wound?' She spoke in a low voice, aware of the driver. 'When did it happen? Was it when you didn't write for weeks? We thought the worst.'

'What's the worst? There was always the chance I'd have my head blown off. Then you'd never have had to see me like this.'

'That's a terrible thing to say.'

'It's terrible to be disfigured.'

She was humbled. 'It's not the scar, Jack. It's the fact that you didn't tell me, didn't let me know what you were going through – as if a scar could change my feelings towards you –'

His face turned from her. She broke off as she felt him clamming up. Here was the old mood, stiff, closed off, like a glaze. She'd gone too far. She'd ruined the reunion. So much remained unsaid, so much she wanted to say.

Up Brunswick Road, along Everton Road and into Cresswell Street. On the top step of Number 80 stood Mam and Pa in the doorway, with William hovering behind.

He paid the driver and ran up the steps. Elizabeth watched them hug him in turn, Mam first.

'Oh Jack! *Cariad*! Your poor face!' cried Mam, weeping.

He held her close for a few moments.

Pa said nothing but moved his pipe from one side of his mouth to the other, then shook Jack's hand. William stood back and turned his attention to Lily, pushing past into the hallway.

They went downstairs into Mam's kitchen, where a celebratory meal had been prepared and a fire filled the grate, a welcome glow on this damp June evening. Jack took up a position in front of the hearth.

'Bring Gwyneth down,' Mam urged, wiping tears away with the edge of her pinafore.

Elizabeth was eager for Jack to see the baby but loath to disturb her sleep and set off the crying and screaming that could last an hour or more. She hurried upstairs and lifted her from the cot. Thank goodness, Gwyneth remained half-asleep. As she brought her down, her thoughts ran back to the arid days after giving birth, the feeling of desolation, a rock pressing her into the earth . . . acute longing for Jack and then no longing at all. Now his first sight of Gwyneth, at two years eight months: rubbing her eyes, hot, her blonde hair darkened by perspiration; rubbing her small straight nose; his replica. Elizabeth passed her to him, passed the moment of birth, the entry and the exit. He held Gwyneth awkwardly on his lap for a few minutes – then returned her as she began to whimper. What was he thinking? What was he feeling? His expression gave no hint.

When she'd settled Gywneth in her cot, they gathered round as Jack pulled open his kitbag. He'd lost nothing of his vitality, she noted, and admired the broadness of his shoulders, accentuated as he'd lost weight. He removed his tunic and rolled up his sleeves; she remembered that old habit of his, rolling them up as high as he could, showing off his muscles; and she smiled at herself for again being captivated by the pale bulging biceps and constant play of the sinews in his arms.

Lily sat on her knee, staring up and frowning at the Daddy she'd been promised. He reached into his kitbag.

'There, Lily. I made this for you.'

She took the doll and held it up for everyone to see. Carved from one piece of wood, it had flaxen hair, two plaits of string glued on. The khaki dress, made from uniform, was held together by three regimental buttons. She sat with the doll on her lap and began to tear at the clothing, trying to undress it.

'Mam, this is for you. I've been carrying it around for a year. Hope it's not dirty.' He brought out an unwrapped piece of lace. 'It's a tablecloth from Wipers. Our name for Ypres. Or I should say what was left of Ypres.'

Mam took the snowy lace and shook it out, marvelling at the intricate design of linked stars.

'Now for your present, Pa. Voila! How's this for a piss-pot?' He pulled a Boche helmet from the kit-bag. 'Of course, I chose one without bullet holes in it.'

They watched as the old man raised the helmet to his head.

Jack stopped him. 'Watch out. I've used it already!'

Laughter; the fire spurting flames from fresh coal shovelled on by Pa, Mam pouring the tea. From the scullery Elizabeth carried in the large Della Lucca platter she'd designed years ago and decorated with holly leaves, berries, fruits of the forest. It was used every Christmas and today was the centrepiece of the table. On it she'd arranged the vegetables – rows of sliced carrots alternating with boiled potatoes, a mound of mixed cabbage and spinach in the centre. Very little meat, in spite of the ration being saved for this special day, ribs of lamb a rare feast. But a rich brown gravy steamed in the blue jug and the air was sharp with the smell of diced beetroot soaked in vinegar, Jack's favourite.

As they ate and swapped anecdotes, Elizabeth felt herself relaxing, adjusting to his presence. At the same time she experienced a sense of disintegration, of coming apart under the old tug of physical desire she now knew as a trap. And love, yes, she still loved him, the pain and ache of it had never gone. Would she again be weak, yield to his demands, the emotional pressures he put upon her, testing her, needing to be the dominant one?

But already she was somehow pushed to the side

of her own being, fracturing the independence she'd forged and enjoyed while he was away.

She caught William staring at her from the other side of the table. Was he reading her thoughts? He too would have to readjust to Jack, accept her new situation.

'And when did you get wounded, lad?' Pa asked after the meal, sitting by the fire, re-lighting his pipe with a taper.

Jack hesitated, paced around the table, cleared his throat.

'Not ready to talk about it yet? Never mind, lad, tell us when y're ready, not before. The wonder is, you weren't killed . . . weren't touched by the wand. What's important is you've got your life ahead – and two lovely children to think about.'

Jack sat down on the opposite side of the hob and propped his foot on the fender. 'It's fine. I do want to tell you, and now's as good a time as any.' He cleared his throat, paused, then spoke quickly, staring into the fire. 'It happened near St Quentin. We were part of the counter-offensive, blocking the German advance on Paris. As Sergeant, my duties included organising a rescue party for one of our tanks which had stalled in the mud. I was co-ordinating my men in a heave-and-pull operation when we came under bombardment by the Boche. An exploding shell caught me. Not serious enough to get sent home, unfortunately! I got patched up pretty quick in a Casualty Clearing Station and was back in action before I knew it. Nothing really. So many had it much worse.'

A strained silence. Elizabeth, her love for him flaring, moved swiftly to his chair and kissed the top of his head. Mam handed him a large mug of tea. 'Thank God, you're back. Mrs Green opposite lost all three of her sons and her stepson.'

As Mam embarked on a litany of those killed or missing, Elizabeth saw Jack's expression stiffen. He stood up abruptly and placed the mug on the table.

'I'm going outside for a breath of air. Coming, Will?'

She followed them out into the scullery, taking some dishes to pile in the sink; the back door was open, their voices coming from the steps up to the yard.

'Woodbine?'

'No thanks.'

'Of course not. The gassing – I'm told it nearly killed you. Well now, Will, my dainty lad, I used to call you some cruel names. Wee Willie Winkie! Bean-pole! No more though, now that we're survivors. Perhaps you'll tell me about your fun with the fucking Huns?'

In the privacy of their own rooms on the first floor, Elizabeth put her arms around Jack as he sat at the table. His bright energy had seeped away from him, his confidence was visibly dimmed. Shoulders slumped, leaning on the table, he stared at the oppo-site wall, now newly bare of her art, hidden away with her pottery in the deep cupboard in case it upset him. She'd tried to make his homecoming perfect. It was the mirror he was staring at, himself in the mirror. Oh, what could she say to reassure him? Before she could speak he got up and, holding her hand, drew her across to the half-empty canvas kitbag lying where he'd flung it down, like a mound of dirty earth.

'Some things in here are for the baby. Souvenirs for when she's older.'

A floppy horse, made of brown wool; an ABC in French; a white sunbonnet with flaps on each side.

He brought out a photograph of himself in uniform, with Sergeant's stripes, mounted in a mother-of-pearl frame.

'Taken a month before I was wounded. I'd been sent to a base camp for training and we – the new NCOs – were being photographed. Didn't know it then. I mean, that this would be the last photo of how I looked. I want Gwyneth and Lily to know what I was like before this.' He gestured to his face. 'Don't try to tell me that it makes no difference, Liz! Don't say anything.' He put his finger across her mouth.

'This is for you.' He handed her something substantial wrapped in red silk.

'Go on, open it.'

She pulled the silk back and discovered a carved madonna and child, about a foot high. The madonna's long hair was arranged around her like a cloak. In her arms she cradled a newborn baby.

'It's you and Gwyneth,' Jack said, and placed his hand on her breast. 'You, as I remembered you, and from the photograph you sent of yourself and the baby. Not as lovely as either of you, of course.'

She was moved but at the same time felt uneasy. Fixed in wood. Fixed in an image. She was no madonna and far from wanting to be one. Anyone who thought that she was didn't know her at all. But she knew she was being unfair.

* * *

That night she undressed by the light of the oil lamp she always kept on for Gwyneth. He watched her as he lay on the bed, naked, stretched out, his hands under his head.

'Leave your nightgown, Liz.'

A command not a plea. She draped it over the bedrail; it was his favourite, the one with small pink floral sprays she'd kept in a drawer since he left.

She unloosed her hair, which cascaded around her shoulders, and slipped onto the bed. He leaned towards her, his voice an excited whisper.

'I've longed for your body, kept myself only for you, kept clean. Look, Liz.' His penis was stirring, a creature with a life of its own. 'The men used to pack into the brothels out there, queuing up for their five-minute poke. Then the syphilis and the clap and all that! But Liz, I never went with the French whores.'

She wanted to say, 'But does that deserve a medal, while I was going through pregnancy and childbirth?'

He'd forgotten the preliminary caresses, the sensitive exploration, the secret intimacies of their love-making. There was no tenderness. She stifled her cries at the searing pain as he thrust into her again and again. It was as though he was taking what was rightly his, what had been denied him for three years. After each climax and ejaculation he remained on top of her, his body going slack, resting, then working up until he was again erect, fingering her breasts, digging into them, kissing her throat. She tried to become aroused, her hands caressing the muscles on his arms and shoulders. She'd always loved to feel their familiar curves, they'd always excited her. Not now. In their new hardness they seemed alien; his skin too, the silky softness gone, the texture of his buttocks roughened. As he pushed deep inside her body, her mind seemed to float above, observing, commenting, assessing.

He fell back onto the mattress into a sleep of exhaustion. She lay next to him, afraid to move, afraid of disturbing him, feeling torn and sore. His penis, now shrunken and moist in its nest of auburn hair, looked so puny, so used, that she almost felt sorry for it. He was lying with his head turned to the right and she was able to examine his face for the first time. She studied him as if drawing his portrait, and realised that never again would he allow her to scrutinise him. The scar was vicious, ugly. She'd overheard him telling William how the shrapnel had sliced through his flesh and opened up his cheek, exposing his teeth. She writhed to think of his pain and suffering, the crude operation, how he must have felt on seeing his face in the mirror when the bandages came off. Jack, proud of his looks to the point of conceit. The other scar, running up his forehead and across his scalp, showed red beneath his newly grown blond hair. It shrieked how close to death he'd come. Little wonder that his face looked harder, his cheeks sunken, the line of his mouth clenched. He'd aged ten years.

17

The next morning she awoke with a start. Jack. The reality of his return rushed in, filling her mind and heart. She reached across but touched only flat sheets and blankets; his side of the bed was empty and cold. Was he with the children? Yes, that would be it, he'd be used to waking early in the army, and had got up to see them. The door to their room was open. He wasn't there. Both children were still asleep; Lily curled like a hibernating dormouse, Gwyneth turned onto her stomach as usual.

She tossed on the lavender blue dress he used to like. Perhaps he was downstairs talking to Mam.

On the landing she almost bumped into William carrying a jug of hot water for shaving. He had a towel over his shoulder, the neck of his striped shirt tucked in.

'Will, have you –'

'Seen Jack? Yes, he's down in his workshop. Been there for the last hour or more.'

He went on towards his room, but changed his mind and turned back to her. She looked distraught.

'Are things all right? I mean, with you and Jack?'

'Yes, don't worry. A bit difficult just yet. To be expected, I suppose.'

'Come to me when you can, when you need to

talk. I know it won't be the same now – now that Jack's here – but when he's out, maybe –'

She touched his arm with its fuzz of golden hair. 'Yes, I'll come when he's out. I think I'll be needing you more than ever.'

'Elizabeth –'

'Ssh, don't get upset. I have to find Jack.'

From the shed next to the vegetable garden came the tick-tack of nails being tapped into wood. She peered through the dusty window. Jack was bent over his joiner's bench working on some picture frames. He was stripped to the waist, his back to her: she took in its perfect, classical shape tapering to narrow hips, his shoulders splendid with their clearly defined deltoid muscles. Braces hung down over his trousers – not his uniform trousers but an old pair in brown check. She could see at a glance that he'd already rearranged the wood, neat stacks of mahoganay next to planks of pine and oak, and at the far end, odd chunks, and pieces of broken chairs.

He was intent on what he was doing and hadn't sensed her at the window. She dodged away to the little gate of the vegetable garden. It was a fine morning, the blue sky only lightly veiled by smoke, as blue a summer day as there could possibly be in the city, and getting hotter. She opened the gate, bent down and pulled up a lettuce and a handful of mint, shaking off the dark crumbly soil and breathing in the loamy smell of earth warmed by the sun.

Should she go into the shed or leave Jack to carry on? Perhaps he expected her to seek him out? It was difficult to know. She stood pinned to the spot. In that moment she was still herself, complete. A move towards him, to cajole, to please, to attract . . . perhaps to be rebuked . . . and she would be less than herself. Here she was, on a warm June morning, the war over, a woman centred in her own being, standing in the sunlit yard with lettuce and mint in her hands. She wanted to prolong the moment. But she was also a woman whose husband had just returned from the war having heroically served 'King and Country'; and she was a wife, wearing a lavender blue dress specially for her man, to attract him.

She rubbed the rough leaves of the mint and inhaled their sweet-sharp odour. A ginger cat picked its way along the top of the rear wall, eyed her and went on. She would hold on to her independence a while longer, hold back from Jack, wear the dress for herself, wear it with pleasure because it suited her.

She stole back into the house and up to the children who were beginning to stir. They would need her attention for the next hour. If Jack wanted to see them let him show it, let him come to their rooms, talk to them, get to know them.

By mid-day, when the hooter blasted in the Corporation Yard, she was fretting that he hadn't appeared. Unable to bear the tension any longer, she hurried down the stairs. Sunlight was angling through the glass of the back door, casting triangles on the wall. She heard sounds from the kitchen below: Jack talking and laughing with his parents. Don't go down, she told herself. Listen. Yes, it was as she thought, Jack keeping up a show of everything being all right, of being his old self, as if the war and the scars hadn't changed him. She wouldn't intrude. Let the old people enjoy these happy moments.

She retreated upstairs where she kept herself busy, cutting bread, preparing the lettuce and the children's eggs for lunch. She called Lily to the table and sat Gwyneth in her high chair. The children had almost finished eating by the time Jack came in, looking a little sheepish, unusually for him, giving him an air of vulnerability. Her hopes rose that he might be affectionate, easy-going – like William. Yet her heart contracted even as she made this comparison – disloyal, she knew, but unbidden.

Jack had washed, and was wearing a white shirt Mam had made and given him as a coming-home gift. He kissed each of them and sat in his place at the end of the table. She poured the children's milk into beakers. Their first meal together as a family, the strangeness of it, the strangeness of peacetime, like being in the promised land. There should have been a sense of liberation, of gaiety, but there wasn't. Jack was tense and mostly silent. She tried to jolly him up, pointing out Gwyneth's little achievements, saying how good it was to have him back, giving him, as she stood behind his chair after placing his tea on the table, that gentle squeeze on his shoulders he'd always liked and responded to. His silence was filled with something she couldn't gauge. It was as though half of him was frozen or lost or left behind at the Front. The war hung in the air but neither of them mentioned it; she would certainly have to avoid questions which might upset him. But she expected questions from him, particularly about the children, about how they'd all managed, the Home Front.

He devoured a large piece of Cheshire, his favourite cheese she'd bought specially for this occasion; he placed another slice on a hunk of bread with lettuce and stuffed it into his mouth. The children watched fascinated as he slurped his tea before he'd finished chewing.

When the children were playing in their room, Elizabeth went to him where he sat on the sofa, touched his hair, gleaming blond and springy after the army crop, kissed his neck. He was stiff and sullen and didn't respond.

'Shall we take the girls to Newsham Park this afternoon? There's a new set of swings and the pond's been refilled. We could buy a sailing boat for Lily on the way.'

'No,' he snapped. 'Forget it. I'm not going out.' From his pocket he took a tin of cigarettes, selecting one and tapping it on the lid several times before lighting it. How deeply he sucked on the cigarette, as if he wanted to consume it whole.

She was disappointed but saw it would be unwise to try to persuade him. Unkind too. His first day home, he was probably disoriented, free from the regulations and discipline of the Army but like a prisoner after years in gaol, not able to adjust to the freedom or know what to do with it. She had begun to clear the table when Lily ran over carrying her carved doll.

'Look. Her name's Katy.'

He smiled. 'That's a nice name.'

'Katy's in the Army, like you.'

Thrusting the doll at him, she shouted excitedly, 'Katy's got a sore face. Like Daddy's.'

He stared at the red scrawls on the doll's cheeks, the bright crayoning.

Hurt and anger showed in Jack's eyes. He sprang up and pushed the doll into Elizabeth's hands. The slam of the door as he left set Gwyneth screaming.

He worked in his shed all the hot afternoon. She heard the hiss of the plane and smelt the odour of newly-shaven wood as she stood outside with a jug of cold lemonade and a glass on a tray, a slice of cake. Four o'clock. The sun still burning through the haze. She knocked on the open door. Jack appeared, flushed and sweating, his scars a livid purple.

'I thought you'd need a drink.' She held out the tray.

He brought out two stools from the shed and they sat in the shade of the high sandstone wall. Above them, the dark leaves and vines of ivy which draped the wall were tangled in bindweed, its white trumpet flowers folded and drooping. In the warm air sounds magnified: dogs barking, cries of children in adjoining yards, the clop-clop of a horse and cart coming up the street, the screech of seagulls flown inland from the river.

He brushed away a fly attracted by the lemonade.

She broke the silence. 'It must feel good to be out of khaki at last.'

'Ay. It's peculiar though, being able to wear anything you like, free to choose.' He quaffed his drink, empty-ing the glass.

'Free to go where you want to, do what you want.' She poured another full glass.

'No, not really. Not when you look like Mary Shelley's monster. Remember the film and the monster

230

catching sight of himself in a mirror, sickened by his face, stumbling out into the night –'

Poor Jack! She sought for something to say, to reassure him. 'Oh, stop that! You're exaggerating. It's only a scar, it's not as if your face is destroyed, not burnt out of recognition like Daniel Oxley's. You're alive and well and strong. The scar will fade with time. So many men have visible wounds after the war. Matthew Riley's lost his arm and William –'

'I thought you'd mention William! He's never looked better. Just think of it, the last two years he's been back here, pampered by you and Mam, while I was going through hell. Yes, bloody living hell –'

'That's not fair. William's lungs are damaged. He gets asthma, can't breathe – and he's not over the shell-shock yet.'

'Yeah. But he looks fine. No one's going to turn away when they see his face, are they? No one's going to shudder.'

'His health could get worse at any time. The doctors have warned him – tuberculosis, pneumonia – perhaps not many years . . . '

She was choked, unable to continue. She took the tray and ran into the house.

That evening, after the meal, Jack stayed in the kitchen with his father, smoking and playing chess. William was out on an excursion to Southport with Matthew. The washing-up done, Elizabeth said goodnight to Mam, who was tired and in pain with arthritis. Upstairs, she tidied up, peeped in at the sleeping children. She would wear the pink, floral nightgown and sit in the chair by the lamp. Tonight would be different. She would take him in her arms, into her tenderness, comfort him, make love.

She waited, reading a novel by Rebecca West, but was unable to concentrate. At midnight she heard the door open.

Jack hardly looked at her. He threw off his clothes and hurled himself into the bed. She climbed in beside him and found herself pinned down as he lifted himself on top of her, shoving her nightgown up over her breasts. In a moment he was erect, intent on his own pleasure. There was nothing of love in it, merely sex, frenzied sex. He was using her to blot things out. This much she understood, but not why he seemed to have stopped loving her.

The next three days and nights followed the same pattern. On the fourth night she resolved to confront him. If he refused to talk she would refuse to be treated like a whore.

Not a word in reply to her protest.

She put her hands on his shoulders and pushed him off. He flung himself onto his side and covered his face with his hands.

'What is it? What's wrong?' She heard her voice tremble. 'Why won't you tell me, talk about it? Is it the war? Why don't you ask about what it was like for us at home, about the children?'

No answer. A muffled weeping. His back was turned to her and he'd moved away. It was as though a crack had opened down the centre of the bed. She thought how he used to cling to her, curl into her shape, cupping his hand around her body, drifting to sleep. Now it was up to her – he needed to be coaxed, comforted. She would press herself close against his back and caress his stomach, he'd always liked that. But as she went to clasp him, he shoved her off and squirmed to the edge of the mattress.

After five minutes or so, she heard his heavy breathing. She lay stiffly, fearing to stir in case she woke him. Some moments later, he began to groan and jerk, shouting out unintelligible words. When the nightmare was over and he was still, she dozed, but woke as he again called out. Now she could distinguish some of the words, the name Hughes and something that sounded like 'keep down', then 'don't move, flat down, you fool' and 'that's it . . . too late' and 'Christ Almighty!' After he'd quietened again, sleeping on his back, she too slept, but only lightly, waking when dawn light filtered through the curtains.

What day? Wednesday. As usual, Jack was already up. She lay there, feeling exhausted. What were those nightmares that haunted him? If only he'd talk to her about them, let her in. She dragged herself from the bed and sighed; an early start, as it was her turn for wash day, Mam always having Monday. She hated it, the back-breaking chore, the reddening of her hands, the choking smell of boiling, the wringing and rinsing, the mangle. Three hours, sometimes four, breaking off only to see to the children, minded by Mam. But at least it wasn't raining and the day promised to be as bright and warm as those before.

* * *

She fingered the sheets on the line strung across the yard. The washing was drying quickly in the heat; she'd take it down before it became too dry for ironing. Aware of Jack in his shed, she filled the wicker laundry basket, folding first the sheets, pillow cases and towels, next the clothing – two shirts, the children's dresses, vests and knickers, two of her own dresses, four aprons, six handkerchiefs.

The shed door was open; Jack stood measuring the side of a picture frame. He frowned as she came in.

'Would you like a sandwich?' she said. 'You've had no breakfast.'

'Thanks.' He brushed the wood shavings into a mound, the creamy-white curls reminding her of Gwyneth's first hair-cut.

At the end of the shed stood two mended high-backed oak chairs. 'Mam will be pleased,' she said, 'she told me how very old they are and that she'd inherited them.'

'That's true.' Jack's voice was flat. He pointed to a neat stack of picture frames. 'I'm going to ask William to take some samples around the photographic shops, the ones who took my frames before the war – there's a big demand for photographs at the moment.'

'Why ask William to do it? Why not go yourself?'

Jack glared at her. 'He'll want to help out. I can be working back here while he gets the orders. I'll give him a percentage.'

'Aren't you going to Harlands? I thought they'd promised to give you your job back?' She'd dared to come out with the question in all their minds.

'Don't you go questioning me! I'll look for work when I'm ready and not before. Bloody hell! Don't you try telling me what to do. You women! Taking men's jobs! You're going beyond yourselves since you got the vote!'

She turned away and closed the shed door behind her. No, she wouldn't be drawn into a quarrel. This was the old Jack whose tactics she knew too well – attack the best method of defence, and attack where it hurts. He'd always resented her involvement with the Cause – for him she'd severed contact with what he called her 'stupid Suffrage friends'. And surely he knew the vote was limited, that she didn't qualify as she wasn't over thirty, wasn't a householder. Clearly, he was hiding his real reason for not going to the Labour Exchange. How could she make him admit to the fact that he feared going out, even down their own street?

18

William folded the greatcoats into a bundle, tied it with string and improvised a handle. He hoisted the load onto his shoulder and took a final gulp of tea. Jack peered around the kitchen door.

'Thanks, Will.'

'Sure you won't come with me?'

'Yeah, I've said not. I mean not!'

'Hot day out there. I'll be back with the money as soon as I can.'

William slipped through the back door, up the cellar steps into the yard and out of the rear gate. Jack's eyes were burning on him, he could sense it, could feel Jack watching him from a rear window of the house, watching him walk into Grant Gardens, down the central path towards the Hippodrome. The weight of the greatcoats, the fierce July heat, trickles of sweat down his face like crawling flies, his breath rasping. He strode on – he wouldn't let Jack see him falter or stop. 'Little nancy brother!' – the old taunts still rang in his mind.

He joined the queue for the one o'clock tram. A relief to drop the greatcoats – he'd be glad to hand them over at the Lime Street office, still more to get a pound for each. He'd give his own pound to Jack, who needed it, with only his unemployed money coming

in and only one order for frames from ten photographic shops. People just didn't have the money, Mr
Sampson had emphasised, pointing to his empty
studio. But it was Elizabeth William was concerned
about, and the children. With food prices still rising,
how could she manage on so little, even with Mam
giving them meals every night?

On the traffic island opposite, the woman with
orange-peel cheeks was selling roses, but her stall was
deserted; neither was her brassy-haired daughter with
her. Who will buy my sweet red roses? Who had the
money for roses?

He heard the rumble of a tram through the haze
down West Derby Road. Picking up the greatcoats, he
was relieved to be on his way.

17th July 1919
I'm writing this as I sit waiting for Matt on the steps
of the Museum. I have just said goodbye to my
greatcoat, and I can't stop thinking about it. I hadn't
expected this sense of bereavement, the pang as I
handed over my old friend and received my pieces of
silver. We'd been through so much together. In the
station office the stink was suffocating, greatcoats
stacked high to the ceiling, awaiting burial –

Only cloth but my body's in it.
Night and day it wrapped my flesh,
Held my spirit, kept me intact.

I can discard you
But not the skin I'm in.
Farewell my friend.
We'll never meet again.

This Summer, the first in peacetime, we've all
been trying to adjust, pick up a new rhythm, jostling
for territory (wasn't this the cause of the war?).
We're like migrating birds returning to their old
feeding and breeding grounds. This last observation
springs from Matt's influence – we've been out along
the shores again, last Friday to New Brighton and
the long coastal stretch where the Irish Sea pushes
in and retreats. Matt talked about his idea of
composing short piano pieces for the left hand,
reflecting the life and movement of bird species from
the great raptors to small birds such as the wren,
including sea birds and water fowl. I never press
him about his progress, only feel a wrench of the
heart recalling that morning when I came down the
path to his door and heard him playing. I stood
outside, listening, feeling like an eavesdropper. The
heavy chords, then the discords, a crashing sound
followed by silence. I heard him sobbing. Eventually
I knocked and he opened the door looking
exhausted. I pretended I'd just arrived. Later we
walked in the park and he told me he still suffers
acute pain in his stump and where his arm was. He
still feels the nerve-ends reaching out through his
hand that isn't there.

He's late today, but I never mind waiting as he
always arrives eventually. Sometimes, though, I
worry that this mourning for the lost part of himself

might have become too much for him to bear, and I'm on the edge of a precipice until I see him again.

From what direction will he come? Usually, if I meet him here, he comes down London Road and across Lime Street, skirting the edge of St George's Plateau, and when he sees me on the Museum steps he breaks into a half-run, waving – it's in moments like this that I feel the strength of our bond.

Looking for him now towards the Empire Theatre and the Station Hotel, I see the buildings all festooned with banners and scarlet cloths. Only two days now to Peace Day; everywhere there's this froth of bunting, decorations looping lamps and balconies, shops and offices draped and frilly. At Blacklers Stores and T.J. Hughes, the windows are crammed with advertisements, Victory mugs and plates, flags in all sizes. Every house is to display at least one flag at the window. We have ours ready, bought by Pa at the market last week.

But none of us will go to London to march in the Parade. Jack's had pressure from his regiment but he's adamant. I couldn't march anyway, even if I wanted to. Matt refuses, with an ironic laugh ('can't swing my arms'). Most of those marching will be those last in, 1918 men, fresh from training, cadets almost. Plenty of work for stonemasons and memorial makers – the poem about this, which I've been working on, is almost finished, just one or two lines still not right.

The Stonemason

'My name is Legion: for we are many' – Mark V.9

He's sure of each new name he carves in marble,
Precision in his chipping out by chisel –

Each hammer tap exact to sculpt a letter.
He's not employed to grieve or show he's bitter

But merely etch the names and regiments,
The years and very finest sentiments.

He has to keep a steady hand and nerve,
Try not to picture faces young, naïve,

Clear-eyed, smooth-skinned beneath their caps and badges,
Consigned to death's red mouth, hell's hostages.

He mustn't think of flesh or the distress
Of mothers, wives, or children's life-long loss.

He's now at work in every town and region
Inscribing names in stone. These names are legion.

21st July 1919

Jack surprised us by going out at last. He applied
for a job making furniture, went for an interview and
came back in a bitter mood. He'd overheard one of
the bosses say 'not Scarface'. Two were taken on but
not him, in spite of his pre-war experience. Elizabeth
bore the brunt of his disappointment. I heard them
shouting at each other while the children sobbed. I

waited outside their door in case she needed me, and would have gone in and dealt with Jack, but all went quiet. Later she spoke to me about his distress, his worry over money, how she'd 'brought him round'. I let her see how concerned I am for her and she took this to mean concern for her physical safety when Jack's in a black mood. She's absolutely certain he'd never hurt her, but of course I meant his other ways of hurting too, and he's already done that.

> Jack, something stabbing through his sleep:
> His cries crack the bedroom wall.
> Elizabeth, scrubbing the face of a doll,
> Tries to erase his wounds of flesh and mind.
> Mam, removing her mask of smiles
> Cannot lift the bone-deep pain.
> Matthew, hearing lost music
> Reaches for something he'll never touch again.
> Me, I'm pacing my cage, hungry
> For something I have never tasted.

That evening I followed Jack to his shed. But I didn't go in or let him know I was there. Through the window I could see him, hunched, sitting on a stool; he was weeping, a shaking shadow, trying to hold himself together. I was in hospital with men in that condition, their nerves snapped. I've been like it myself. But Jack – what monstrous pride – he won't admit to anything that seems like weakness in himself, or imperfection. Those scars – he's putting Elizabeth through a bad time. The expression in her eyes tells me that, but she says nothing. Jack seems to have built a wall around her.

19

Three open-topped army lorries loaded with soldiers rumbled down London Road towards Lime Street.

'Lads from the Nottingham and South Staffordshires.' William watched the convoy as it slowed near a horse and cart. 'Regulars, and some Derby lads as well, according to the newspapers.'

'Wouldn't have thought it possible. Any of it!' Matthew's voice rose in disbelief.

'And only two weeks since the Peace Day celebrations. What a farce!' His face flushed, William tugged at his shirt collar, removed his tie and shoved it into a pocket of his jacket. Dock strikes, a transport strike, now the Police on strike and the Army brought in to control the looting and riots. The bloody Police! What was the strike about anyway? More pay, defence of their new union, so the news said – and spread here from London.

They walked on down the road where police volunteers were breaking up knots of people who stood about, staring at the wrecked and raided shops.

'Bloody hell!' Matt shrieked as a young lad was thrown to the ground.

'Ssh! Be careful! They might think you're a ringleader.' William restrained him, always fearful now for Matt's safety since he'd become active in the cause of men like themselves, disabled by the war, many thousands who'd lost their livelihoods. Last month he'd led a protest march around the city and slowed the traffic around the Labour Exchange. And a week ago he'd tried to punch a civil servant who told him that if he'd had the top of his arm removed as well as the rest he'd have received a bigger pension. Matt had mimicked the mincing voice – *And, after all, you do get more for a right arm than a left.*

Police volunteers stood guard near the broken glass and strewn wreckage from shops looted the previous night. All the windows were out at Lartache and the shelves empty of jewellery. In front of T.J. Hughes torn clothing littered the ground.

William edged Matthew off the pavement and they crossed to the other side of the wide road. From the direction of Lime Street a troop of soldiers advanced towards the shops. That half-forgotten sound, the mechanistic tramp-tramp. William was back on the dusty road to Breilly, feeling the utter weariness, trying to keep in step and failing.

'Christ! They've got bayonets fixed! Going too far, that is!' Matt shouted.

'Keep your voice down!'

His mouth dry, throat raw, William longed to stop and rest. Only a few hundred yards and they'd reach the Steble Fountain; he'd sit there and bathe his face. This humid, overcast day. He'd never liked August Bank Holiday. He'd never liked the heat, the wet heat, cloying, making him feel weak, subjugated to its clammy paws. Recurring fever, but he'd not fallen to the killer influenza, neither had any of the family.

Matthew tugged at his coat. 'Did you hear about old Mrs Price from your street?'

'No. What?'

'Arrested. Caught outside Owen Owen with one shoe and a coat-hanger in her hands! They're rounding up anyone!'

'Come along there! Move on!' A grey-moustached, corpulent policeman pointed his baton at a few men standing on the street corner.

'Caldwell's new old men,' William whispered. 'The retired brigade taken back on. Those on strike won't get their jobs back.'

'That one over there looks like a volunteer.'

A young policeman stood outside a smashed-in furniture shop. Clutching his baton to his chest, he glanced nervously up and down the road. Something about his white face and skinny body reminded William of Peter. That last glimpse of him, stricken, waiting for the gas to bite.

They pressed on to Lime Street and veered right towards the Steble Fountain. No hope of resting there. A tank crouched like a massive toad at the foot of Wellington's Column, guns poking out, and other tanks squatted on St George's Plateau.

William looked up at the Iron Duke high on his pedestal. What would the hero of Waterloo think of this 'land fit for heroes'? Armoured vehicles, troops, bayonets threatening the people, the demobbed, the vast new army of unemployed ex-soldiers.

Matt nudged him. 'Jesus! They've taken over St George's Hall!'

Soldiers were coming and going on the steps. And on the plateau, near the statue of Prince Albert, a sergeant major shrieked his commands, putting a platoon through drill. It could have been a scene from a theatrical satire, William thought, but the reality was grim and dangerous. Military Police stood on guard at the edge of the plateau.

'Better get out of their way! Come on!'

He pulled Matt's coat and they crossed the road to the museum steps, a vantage point where a small crowd had gathered. They stood half way up the steep flight. How bizarre. The lawns of St John's Gardens smothered with Army tents, the Boer War Memorial surrounded by canvas latrines.

As a convoy of armoured lorries crawled up William Brown Street, the crowd surged forward. Some of the men were ex-soldiers, still wearing uniform, buttons and badges missing. At the foot of the steps a fledgling police constable hovered.

'Fucking Police! Should be ashamed of yourselves!' A gaunt, grizzled man shouted and spat on the ground. 'On strike! We weren't allowed to strike in the Army!'

'Not all of them are on strike,' bellowed someone further up the steps. 'Be fair. A few hundred, maybe.'

The ex-soldier shouted back. 'Rubbish! More than a few hundred. Must be. Why do they need the military then?'

A newspaper lad arrived with his cartload of the *Express*. 'Looting. Man shot dead!' The headlines on his placard brought a rush to buy copies.

William craned over the shoulder of a man in front of him, peering at the copy he'd just purchased.

'Shot in Love Lane.' He relayed the news to Matthew. 'A bad show. Soldiers charged some looters at the bonded whisky store. One man killed.'

'Bloody mad!' Matthew's comment was echoed by those around them.

Rain began to pelt, drenching them in seconds; the cobbles shone, water streamed in black rivulets down William Brown Street. They joined the people heading towards the river, stopping now and then to shelter in doorways. The tram strike hadn't deterred the Bank Holiday crowds but Dale Street was strangely empty of traffic. By the time they reached the Town Hall the rain had eased off. William leaned against the soot-grimed stone. Pigeons fluttered above, landing on the ledges and balcony, whitened with birdlime.

'I need to rest a few moments. Damn breathing's rough.'

Matthew spun round. 'Sorry, lad. Going too fast!' He took a brown paper bag from his pocket. 'Let's share this!' He tossed the bag across and William caught it.

'An orange! Haven't seen one for years.'

'Spanish. Bloody shame, they're rotting in the docks.'

William tore off the skin. It came away readily, releasing the tang. He divided the orange, gave a half to Matthew and sank his teeth into the pith, the sharp juice easing his throat. Fruit from paradise. Pre-war, lines of ships had queued to enter the Mersey, bringing fruit from faraway. Suddenly he felt the thrill of an intuition he'd experienced years ago, looking from Everton Brow one bright spring morning towards the mouth of the river . . . an intuition of distant ports, the far west, blue skies, Caribbean islands; a waft beckoning him.

'Remember our plans to travel, Matt? We could still go.'

Matthew looked surprised. 'I suppose so. I could travel light. A rucksack maybe. Wales first then Ireland, I think we said?'

'And after that Sweden? And then America?'

Matthew laughed and gave a little jig. 'Amazing what an orange can do!'

They were about to move on when a unit of a dozen soldiers marched around the corner, patrolling the Town Hall, followed by a motley group of boys, small shadow-soldiers trying to keep in step. Lured to be a soldier-lad, thought William, perhaps to die in 'fields where glory does not stay' – Housman's words and sad cadences never failed to affect him.

In companionable silence they trudged downhill towards the Pier Head as the rain, with renewed ferocity, soaked them to the skin. Without trams, the roads were uncannily quiet except for the occasional swoosh of a passing motor-car or lorry, or the clatter of hooves and cartwheels over the cobbles. They walked under the Overhead Railway and approached the massive Royal Liver Building. William looked up, as he always did, at the two Liver birds tethered on top of their towers, today swathed in mist, except for the tips of their great wings reaching out like suppli-cating hands. Already a belief was growing that as long as they remained on their stone perches Liverpool would not be destroyed. He thought of the Leaning Virgin of Albert, the birth of legends.

At the Pier Head they were almost bowled over by people running past them, mostly men, but boys and women too, hurrying towards the landing stage and its covered gangways now at a steep angle to the river in the low tide.

'Take it easy, Billy!' Matthew glanced at him anxiously.

'O.K. I'm all right, really I am,' he insisted, his heart singing because of Matt's concern.

Along the railings by the empty tram bays, beggars held out tins and plates. Matthew placed some pennies in the tin of a man without legs who lolled by a cart, MONS 1914 scrawled in red on its side. One of several child beggars came up to William and tugged at his coat. Her face was pale and dirty, her hair that should have been flaxen, a tangled, dingy mass; he gave her money, and some biscuits and sweets.

As they entered the covered gangway, William relished the tangy smell of the Mersey, the tarry ozone. They hurtled down the slope, impelled by gravity, and emerged, exhilarated, onto the landing stage. Shouts and angry murmurs came from the crowds gazing at the middle of the river. A battleship and two destroyers were anchored, like grey locusts still but watchful. Ferries, as though aware of their midget size, hooted deferentially as they neared the warships.

'There's a space over there.' William indicated a gap near the New Brighton Ferry Terminal. They stood by the chains, staring at the scene on the river.

Next to William a bulky, bearded man trained a huge pair of binoculars on the ships. 'Want to look?' He offered the binoculars. 'I served on the *Valiant*. Never thought I'd see her in the Mersey!'

'Thanks.' William took the heavy field glasses and held them to his eyes but the lenses gave only a grey blur.

'Here, let me show you. I'm Harrison, by the way. Ex-Petty Officer.' He swivelled the focus wheel. 'Tell me when.'

'That's it!' The battleship *HMS Valiant* became clear. Like being on deck, William thought. He focused on the impressive length and diameter of its guns. No wonder these ships were called Dreadnoughts. Now the two destroyers . . . their names . . . *HMS Venomous* and *HMS Whitley*.

'Steamed here in no time from Scapa Flow.' Harrison clearly took a personal pride in the achievement. 'Government order. In case of riots in the port.'

William picked out a small boat coming towards the warships, with about twenty sailors on board. Its arrival provoked a stir in the watching crowd.

'That's the day shift returned from guarding the Albert Dock,' Harrison informed him. 'There's a round-the-clock-watch on all the docks.'

William had seen enough. He lowered the field glasses. 'Thanks very much,' he said, handing them back. He turned to speak to Matthew, but he wasn't there.

He tapped Harrison on the arm. 'Did you see my friend leave?'

'No. Sorry. Can't help.'

William scanned the people packing the half-mile landing stage. Perhaps Matt had moved further along for a better view of the warships? Why hadn't he said so? No sign of him to the left or the right.

Running in panic, William was gouged by a huge sense of loss. He was back at the Somme, turning over a dead man.

A crowd had gathered around a speaker on a soap box. Matthew might be among them, listening to the man hurling protest at the police for striking, the government for mass unemployment and broken promises. William pushed through the sodden people, shoving aside two men holding a drenched banner. Rebuked by women under umbrellas, he took a punch on his shoulder, a thump on his back.

It was hopeless: Matthew wasn't there or anywhere along the stage. All the people looked the same and in a haze. The ground spun. He touched the cold, wet iron of a bollard and held on to it. The Liver clock chimed four: half an hour had passed since he'd begun searching.

He'd keep on looking. He had to. Perhaps Matt had gone back up the gangway? Surely he wouldn't have gone home, without a word?

Was that him leaning against the rail? Yes, there he stood, in the shelter of the gangway.

'What is it?' William gasped. 'Why didn't you tell me you were going?'

'I'm not going! I'm fine.' But his expression suggested otherwise and the pallor of his face, his eyes sharp with pain, the way he clutched his empty sleeve, pulling it across his body.

'No, you're not fine at all. You'd never have left me like that.'

Matthew glared, then burst out, 'Sorry!'

'Look, I know you're in pain. You should have told me –'

'It's the damp. Gets inside this bit of arm. Like thousands of termites gnawing and biting, and going on and on gnawing, even where there's nothing, as if they'd eaten my arm away.' Matthew's voice became a whisper. 'Standing there by the river I wanted to throw myself in.'

Why hadn't he taken more care of Matt? Why hadn't he seen this coming on? 'I'm a stupid ass. You must have been in pain all afternoon.'

'Don't blame yourself! It's been throbbing for days now. Got worse after that last downpour.' Matt cradled his stump in his left hand, swaying a little from side to side.

'Let's go home. I'll get us a cab.'

Hot *labskaus*, beer, the warmth of the kitchen fire: he'd made sure that Matt had all the home comforts he could give, including a change of clothing. And Elizabeth had helped by making up a bed for him in the spare room. Pleased to be kept busy, she'd said, on edge because Jack had gone looking for work at a furniture factory on the dock road.

After dinner they sat with Pa who wanted to hear again and again about the Police strike, the tanks on St George's Plateau and the incredible scene of warships in the Mersey. Matt spoke animatedly, enthralling the old man who kept interrupting, asking questions and scratching his grey-blond head with the stem of his pipe.

Later, alone by the fire, they watched the amber glow reflected in their glasses of beer.

Matt leaned forward, grinning a little sheepishly. 'Sorry I gave you a fright this afternoon.'

His face was half in shadow, the other half lit by firelight. Still gaunt, William thought, the high cheekbones adding to this emaciated effect. He was swamped by William's sweater, shrugged into it.

'I should have warned you, Billy –'

'No. I should have realised. I'm still disgusted with myself.'

Matt jerked his head towards his stump. 'You see, I ought to have had that third operation but I just couldn't face it. I said I'd take my chance. They warned me of the signs – as if I didn't know – the blackish colour, the sickly warmth, stabbing pain, the smell.' He broke off, looking away from William into the fire, then back again. 'Yes, the smell! The putrified bloody stench! Every day I wake up thinking I can smell gangrene. I look in the mirror, examining this bit of arm, searching along the seam for unhealthy grey. I dread the morning, the mirror . . . and I dread the night too, going to sleep, because I dream of the death of my arm, my hand . . . thrown into an incinerator. I watch the ashes, not floating upwards but falling into a cesspit.'

He drained his glass. William sought for words but remained silent, not able to express the love and pity that whelmed up. He poured more beer into Matthew's glass and his own.

'And every day, every day and every night I'm struggling. One arm and a bit. From the moment I get up. Shaving, washing, squirming into my clothes, cooking my food, clumsy, dropping things, looking ridiculous. I'm glad that I'm alone. No one to watch me, no one to see me looking ridiculous, lop-sided, useless –'

'Nobody would think that. You know I wouldn't.'

'It's pride, Billy. My suppurating pride. Not just that.

Some nights I dream I'm sitting at the piano playing; some mornings I wake up dreaming music, a piece half-formed in my mind, often a complete sonata. Yeah, I've tried to play – it rips me up – my ghost hand reaching out, yearning to press the keys, mad to reach the keys. Then I run out into the park, keep running, avoid the lake when it beckons.' He paused. 'There was a thrush I used to look for. It hopped on one leg. I fed it every day, then one morning I found it dead, savaged. Survival of the fittest!'

'You know I want to help. I'd do anything for you. You know that. Won't you live here for a while?'

'No. I have to get through on my own.'

That night, when they went up to the bedroom, William fetched a jug of water and a glass, and an extra pillow. His heart clenched, seeing Matt's face white with pain as he slid under the blankets. He lay next to him, tenderly stroking his hair, then holding him in his arms until he slept.

The next day a letter arrived from Aunt Mair to Mam. Her manager, Big Harri, had hurt his back and she needed help at Bryn Tirion. William might want a change and would certainly benefit from the pure Welsh air. Would he be able to come?

20

William stopped to rest on the hill path winding between banks of heather and bracken. A few yards ahead of him, Matthew stood waiting. Below them the Vale of Clwyd stretched in green distance towards the blue rim of the sea. To be here, on the slopes of Moel Famau, and with Matt. He'd hoped for this chance, longed for these moments, this place.

They moved on and reached an outcrop of rocks. William leaned against a boulder of ancient grey limestone.

'I'll wait here. You go on.' He knew Matt was eager to reach the summit where the ruins of a tower provided a vantage point for observing kestrels.

'You are all right aren't you, Billy?'

'Perfectly. I'll rest, then I'll be able to enjoy the walk back.'

He watched Matt ascend the path until he disappeared around the next shoulder of the hill. No other walkers were visible on this stretch, although some had been ahead of them earlier on. The evening was fine, with a warm southerly breeze moving the ferns and tall grasses, bending them in waves of green. At his feet a line of ants was making its way into a crevice of the rock – a battalion on a manoeuvre. A moment later they were driven back by an occupying army, advancing from the crevice, outnumbering the invaders, several ants to every one of the intruders, their strong jaws tearing heads from bodies, ripping them apart. The viciousness of insects. Little difference between their activities and those of humans, warfare not unnatural but simply part of the natural order. He didn't like the thought, didn't want to argue with it, most of all he didn't want to be reminded of the war, the blasted war, not here, not now.

He rejoined the path to the summit and walked slowly up towards the curve of the hill. He wanted to catch sight of Matt. The wind blew more fiercely the higher he went and leaned on him, pushing him back. He reached the bend, panting, and flung himself on the grass beside the tufty clumps of heather. How clear and sweet the air was at this altitude; he breathed in greedily, grateful for these last three weeks. Where was Matt? He sat up and scanned the higher path, a white thread between banks of heather. A solitary figure, familiar even at this distance, was ascending the steepest slope beneath the tower ruins.

The wind buffeted, sending clouds scurrying over the hill range, their shadows sliding, shape-shifting across the green and purple flanks of Moel Famau. Matt was moving forward on the sunlit height, cloud-shadows racing towards him, swooping like the wings of a gigantic bird, darkening everything below. He willed them to glide away, miss the path where Matt was walking, leave Matt in the sunlight.

—◈—

Bryn Tirion
5th September 1919

Dearest Mam,

You'll be pleased to hear that Mair has been looking after her nephew splendidly, in fact spoiling him. He is gaining weight, relishes her Welsh cakes and butter and tales of your wild girlhood (more of this when I come home!).

Last week we all three – Mair, myself and Matt – attended a recital at St Asaph Cathedral. Mair took us in the trap. You can picture her, tall and wiry, greying now but still a dark Welsh beauty, in full command of Benjo, her chestnut stallion, who pulled us admirably, and seemingly without effort, all the way from Cilcain through Afonwen to St Asaph, going at a fair speed, and the warm wind was in our hair, refreshing and stimulating. The recital was excellent: first a harpist, then a soprano accompanied on the piano by Ifor Morris from the Denbigh Music Society.

Mair told us of the time you and she played a duet at the Corwen Eisteddfod and won a prize. Then off you went together on a shopping jaunt to Rhyl and bought new hats. She's sure you will have remembered what happened there . . . ?

Big Harri's big voice gives us orders from flat on his back on the slate floor of the kitchen. He'll be recovered soon, as he makes good progress and wants to be fit for the auction, buying in the new stock of sheep. Good that Aunt Mair has such an efficient manager. She's making up a parcel of good things for Lily and Gwyneth, including eggs from her hens, and butter, and says to tell you she's sending it by carrier tomorrow. She has just called across the kitchen telling me not to

forget to give you her love and, of course, cofion cynnes
from her and Harri to Pa.

Your loving son,
Gwilym

P.S. Good to hear that Jack's got work – and with over-
time promised.

———

He lingered in the orchard as twilight came on and
with it the piercing birdsong he loved for its intensity,
the thrilling ethereal sound; feared for its aching love-
liness, a plaint for all living things, for the pathos and
fragility of life.

He wanted to write, record these thoughts in his
journal, talk to Elizabeth on his return. He could be
expansive with her, but with her only. Yes, he could
talk with Matt, but only so much, only so far, then he'd
be cut off with a laugh or a quip if he 'went on' too
long or too deeply into what Matt called his 'disquisi-
tions'.

Elizabeth. How was she coping with Jack, and was
her marriage easier now that he had regular work? Not
questions he could ask in a letter.

———

Bryn Tirion
Sunday, 15th September 1919

Dear Elizabeth,

I hope you and the girls are well and enjoying
this Indian Summer. Soon it will be Gwyneth's third

birthday, and I've been thinking about a present for her. There are some craft stalls at Mold Market and I've ordered a little pinafore for her, woven with a design of lambs. Also a Welsh doll for Lily to add to her collection and so she won't feel left out.

Mam will have let you read my last letter with news of the recital.

Now Matt has found Aunt Mair's old piano in the room that used to be Uncle Iolo's study. The best news is this – she brought in the tuner and Matt has been playing.

I can't begin to tell you what this means for him and how I rejoice. He's trying out some new compositions using chords, inspired by the moods of nature and the life of small creatures here in the Clwydian hills. One of his compositions depicts a drama we both observed in a copse half way up Moel Famau – bass chords for the raptor approaching – a hawk hovering over the hillside – lighter chords for the pheasant who hurries back towards the wood in fearful flight. Matt is increasingly adept with his left hand.

This has been a time of healing for us. Physically, I'm breathing without a wheeze, and Matt is flourishing too. He goes through each day free of the pain, except on one occasion – a cold wet afternoon when we helped Aunt Mair in the barn. Spiritually too (even more), it's been a perfect time for us. An exhilarating harmony, in every way. We work in unison. While I cut the branches, Matt picks them up and hurls them into the cart. While I shake apples from the boughs, Matt collects them in the basket. While I fill gaps in the hedge with brushwood, Matt gathers the left-over twigs for kindling. I make sure he doesn't work too long or *too hard. There's a freedom such as we've never before experienced.*

Sunday in Wales has a broody, solemn atmosphere that seems to infiltrate everything and everything breathes it out, especially the hills. This evening, in the dusk, the hills seem to loom closer, not ominous but protective presences.

I enclose two poems, one written for the girls and one especially for you.

Yours ever,
William

For Lily and Gwyneth

The Wind

A Big Wind striding up the hill
Seizes hold of your Uncle Will.
The Big Wind rocks him on his toes
And wets his nose, poor Uncle Will.

This wind flings Uncle by his coat –
He fears he'll be whisked off the hill and float.
All trees, all grasses bow low to the ground
As Big Wind flies by with a roaring sound.

The sheep, the cows, the dancing cats
Feel the wind as they lose their hats;
While the pigs are happy and twirl their tails:
They always rejoice when they hear of gales

Because only they can see the Big Wind –
Yes, only pigs can see the wind.

Your poem (I have been re-reading The Mabino-gion*).*

Rhiannon

Once he had seen her, standing there
Under the canopy of trees and stars,
No other woman would replace her
In his heart. So Pwyll pledged
He would wait, stifling his pleas,
Keeping watch at a distance
In case she needed him,
In case she beckoned.

Bryn Tirion
22nd September 1919

Dearest Mam

A note to let you know that we're absolutely sure Harri's back is strong again and that he and Mair can manage without us.

So I'll be home soon, Mam, and will let you know exactly when.

Your loving son, Gwilym

—◇—

He put down his pen and sighed. He'd never been more reluctant to return. To stay here in Wales was too much to hope for, even though Aunt Mair would readily keep him on and Matt as well. To live the rest of his days in these hills – the longing tugged at him and was physical, a gnawing in his stomach. But he would have to quench these hopes and these feelings – Matt couldn't disguise his eagerness to 'get back home'. How often his talk turned to demonstrations, to making the authorities do something for disabled ex-soldiers, and to his idea for workshops like those at Alder Hey where useful new crafts and trades could be taught. Well, whatever the future held, he wouldn't abandon Matt, even if staying in Liverpool meant he'd be shortening his life.

Their last day. William welcomed Aunt Mair's suggestion of a bonfire – gathering some of the dead branches they'd cleared from the woods and hedges might help to ease his tension. And Mair promised them a farewell supper around the flames.

The morning mist cleared, leaving a cloudless sky, clarity of light and air. In the sloping field at the edge of the woods, William smelt something rank – signal of the changing season, the decay of vegetation, although many of the trees were only just beginning to surrender their green to yellow and orange.

He and Matthew toiled in the heat all morning and into the afternoon, dragging the branches into an enclosure close to the wall of the farmyard. Sweating, they removed their shirts, their bodies gleaming, braces hanging down over their trousers. When they'd built the bonfire, completing the wigwam, they stripped near the stables and hosed each other down, larking and shrieking like boys. Afterwards they sat on their clothes, leaning against the stable wall, drying and enjoying the warmth on their skin.

* * *

Matthew had been out for an hour on a final walk in the cool of early evening. He'd already packed and left his suitcase and rucksack by the front door in the hall, ready for departure. William was still gathering his books and papers and arranging his clothing in the suitcase. Where was his copy of Borrow? Perhaps on the window ledge? He found the book there with his maps and newspaper cuttings and the small oil lamp Matt had bought for him in St Asaph. Through the half-open window he heard a thrush singing in the orchard, haunting; it voiced his yearning to stay.

Matt was striding up the path into the farmyard, over his left shoulder a cloak, Aunt Mair's old cloak of Welsh tartan which she'd given to him, a token of her affection. How fine he looked, what energy in his stride, his dark brown hair grown quite long and wavy. With a tuneful whistling, he crossed the farm-yard.

William caught him as he reached the yard door. 'Look at these beauties.' He pointed to a large pottery bowl on the doorstep, filled with potatoes. 'Mair prepared them to bake in the fire – they're partly cooked already.'

Together they nestled the potatoes strategically in the bonfire and applied lit tapers to the base.

The flames burst higher, hawthorn and holly branches quickly consumed. William placed further kindling around the branches of oak, slower to burn. The voraciousness of fire, hungering to be fed, fire used for creation or destruction. He was trapped in a wood of charred trees and bodies, black smoke, the crackle and spit of fire. The image gave way to the bonfire roaring in front of him and the shouts of Matt from the farmhouse that the meal was ready.

He arranged four wooden stools around the fire and forked the potatoes, their skins browned, turning them over, savouring the aroma, the earthy, smoky smell which would be perfectly matched by the taste. Aunt Mair arrived with plates of ham and a bowl of mixed carrots and cabbage; Harri followed, leaning on his stick, and Matt carrying the knives and forks.

Later, when they were all drinking beer in the kitchen, William went back outside to rake the ashes. In the dusk, he stared with longing at the familiar outline of the hills – never had they been dearer to him, the known shapes greeting him like a loved relative or friend; hills which were boundaries he accepted and by which he knew himself; hills always holding the promise of beyond. He soaked in these last impressions, his favourite smell of woodsmoke, distant lights of farmhouses and cottages, scattered sounds – the sharp bark of a fox, the hunting cry of an owl, the squeal of a weasel – small, clear sounds tossed in the pool of night.

21

William sat on the crowded tram, relieved to have found a seat in the lower deck. He felt shaky today, feverish, his fingers restless. Through windows bleared with dirt and dust, he gazed at streets fading into hazy distance. Two years since he'd left Bryn Tirion – and during two winters with their dense, acrid fogs – he'd fought through bouts of bronchitis and asthma. More than bronchitis he dreaded the asthma attacks, increasingly frequent, feared his lungs were going to burst. Fighting to write poems, fighting for air like a landed fish, like the trout Matt had caught in the river Alun – how it threshed about gasping on the bank, until Matt released it back into its element. He'd have gone back to live at Bryn Tirion, as Aunt Mair urged in her letters, but Matt needed him and wouldn't leave Liverpool. Elizabeth too, in her way, still seemed to need him. She'd confided to him last night a quarrel with Jack about her visit to an art exhibition – and she would have said more, he knew, but as usual held her worries back.

His stop. He left the tram and hurried across Lime Street towards St George's Hall and the unemployed demonstration. A massive crowd on the plateau, the largest he'd ever seen, chanted slogans, waving their banners. As he approached a section of the crowd bulged and surged over the pavement like a wave.

Rain on the September wind, not yet spilled. Spits of rain on his face, and his cap tugged by the gusts. He was here only because Matt had urged him to come. He'd missed the last demonstration because it involved marching. What good did marching do? Like being back at the Front. That final march in the mist, collapsing, being dragged off, accused of feigning, staring into the pale amber eyes of the medical officer.

He eased his way through the crowd towards his lion. Matt would be waiting for him, up on the lion's back. The thrill of anticipation when meeting Matt. Yes, there he was, sitting astride the lion and waving to him. As he approached, two other men slid off its back and jumped down into the crowd.

'I saw Tom Peters last night,' he called up to Matt. 'On his way to the Crown. He's going to speak if he's given the chance.'

A contingent from the Dingle burst into a protest song, shaking their banner, answered by a Bootle group on the other side of the plateau whose singing was snatched and flung on the wind like loose ribbons. William couldn't make out the words but it took his mind back to the buoyant singing of the Pals in 1914 as they marched along Dale Street. Only the Dingle lads didn't sound buoyant at all, but angry and hoarse.

The crowd hushed as the Unemployed Workers' Committee stepped onto a platform improvised on the steps of the Hall. A fuzzy-haired young clergyman gesticulated to the pug-faced leader and a woman organiser whose blonde-grey hair streamed out from under her tam o'shanter.

Placing his feet on the edge of the lion's plinth William tried to clamber up but swayed and almost fell.

'Up you go!' Shoved by several men onto the lion's back, he felt Matt clasping him. The cool stone of the lion. Slumped along it, facing upwards, coughing, lungs hurting, lights wheeling across his vision.

'Hold on, Billy. You'll be all right!' Matt's voice calmed him. 'Steady. Don't panic, try the slow breathing.'

'Fellow workers . . . since the return to peace . . .' the voice of the first speaker, intoning statistics of the unemployed, came across on the megaphone only to fade on the blustery wind.

Drowning . . . he must reach the surface of the water, try for a bit of air.

'Billy, don't fight it! Try to relax. Give yourself a chance.'

He closed his eyes but still saw Matt's face, his worried look, the way his left sleeve hung flat and empty from the elbow down and swayed when he moved, the personal flag of protest he refused now to pin away.

The roar of the crowd, like a storm in a wood, pierced by a higher sound, the clergyman's emotional cadences, more *hwyl* than speech, such as William had heard in the chapels of Flintshire. Then cheering as another speaker took the megaphone.

Gradually his breathing became easier. Matt helped him to prop himself against the lion's head and mane.

'It's that bastard. Barry Edwards, the Police Strike leader.' Matt booed.

'Shut your fucking gob!' One of an angry group

nearby raised a clenched fist; another lunged towards the plinth but was held back by the rest.

'Quiet, Matt. Keep it.' William held his shoulders, pulled him closer and they sat one in front of the other. He was glad he was here to keep Matt out of trouble – he'd become too vocal lately and had already been given a police warning, his name noted. He was glad he hadn't let Matt down, in spite of Elizabeth urging him to stay back. He'd been surprised by the concern in her voice, the way she'd stopped him at the door, urgent, begging almost. She'd even followed him out to the back gate trying to persuade him not to go.

Edwards, underway, extolled the Labour Party and the crowd went quiet as if listening to a sermon, revering this man who'd been sacked from the Police.

Matt pointed to the lines of mounted police advancing at a steady pace, a slow clatter, along Lime Street. Within a short time they ringed the plateau, tall and threatening on their huge glossy horses.

A man in a raincoat leaning against a lamp-post seemed to be taking down the Police Striker's speech in a notebook. He was joined by another man who'd filtered through the crowd. The pair then strolled towards Wellington's Column.

'Looks like plain-clothes detectives,' Matt murmured, shifting his position.

'Or reporters,' William suggested, 'Tweedle-dum and Tweedle-dee.'

Matt slipped as he manoeuvred on the lion's back. William held him. Hell! He knew the signs. That tugging of the empty sleeve and the rocking from side to side. Matt in pain. His restlessness, the need to keep moving, driven by needles, his stump gnawing. Only two Sundays ago, when Matt was playing Mam's piano, he'd let out a scream and ran from the room, then came back apologetic, admitting to the pain, how his lost arm and hand wanted to play and shot knives down from his shoulder to non-existent fingertips.

'Do you feel ready to move off, Billy? I can see Tom over there.'

William would have preferred to stay where he was and rest for at least another half-hour, but he slid down from the lion and followed Matt.

Tom Peters towered bare-headed over the sea of caps, his ginger hair clashing with a bright red scarf wound several times around his throat. As towards a beacon, they edged forward to Tom on the far perimeter of the crowd, threading their way through the tight-pressed bodies. A tram clanged by, people on the open-top deck cheering the demonstrators.

They reached the edge of the plateau. Tom joined them as they stopped by an organ-grinder parked on the pavement near the Steble Fountain. The fat Italian proffered his monkey for Matthew to hold while he unwrapped a sandwich, and in a flash it jumped onto his shoulder. Matt laughed and the monkey fixed its gaze on William as he bent over to tie his bootlace, now so thin that it snapped when he tugged on it. The dizziness again, the monkey's shrivelled face, its black accusing eyes, like Captain Barlow's, the pink-crab hands of the organ-grinder.

William swayed across to the fountain and sat hunched on the stone rim. Wind rippled the surface of the water, seagulls screamed. He shivered as the chill of the granite penetrated his flesh. Only a month ago in intense heat the fountain had been filled with children bathing and splashing, children without shoes, who'd never had shoes. Boys mainly. *O the ragged boys* – a poem he'd begun but never finished –

O the ragged boys of Summer
Bathe their feet in fountain water
When the cobblestones are burning
And their life's a shining morning
O the ragged boys of Summer . . .

There were other lines he'd struggled with, how did they go – yes, something like –

But they have no boots for walking
Will they have a chance of working?
Now they dangle feet in water
O the ragged boys of Summer.

No, these last lines were not enough. He wanted to show more of the poverty of their lives, unable to escape, stuck like flies on arsenic paper.

He'd ask Elizabeth to read it, that evening maybe, when the girls had settled and before Jack came home from work. Would he ever be able to write again? And what could he achieve like this, trapped inside every breath he took, when every next breath might be a searing flame?

He leaned into the water, splashing his face and hair. *Pro patria mori* – sunrise, ethereal dawn light before the trumpet, stand-to. Someone shouting his name. He struggled to his feet as Matt and Tom came towards him.

'Let's not stay to the end, Billy. Tell me when you want to go and we'll –'

Matt was interrupted by Tom, laughing as he pointed to the platform.

'Lady Do-Good, if you please.'

The woman organiser adjusted her tam o'shanter and looked worriedly at the unemployed, many now muttering among themselves, wary, not linking arms as they had before.

'Families are facing starvation. No food. No fuel. No money for the rent. The Poor Relief must be raised,' she began, but her words were lost to William on the fringe of the plateau. The wind was strengthening, a malty smell pervading, blown from nearby breweries.

Edwards took over. 'Nothing new to report. No offer of work schemes, no relief –'

He was interrupted by a waiting speaker who snatched the megaphone, a young man in dungarees, his cap pushed jauntily to the back of his head.

'Come on, lads!' he shouted. 'We're wasting our time standing here like a gang of dummies. Let's get on the move and show them. At least we'll be doing some-thing. Group up now for a march around the shops.'

Edwards shoved the young man aside and took the megaphone. 'No! It's too late to march now. Let's take a short walk instead – over there!' He pointed to the Walker Art Gallery. 'We'll all be art critics this after-noon. We'll go across and look at the pictures in the gallery. Those places are as much for us as for anybody else. They belong to the public. They belong to us! Let's go!'

Signalling to the crowd to follow him, Edwards moved off down the steps. They poured after him, accompanied by the clergyman and the woman organiser, crossing the tram-lines towards the gallery. William saw Matt and Tom ahead of him swept along with the crowd. He felt himself being carried forward on the surge of people to the short flight of gallery steps. He glimpsed Tom ahead, among those squeezing through the vestibule doors. Matt would be with him. A bottleneck at the entrance. He couldn't move, wedged between two men, one stinking of stale beer. He glanced at the soot-stained statues on either side of the steps, Michelangelo and Raphael in thoughtful poses, and he was seized by a longing for a quiet landscape in another country. Behind him came a rising tide of screams, a boy shrieking, 'It's a trap!'

He turned and saw hundreds of police with batons running out of the Sessions Court adjacent to the Gallery, hurling themselves on the crowd, lashing out at them, clubbing their heads and bodies. Some people were fleeing, their arms over their heads like troops surrendering. Others fell to the ground and were trampled. Mounted police turned their horses sideways, the wall of horseflesh making this like an arena.

'Ambush! God help us!' Someone shouted hysterically. It was the man in dungarees. Two policemen reached him, cut him down.

A mass of bodies heaved and William was half-lifted through the gallery doors into the foyer, managing to protect his chest by locking his arms in front of him. Piercing screams, shouts and police came at them, police flailing batons, striking, slashing. Christ! A massacre. Police and more police, who seemed to seep out of the walls, to step out of the pictures.

All around him he hears dull thuds as the batons split skull after skull, blood spurting, spattering the panels and doors. Bodies fall, tangling, jerking, locking together, squirming on the ground. He's spinning, slipping on the blood greasing the floor. He grasps hold of a pillar. Nowhere to hide. Matt. Where's Matt?

On the ground, unable to move, he's trapped beneath the body of an old man. He sees pigeons flutter through the open windows and men follow them, diving out into the side street. Police snap the windows down, swinging blows at heads and shoulders, kicking, punching. He sees Edwards stagger, clubbed by three police who jeer and batter his head and, as he falls, strike him again and stamp on his face. Matt, where's Matt? He lifts himself free, is half off the floor. There's the clergyman holding up his arms, sobbing, blood cascading from his half-severed ear, urine seeping down his trousers. And Matt is lying near the staircase, his face as white as the statues, and a policeman leaning over him with a crimsoned baton. Must reach Matt. He tries to move, can't . . . more police . . . they're glutting on blood like trench flies. A blow chops his head as he slips sideways . . . the Boche. Helmeted, heavily moustached, a policeman scowls above him. He lies full-length; next to him a woman moans, her blonde-grey hair streaked red. He's sinking in mud, clutching at air, gas fills the trench, his lungs are on fire.

A cold wet cloth across his eyes and forehead, darkness yet not deep dark, somewhere a blue light, a star perhaps, but no, it is in the room. Where is the room?

Why are there no walls? Groans, from left and right, one calling Jesus, another calling for his mother. Someone in white comes close, bends over him.

'Well, you've come round at last,' she whispers. 'Only four stitches. You were lucky.'

She doesn't know he's writing, writing in his head, his journal in his head . . . he's got to remember, describe what happened, what was it that happened? He tries to focus on her face, but can't. Her voice comes from a hinterland of bedscreens. She calls to another nurse down the ward, an Irish voice. Now he's beginning to remember – the bodies piled on each other like sacks of rotting vegetables, the surprise attack giving them no chance. No, not the Front. The gallery. Screams and cries. A helmeted face staring down at him, weapon raised to strike again, the face of a mad beast, and up there on the wall is a picture of paradise – fields, horses, mountains. The gallery. He sees it more clearly now, the police, the ambush. His head aches, the bandages are criss-crossed in bands under his chin. He must find Matt. He tries to speak. Matthew Riley, is he here?

'There, you must rest. Rest.' Her Irish tones soothe. 'Don't attempt anything at all. Give yourself a chance.' She lifts him higher on the pillows.

He's desperate for news of Matt. Is he alive? She hasn't mentioned the dead. How many dead?

'That's better. You've a way to go yet.' She smooths his forehead with the damp cloth, dipping into a bowl on a trolley, squeezing, wringing. 'You were a lucky one, weren't you now. Your shoulder's hurt though – no, don't try to speak – I told you, first things first. Mary, Mother o'God, you'll be choking again if you carry on like this. That's it. Quiet now. Nearly dislocated. Trodden on like as not. Many of you were trampled almost to death. A wonder that no one died. A miracle. Thanks be to St Patrick and St Paul and all the saints come to that.'

Now he can rest. He'll ask the nurse to find Matt. How badly was he hurt?

Already he can focus, everything clearer, like through a clean window. This nurse. He likes the shape of her face, a long face, firm jaw, the lovely lines that run down each cheek, deeper when she smiles. What colour are her eyes? Difficult to tell until she comes close. Perhaps dark grey, Irish grey, but with very little of the white showing. As she smiles her eyes shine, become half-moons.

'Nurse. My friend, Matthew Riley. Please find him.'

'What's that you're trying to say? I'll not tell you again, save your breath for recovery. There, your wheezing's started up again!' She keeps her hand on his until his breathing quietens. 'When you get out of here you'll need to go somewhere that's free of fog and smoke – the countryside, the coast – and spend most of every day outdoors. As much clean air as you can get! Now, just whisper – your name and your address. We can let your relatives know you're safe.'

Sleeping . . . how long? Dreaming. He remembers the dream. A lion dream. The old Queen is in it. She is on her horse, young again, straight-backed, side-saddle, a plume in her hat, and there, nearby, is Albert on his horse. They are the plateau statues come alive. They ride towards the mounted police, ordering them back.

The police won't stop and charge their horses at the crowd. He watches it happening as he hides behind his lion's plinth. Like a cavalry charge, the police press forward, men and women trampled under the hooves. His lion comes alive too, snarling and roaring at the police and their horses. Magnificent, he stands up on the plinth, shakes his mane and tenses his haunches ready to leap, all the time snarling, showing his great teeth. And then, with his lion he slides into a landscape of rocks and ravines, sublime, a static landscape, the painting in the gallery. His lion takes up a position about to spring at a horse – it is the huge police horse now harnessed to a rock and terrified. He becomes Mr Stubbs, brush in hand, embellishing the lion and the horse with his glance.

He understands the dream, knows its meaning – nothing now will hold him back from writing. He is the artist creating his picture, designing his future. The lion awaits his command and will not spring until he signals. The horse is fixed by fear – he can release him and he can release the rain from the heavy clouds over the ravine. The choice is his. And he is saying all this over and over to himself. The choice, the choice is his.

His head hurts. Sleep. More sleep. Afternoon drowsing. A dream? Elizabeth's face very close to his, he can feel her breath on his cheek . . . she has that stricken look he's seen before . . . her lips against his cheek, her lips on his, soft and warm . . . she holds his hand, kisses it again and again.

* * *

Two familiar faces. Mam and Jack, bending over him. He tries a smile and says he's well, but he can't speak to them for long. Light spears his eyes and he drifts into sleep. They leave paper and a supply of pencils sent by Elizabeth, all the pencils newly sharpened, and three oranges, apples, a golden cake rich with sultanas.

He holds a pencil. How reassuring it feels. Like coming home. He tries to write – his letters waver and wander across the page. He manages Matt's name and gives the page to Nurse O'Keefe. She reads it, frowning.

An hour later she arrives at his bedside with fresh bandages.

'I've got news for you. Your friend's in the next ward and he's recovered consciousness.'

22

The fog was almost palpable, yellow-grey, and becoming denser with every hour that passed of the late November day. Elizabeth looked down at the street where gas lamps shed an eerie, diffused light. She stared through window panes beaded with dirty moisture like everything outside. Familiar shapes of houses and rooftops were lost, dim figures passed on the pavement; a man and woman groped along, huddled together, a child holding the woman's hand. From the river, fog horns boomed their warnings. About to draw the curtains, she hesitated. Another hour and a half before Jack would be back from work. She shuddered at the thought of an accident in the fog – huge iron cart-wheels, slippery dock roads. She'd pleaded with him not to accept the overtime, insisted they could manage, but he was adamant, said he couldn't refuse and it would bring in extra money for Christmas. Leave the curtains open, she told herself, the lit window would be like a beacon, guiding him when he came up the street.

The pottery clock on the mantelpiece chimed six. She paced around the room, cleared the table of the children's supper dishes, tidied their toys and books. Then she peeped in at them, settled earlier than usual; both asleep now, thank goodness. A fierce poking of the fire brought spurts of flame licking around the fresh pieces of coal she'd placed on top. Was the room warm enough? William would be here at any moment – she'd asked him to come, and as usual he'd accepted eagerly. If only he'd hurry up – she wanted to get this over with, brooding on it all day and all last night, hardly sleeping. What she had to say to him would not be easy for her, although she'd rehearsed it. She could influence him, she knew. He always listened to her advice. But could she carry it through, could she bear to lose him?

A light tap at the door. He stood there, hesitant as usual.

'For goodness sake, come in from that draughty corridor.'

He followed her across to the sofa in front of the fire.

'Tea?' This in a tone more formal than she'd intended, more severe.

He nodded, and gave her that half-shy, half-quizzical glance which never failed to snatch at her heart. He was wearing his old navy cable-knit jumper – her favourite – it set off his blondness and enhanced the blue of his eyes. He'd pulled the polo neck well up, framing his face. She mustn't let him see her appraising him, admiring his 'Viking look' that they used to joke about and she'd come to love.

Her hands shook as she held the teapot and poured hot water into it from the kettle on the hob. How could she bear not to see him every day, not to know how he was and what he was writing, not to talk, as she could only with him, sure of his understanding, their exchange of a wordless thought? His absence would weigh heavily on her heart – and on the house.

'Aunt Mair's letter, Will.' She sat next to him on the sofa. 'I've read it. Mam showed it to me. I said I thought you should accept the offer. Don't hesitate. Go, this time. Go.'

She'd blurted it out. The only way – blunt, direct, showing no emotion.

William looked stunned, as if she'd struck him.

'But I thought you needed me here. Don't you need me?' He flushed. 'As your friend, I mean.'

This was the moment and the question she'd dreaded.

'No. Yes! Of course I need your friendship. But not at the cost of your health.'

'I'll risk that if you need me.'

'No, you won't. You've been ill already and it's not even winter yet. This fog today's a warning. A real pea-souper and plenty of them to come. Another winter here might kill you.' She heard the sharp edge on her voice.

William shrugged and looked away, hurt in his eyes.

She mustn't waver. Keep a tight rein on herself.

'What of you and Jack? His moods. He might get worse. What if –'

'But we're all right now!' A necessary lie, she thought, as they were not all right, far from it. Oh, she'd tried to get close again to Jack, manoeuvred around him, given in to his wishes every time, but too often he seemed like a stranger. She hadn't given up trying, though, hadn't given up hoping they would find each other again. 'Jack's still adjusting and can be difficult. But things are better between us. I promise you. Perfectly all right.'

William looked unconvinced. He tried to catch hold of her hand but she'd anticipated this, neatly evading him as she rose from the sofa. No, his touch would undo her.

'I've forgotten the tea.' With forced light-hearted-ness, she chatted on as she poured it into the two mugs. 'What a wonderful opportunity, Will. To live and work permanently at Bryn Tirion! Mair expanding the farm. A generous wage as well as food and your own rooms.'

'Yes, I know. But not seeing you month after month?'

'You could easily come back on visits to see us all. You would, I know. Mam and Pa would expect that.'

He still looked utterly miserable.

'You didn't want to leave Bryn Tirion last time. You told me how you felt then. Your love of Wales and the Clwydians? Mair will need to know soon, Will.'

'There's nowhere I'd rather be. That's true. She's given me till the end of the month to decide.'

They sipped their tea in silence for a few minutes. To hold him and be held by him, this longing she'd felt so often in the last few years, and resisted. She'd struggled to suppress and deny her love for him. She dare not let him glimpse the depth of her feelings – it would only damage him to know. And now she was losing him, pushing him away.

'Mair's certainly doing well – all those extra acres. They'll need your help – she and Harri will have to look for someone else if you dither.'

'She'll have no problem finding someone locally. Elizabeth –'

'And Matt. She's invited him too. Says you're like

the sons she never had. Do you think he'd be willing to go?'

He ran his long fingers through his hair. 'I'll be talking to him about it tomorrow.'

'What about his work for the disabled?'

'He's given up. Couldn't get any support for his workshop schemes. And lately – since leaving hospital – he's been depressed.'

'So, do you think he'd be willing now to leave Liverpool?'

'Yes, he'd want to be with me.' He said this looking steadily into her eyes, as if probing her deepest feelings. She turned her face away and stood up. Always she'd concealed this sting of jealousy about his devotion to Matt, something she'd never questioned, she had no right, no claim.

Poking the fire, she sent hot coals spinning into the hearth. From the children's room came a faint crying, a snuffling and stirring. She welcomed the diversion.

'Sorry, Will. It's probably Lily. She's got a cold. I'll have to see to her. And Jack will be home soon –'

'Of course. I'll go.'

'Accept Aunt Mair's offer!' She flung the words at him as he went across the room. Turning round with a perplexed look, he seemed about to say something. Then he left, gently closing the door.

23

Bryn Tirion
12th June 1922

My dear Elizabeth,

Here's some unexpected news. Aunt Mair is to marry Big Harri. It is planned for the Autumn and, because they'll need privacy, Matt and I decided to move out of the farmhouse. Aunt Mair didn't suggest it, but better it will be for us. We're presently restoring one of the farm cottages and Harri is helping us. It's almost finished! We've repaired the roof and now we're putting up shelves and cupboards. There's no sign of damp, you'll be pleased to hear. Now the plan is to move in next week or the week after.

How are you, and Lily and Gwyneth? Please write to me soon and enclose drawings of the girls. I cannot say how keenly you're missed. Dare I ask you to think about coming here for a few days? I could wire you money for the train fare and meet you at the junction for Mold. <u>Please</u> come, perhaps next month? We could put you up at the cottage, and it would be a little holiday for you all.

I'm reading a lot of poets. I've discovered the work of Gerard Manley Hopkins, a Victorian who died in 1887 but wasn't published until 1918. He lived here in the Clwydian hills for a time, training to be a priest. Matt and I have been to see the college at Tremeirchion where he studied. He was inspired by the Welsh countryside, so, as you can understand, I'm drawn to him for that, also because he was a tortured spirit. And, of course I'm still reading Sassoon. All this between my milk rounds and farm work. I can speak Welsh quite fluently now and the people are very kind here, helping me through when I stumble over words and get stuck! But invariably they correct my pronunciation!

Matt has completed his Concerto for the Birds *for the left hand. He's hoping to perform it at the Denbigh Music Society this Autumn. Now he's working on another concerto inspired by the sea and Hopkins' 'The Wreck of the Deutschland'.*

This week we bought some furniture at the Flint Auction Rooms. A deal table (good size), and four chairs, also a Wilton carpet, worn in places, but ruby red with a clever design like a Turkish carpet. Matt sends you greetings.

Always
Your friend William

Elizabeth read the letter yet again, folded and placed it with the train timetable in her holdall on the bed. She began to pack three neat piles of clothing – her own, Lily's and Gwyneth's. The bedroom door opened. Jack. She'd dreaded his return from work.

He came in, closed the door firmly behind him and leaned against it.

'I thought I'd made it clear that you couldn't go!' The venom in his voice frightened her.

She flinched but was resolute. 'I think I made it clear that we are going. Whatever you say. Whatever you're thinking.'

Jack lunged at the holdall and tossed everything out of it onto the floor – clothing, toys, books and some little gifts. Oh, no, her wedding present for Mair and Harri – the blue and yellow ochre bowl she'd made at the Della Lucca. She picked it up and felt the broken pieces inside the wrapping. Flinging it on the bed, she wanted to scream at Jack.

Seizing her shoulders, he shouted, 'You're not going! I forbid it.'

Forbid. The word inflamed her. And she saw in that moment her father's red face and raised fists, her mother cowering.

From the children's room came a cry she recognised as Gwyneth's.

'You've disturbed the girls, shouting like that. They've been excited all day and I've only just got them settled.'

He hissed, 'I won't allow you to take the girls away. Defy me and accept the consequences. You'll lose us all.'

Not this. She'd heard of women who'd lost their children and home, whose husbands had thrown them out, whether or not they were guilty of anything.

She drew in her breath, feeling as though she'd been punched in the stomach.

'Won't allow? Lose us all? What do you mean by that, Jack?'

'I mean what I said. I won't allow you to take the girls. Go yourself, but if you do don't bother to come back!'

She reeled, sought in desperation for something to make him see reason.

'How are you going to tell Mam that you've stopped me from taking the children to visit her sister? She's delighted that they're to have a few days in Wales . . . that . . . that her grandchildren will see her country. She's written a letter for me to give to your Aunt Mair.'

Jack looked furious. She swept on. 'Go on then. Do it now. Tell Mam you're forbidding us to go. Explain why.'

She bent down to pick up the scattered clothes and toys. His hand gripped her wrist, his fingers dug in and hurt. He pushed her to the floor and flung himself on top of her. She lay pinned, his full weight on her.

'Jack, be reasonable,' she gasped. 'I told you before – just four days, a holiday for the girls, fresh air, they'll see their relatives –'

'You mean William! Uncle bloody William!'

His old animosity to William – his jealousy – flared and licked them in its flame.

'Mamma!' Lily's cry, followed by Gwyneth's tearful wail.

'You're frightening them!'

Jack released her and she struggled to her feet. But he came at her again, his face contorted.

'I'm working my hands raw for you, taking all this overtime to get more money, and you dare to defy me!'

'But it's only a visit and it won't be costing us anything, William sent the money for the fares and we won't need to buy food – you know this. Why –'

She moved towards him, though still fearful and trembling, wanting somehow to hold him, comfort him. He shoved her off and turned away from her to the door.

'That's it then!' His voice was choked as he left. 'I'll sleep in the spare room tonight.'

Later, after she'd reassured the children, she went to find him, console him, but the door was locked. She tapped. There was no reply.

Unable to sleep, she saw Jack's tight face and icy eyes, and his words bit deep . . . forbid you to go . . . won't allow you to take the girls . . . don't bother to come back. Twice she crept along the landing, desperate to heal the rift, but still the door was locked.

In a tormented half-sleep she told herself she would get up early, catch Jack before he left for work. But just as light began to creep beneath the curtains, she sank, exhausted, into unconsciousness.

Lily and Gwyneth jumped down from the carriage seat, tired of waiting for the train to move off. The late July afternoon was hot and the upholstery itched their legs. Elizabeth took out two paper twists of sweets from her bag, one for each child. They stood at the window eating the jellied fruits.

Elizabeth tucked William's travel instructions into her coat pocket and picked up her library book. Her hands were tense as she opened it and flicked through the pages, unable to focus on the print. If only the train would leave. Jack might come running along the platform and she couldn't face another quarrel now – but even so, she half hoped to see him and couldn't stop looking out. Foolish thought. Her letter to him was safe with Mam who'd give it to him when he got home that evening, and he'd read it and know that she'd wanted to see him before he left for work, that she'd wanted to tell him she was sorry he was upset. He would read it and know that she loved him.

She pictured his face, twisted with a jealousy of William that bordered on hatred, and she pitied him. Yes, she longed to see William again, to be with him, to talk, to be herself as she always felt most fully herself with him. And now there was her fear that this might be the last time. How careful she would have to be during the next five days not to let him sense anything other than the old easy affection. And she would wrestle as ever with the guilt, knowing her love for him was a betrayal of Jack in her heart and mind.

But on her return she would soothe Jack, reassure him; he'd see how the girls had benefited from the holiday. And by then she'd know for sure whether she was pregnant again, as it would be two months. She'd break the news to Jack as soon as they got back, and though she anticipated his first reaction, 'not another mouth to feed', she knew she could bring him round – this baby might be the boy he'd always wanted, and they would name the child after him.

The whistle shrilled at last and the girls clung to her, one on each side. She held them close as the train juddered and clanked out of Seacombe Station. It gathered speed and before long was cutting through the Wirral countryside, the lush flat fields edged by woods; and as the girls stared fascinated, she pointed out the rosy sandstone farmhouses, cows grazing and flocks of sheep – animals they'd only ever seen in picture books.

By the time they reached Neston, Gwyneth and Lily were slumped against her, sleeping. Her thoughts revolved. With a stabbing regret she recalled William's young, hopeful face outside the Della Lucca Studio, how she used to avoid him; his depression after she'd rejected him; how he'd drunk too much at her wedding; his return from the Front, convalescent, hollow-eyed, wasted. Her portraits and sketches of him, the one photograph, in uniform, and his letters and poems, were all she would have of him in the years ahead.

So near now, the Wales he loved, there across the Dee, the hills in varying greens stretching the whole length of the estuary. And already he would be waiting for them at Hope Exchange station.

As the train drew away from Burton Point, she took in the shapes and shades of land and water and where land was part of water, the sandbanks and the gleam of the marshes, the river flowing out to meet the Irish Sea. A flock of birds rose from the salt beds, their wings black then silvered by the sunlight as they wheeled and turned as one against the towering clouds.

Acknowledgements

A selection of the poems and journal writings of 'Private William Manderson' first appeared in my war-themed collection *Song of the Butcher Bird* (Flambard, 2007).

'The Stonemason' was published in *The Wilfred Owen Association Newsletter*, 2007 (ed. Merryn Williams).

When writing *Clay* and researching extensively, I received help of various kinds which I would like to acknowledge here.

I wish to thank staff at the Imperial War Museum, where I spent weeks reading unpublished letters, diaries and memoirs of Great War soldiers and rare published material in the Department of Documents; also exploring the Sound Archive, Photographic Collection, War Art Collection and exhibitions such as 'The Trench' and 'Anthem for Doomed Youth: 12 Soldier Poets of the First World War'.

I am grateful to the Wellcome Foundation, Dr Joanna Burke and the extraordinary exhibition, 'Medicine Man' (British Museum, 2003); the Red Cross Museum and archivist Helen Pugh; Museums of the Cheshire Regiment, the Royal Welch Fusiliers and the King's Liverpool Regiment; Port Sunlight Trust and Unilever Archives; and staff at the Local Studies Departments of Birkenhead and Liverpool Central Libraries. Thanks also for assistance to Simon Gotts, Information Librarian at Flintshire Library Services;

Keith Chandler, Principal of Burton Manor College; Colin Simpson, Curator of Wirral Museum and Williamson Art Gallery; the helpful librarians at West Kirby and Heswall Libraries (Wirral) and at Ruthin Library (Denbighshire).

Special thanks to Dr Jenny Newman, novelist and discerning editor, for her invaluable advice, constant encouragement and friendship. My thanks are also due to James Friel, Dr Aileen La Tourette, Dr Tamsin Spargo, the late Dr Edmund Cusick, Gareth Creer, Dr Jo Croft, Professor Timothy Ashplant, David Jackson, Amanda Greening and Cathy Pepp at Liverpool John Moores University.

I am very grateful to the novelist and poet Professor Alan Wall and to Dr Gill Davies, who were among the first to read *Clay*.

For their support I wish to thank my many writer friends, including David Evans, Michael Carson, Clare Dudman, Jan Bengree, Nancy Roberts (USA), Lynn Pegler and the writers in my workshops; also my friends in the Wilfred Owen Association and the Mary Webb Society (of which I am President); staff at Academi (Welsh National Literature Promotion and Society of Authors); Sally Baker and everyone at Tŷ Newydd (the National Writers' Centre for Wales) where, in this inspirational environment, I worked on part of the manuscript of *Clay*.

To my family, love and appreciation always.

And for publishing the book, warm thanks to Will Mackie, Peter Lewis, Margaret Lewis and all at Flambard.

Note on the Author

Gladys Mary Coles is a novelist, poet, historian and editor, internationally known for her biographical and critical work on Mary Webb. She has received many prizes and awards, and was selected to represent Britain in the Euro-Literature Project. Her poetry collections include *Song of the Butcher Bird* and *The Echoing Green*, both published by Flambard. She has a PhD in Creative Writing, tutors workshops across Britain, for the Arvon Foundation and Tŷ Newydd, and teaches at Liverpool's universities. She lives on the Dee Estuary and in Wales. *Clay* is her first novel.